A Rather Peculiar Poisoning

Chrystal Schleyer

ISBN-13: 978-0-7783-8795-4

A Rather Peculiar Poisoning

Park Row Books
22 Adelaide St. West, 41st Floor
Toronto, Ontario M5H 4E3, Canada
ParkRowBooks.com

HarperCollins Publishers
Macken House, 39/40 Mayor Street Upper,
Dublin 1, D01 C9W8, Ireland
www.HarperCollins.com

Printed in U.S.A.

To David,

For someone so full of words, I never have enough for you,
so I'll leave you the four that weigh the most.

I love you. Always.

1

Asquith Manor
Afternoon
May 9th, 1910

The wind whipped at the lake, turning it choppy and dark as if all the water had been replaced with crushed silk dyed an oyster gray.

It was a terrible start to the party.

And threatened to be a poor week for the guests.

Sadie stared outside where fog clung close to the earth, blurring the grounds until it seemed as if pale froth had spilled itself out over the grass. And at the lake's bank, the forest swayed a warning.

She turned away from the greenhouse's long wall where the storm gathered beyond the ornate glass and gold metal. The gilded frame tangled into curves along the edges of the windows, and the thin panes rattled as the wind let out a low howl.

But in the humid greenhouse, life permeated the space in the small scents of soft dirt and fresh growth and clean citrus, and the coming storm seemed far from reaching her. The cozy room calmed her. Besides, she had a warm hearth and a busy kitchen waiting for her. She'd let the guests worry over the sharp winds, the thick fog.

A basket hung from one of her arms, holding a pile of huckleberries, their color so dark they looked as if drops of ink had pooled together in the nooks of the worn wicker. Soon, they'd be simmered down, crushed up, and drenched in sugar until they formed a sweet compote laced with cinnamon.

Sadie left the gathering storm quickly and swept through the door leading back into Asquith manor. After all, Deighton was known for its lush land that bloomed in summer, brought about only by these very spring storms. She'd have to get used to them. She pushed the dark clouds from her mind—even as they bent so low, they seemed near enough to whisper a warning in her ear.

Smooth wooden walls muted the thunder as Sadie stepped quickly down the hall, sinking deeper into the heart of the manor. She focused on the steps in front of her, the solid bricks beneath her feet. The Asquith estate was grand and well-built, nothing like the cottage she'd grown up in where thin wooden walls let in the wind and a thatched roof dripped rain. Here, there was so much stone, the stalwart manor seemed as if it threw its chest out to the storm, dared it to rage.

Still, Sadie had never experienced such harsh weather before, and a finicky thought wouldn't leave her mind. "Aunt—" she started to say as she entered the kitchen before correcting herself. "I mean, Cook . . ."

Aunt Agnes turned to Sadie. Copper curls were piled atop her head. A few escaped as she moved before a large cast-iron stove, the flames inside warming the room until Agnes's pale cheeks flushed. "Lachlan isn't so formal that you can't call me Aunt. He'll not care whether you call me Aunt, Cook, or Lady of the Kitchen"—she smiled, and the freckles scattered across her face danced—"So long as his food is served on time and you work hard, Sadie. It's a good home here."

Sadie nodded. She knew her position was a coveted one.

Lachlan Asquith was a generous employer, and if her aunt hadn't been his cook, Sadie wouldn't be Asquith's new help. She did wonder, though, why the last kitchen maid had left. No one talked of her but in whispers, and Sadie wondered if it was to spare her feelings. Was the last maid—Betty, they'd called her—as skilled as her aunt? What did Agnes think of trading Betty, who she'd worked alongside for years, for . . . *her*?

"Now then, what did you want?" Agnes asked, interrupting her thoughts. "Did you get the huckleberries?" She turned to the stove, stirring a pot, then faced Sadie and the large worktable standing between them. Pastry dough waited on its flour-dusted wood for her.

"Plenty." Sadie lifted her shoulder, showing the basket hanging in the crook of her elbow. "I was just wondering why Easton and Weston picked such a miserable week for the party. I mean, if these storms are normal for spring . . . why not wait until summer?"

She didn't add that she thought their names were ridiculous. Easton and Weston. East and west. But from what she'd heard of them, she supposed the silly names suited the twins. She'd been told more than once how they were as opposite in personality as they were in their names even though they looked exactly alike. Having been there only a few days and her time spent mostly in the kitchen or the servants' quarters, Sadie had yet to see them herself and make her own judgment.

"The weather is strange this year." Agnes glanced to the back door, where a glass window rested in thick wood. Rain had started, pouring in sheets. The grounds out there would be covered in mud in no time if they weren't already. "Normally the spring storms have passed by now. It's not usual to have such a fierce one this late in the season." She wiped her hands on her apron, leaving snowy smudges across the coarse gray fabric. "But no matter, it'll be the fanciest engagement party Deighton has seen since Lachlan and Roslin." Agnes dipped her head, touched her heart. "Rest her soul." She reached beneath the worktable, bringing up a pale bowl and setting it next to the waiting dough. "I'm sure everyone will be talking about it for weeks, so"—she tipped her head to the basket hanging from Sadie's arm—"Let's make sure the food is highly praised. Dump the huckleberries in here."

And as Sadie poured the basket of dark berries into the clean white bowl, Agnes screamed.

The older woman clamped her mouth shut, her eyes flying between Sadie, the bowl, and the hallway.

"Child!" Agnes took a small step back, nearly bumping into the hot iron stove behind her, and dropped her voice to a whisper. "You've gone and plucked nightshade." Her gaze shot to Sadie's mouth, fear widening her hazel eyes until the black of her pupils nearly swallowed the ambers and olives of her irises. "You haven't eaten one, have you?" She leaned forward, her middle pressing into the table between them. "You haven't picked a bite for yourself while gathering them, right?" She stared at Sadie's lips.

Sadie brought a hand to her mouth, shaking her head, the word *nightshade* rolling and rolling and rolling through her thoughts. Her heart picked up, beating beneath her thin ribs until she felt its rhythm in her throat. She'd held nightshade. In her hand. A handful of sweet berries. That's all it would've taken.

"Why do they have nightshade growing in the greenhouse!" She stared at the shiny dark fruit.

Agnes' voice was low. "You went to the wrong greenhouse." She picked up the bowl, her calloused hands shaking.

A single berry fell to the wooden counter, rolling until it dropped onto the bricks at Sadie's feet. She bent, picked it up, and watched as dark juice stained her fingertips.

"Come. We need to get rid of this." Agnes cradled the bowl against her body and turned to the stove, opening its small cast-iron door where flames burned inside. "If anyone found out where you'd been, we'd both be looking for new employment." She tossed the berries into the fire. "No one can know about this."

"But we can't lie." Sadie swallowed hard, her throat bobbing. "It was an accident. Wouldn't they understand? You just said Mr. Asquith is agreeable!"

"No." Agnes' voice was hard. "They wouldn't. Lachlan may be easygoing about titles, but not about entering the poison garden."

"Poison . . . garden?" Sadie's attention flew between her aunt and the berry in her palm. "But . . . what if someone had seen me in there? I'd be caught in a lie. That would be worse!"

Agnes leaned across the table separating them. Her voice narrowed to a whisper. "*Did* anyone see you?"

"I . . . I don't know." Sadie shook her head. "I didn't pay attention."

"We'll assume no one did then." Agnes leaned back, her head tilted, spilling her copper curls over her left ear. "I think someone would've come by now if they had." She nodded, and Sadie wasn't sure if she were trying to convince herself or her. "I know you've your morals, Sadie, and that's good, but . . . it's not really a lie. We just . . . we just don't say anything at all." She stared at her, hazel eyes bright, burning. "You understand? No one can know."

"Know what?" A soft voice slid through the kitchen. It drifted along the air behind Sadie's right shoulder. And slipped icy fear into the warm room.

2
The Heiress

Afternoon
May 9th, 1910

The dark sky grumbled, matching Della's mood, as their car approached Asquith manor.

"Take the scowl off your face," her mother hissed. "You're twenty-two, not a child. Stop pouting like one." She straightened a large ruby ring, crowned with black diamonds, on her finger, dusting it off as if the polished stones needed it. "You're to be a lady with the name of this place soon. Can you not even pretend to be happy about it?"

Della wasn't sure why her mother took the time to reprimand her when the old woman's face mirrored hers. Her mother's lips pinched, turning downward and creasing the corners even more than they already were. Her eyes—a blue so dark they resembled the very bottom of the seas—narrowed on Della. Neither of their expressions looked fit for a party.

She turned to her mother, threading the emerald ribbon at her waist between her fingers. Della was draped in a silk gown that swept to her ankles. It was tight—too tight, accenting the curves at her waist rather than hiding them like her mother thought it would. Not that Della cared. She didn't care if her mother thought her too round or if Weston wouldn't be pleased with his fiancée or what anyone else thought about her. She only wanted out of this engagement, but her mother ground her desires underfoot as easily as a spent cigarette.

Della tipped her chin up, staring out the car window as they made their way down the long drive to the manor. "Why don't you marry the widower and be the lady of Asquith yourself then?" When she glanced to her mother, the old woman rolled her eyes.

"Can't you see I'm doing this for you? It's the perfect match. A second son who needs a fortune. And you need a name." She fluttered a hand. "Besides, Lachlan Asquith is still deeply in love with his dead wife." She leaned close. "Obsessively so, some say."

Della ignored her mother's gossip. Having been the center of talk more often than she'd like to admit, she hated her mother's backbiting words, her love of secrets.

"And on top of that," her mother went on, oblivious to the way Della's lips twisted at the conversation slithering through the car, "I'm too old to remarry." She glanced at Della from the corner of her eye, the same look that accompanied a complaint from her mother that Della was getting too old as well. *Spinster*, it whispered too loudly. "What a burdensome endeavor it would be at my age. I've grown much too independent for that life."

And that was Della's problem as well. She was more like her mother than either wanted to admit. Della desired the same freedom—to choose her own husband like her mother had, or to not choose anyone at all.

"I don't need the Asquith name," she said quietly, fiddling with the ribbon, tightening it around her finger then releasing it. Once. Twice. "You could just let me inherit without . . . *him*."

"And watch you grow old with no one but me?" Her mother shook her head, and her waves of buttercup-colored hair brushed shoulders wrapped in fox fur. "I won't be around forever. What a lonely life that would be, Della."

Della snapped her mouth shut even as words clawed to leave her tongue. They'd had this conversation already, and here it ended, with the two of them approaching Asquith manor during a storm that rumbled so loudly it rippled deep into Della's bones, electrifying her veins as surely as the lightning searing the sky.

"We're here." Her mother patted one jeweled hand over Della's. "Do try to look like you aren't attending your own funeral."

And with that, her mother exited the car, a footman opening the door and holding an umbrella out to her. A second servant appeared the moment her mother was gone, waiting for Della.

She took a deep breath and shimmied from the pale leather seats into a night that raged as much as she wished she could. Della straightened her spine, not yet willing to acquiesce to her mother's plans.

Just meet him, her mother had said. *Meet him and if he doesn't suit . . .* Her mother had lifted a shoulder, yet here Della was walking toward large wooden doors held open on either side by servants to meet Weston for the very first time . . . at their own engagement party.

Well, she'd meet him.

But that was it.

Rain splattered Della's arms, the edges of her silk gown, as she slipped out from beneath the umbrella and into Asquith manor behind her mother. Electric light danced along the entryway's walls while a candlelit chandelier hung overhead, warming the large space.

A small crowd stood before her, the flickering lights casting shadows long and short over their faces: an old man in a fine suit up front, servants in the back with their clothing pressed crisply, and to the right . . . two faces that mirrored each other more than Della's scowl matched her mother's.

Easton and Weston.

One of them—Weston, she assumed—stepped forward. Rich brown eyes trailed from her swept-back pale hair to her heeled slippers dusted with three small diamonds across the tops. Then his gaze met hers.

A smile slid from his mouth, and Della let out a forced breath, easing the grimace off her face that had taken up residence ever since her mother had first announced plans of marrying her off.

"Mrs. Drewitt." A voice like worn leather—cracking around the edges—broke the silence. "Happy to see you arrived safely despite this unusual weather."

The other twin peered around Weston, searching the door behind Della and her mother. "Now if only my bride would show up."

"Not to worry, Easton. Ms. Sutcliffe will be along shortly, safe and sound, as always, but we've guests here now." Mr. Asquith spread an arm out and turned to them. "Care to retire to your rooms for a bit after your long ride?"

"That would be lovely, Mr. Asquith." Della's mother smiled then glanced back at her, tipping her head to the younger twin as if Della could forget Weston stood beside her.

Della grinned, and hoped her lips remembered how to lift. "Thank you, Mr.—"

"Wes." He bowed slightly. "If we're to marry, I think it's safe to say you can call me Wes."

"It's Weston, not Wes," Easton muttered, then louder added, "You're an Asquith, not a farm boy."

Mr. Asquith cleared his throat with a slight shake of his

head at the twins, a scowl marring the space between his eyes. He turned from them to Della and her mother, smoothing out his features before smiling. His lips pulled tight until the already deep lines beside his mouth cut canyons into his skin.

"Never mind them." He cast one more quick glance between his sons before grinning at Della's mother. "You'll find us much more relaxed here at Asquith manor than the city permits." He bent, dipping his head down to reach her mother's height. "It's the country air." He looked back at Della, then with a wink turned to her mother. "Feel free to call us by our given names, Caroline."

"It's just Wes," the younger twin whispered, pulling Della's attention away from the way her mother smirked at Mr. Asquith. Della looked at Wes as he leaned close and added, "And it's not the air out here, but the lack of gossip columns in the papers." He winked, and a small, shy smile curled up one cheek.

"I'm glad for that," she answered as softly as he had so her mother wouldn't catch their conversation. "Mother loves gossip columns." Della paused, pursing her lips a moment. "But I hate them."

Wes nodded. "Have they not been particularly kind to you?"

Della tipped her head close to him. "They say we're scoundrels and could have only made our money through nefarious means just because we didn't inherit it. But my father worked hard." She leaned back, thinking. "And honestly." Watching the way his eyes skimmed over her, she added, "What do you say?"

Wes looked at her, and she stared back. His crisp black suit was as dark and orderly as his perfectly combed hair. "Why should I care how you became rich?"

She stepped away from him. "So long as I am rich, though." It wasn't a question, and as Della chipped the words from her teeth, her lips twisted as if the frown she knew so well would never leave her alone again.

Wes stepped forward with a sigh. "And so long as I have the Asquith name." He raised one inky eyebrow.

She didn't answer. For a moment, they watched each other. And Della didn't miss the clench in his jaw, the hardness of his spine.

"Come along," her mother said from where she and Mr. Asquith had already meandered to.

Wes offered her a rigid elbow, and she took it just as stiffly, while a fast grin still swooped across her mother's thin lips at the gesture. Della looked down, focusing on the creamy marble tiles beneath her feet, not wanting the satisfaction dripping from her mother to leak onto her.

They stepped down the narrow hall together, leaving Easton at the manor's entrance, presumably to wait for his fiancée, with the servants still lined up beside him to collect the bags.

Wes sighed again, and then tugged his free hand through his hair. "Sorry." He scratched the back of his neck. "It's not your fault I was born eight minutes too late."

Della pulled in a long breath, shrugged one shoulder. "And it's not your fault my mother won't let me inherit without your name."

Wes glanced down the long hall as his father opened a door at its end for the older Drewitt woman at his side. "Would she really keep it all from you?"

Della watched her mother sweep into the room Mr. Asquith had opened, and hoped she wouldn't be sharing it with her. She nodded. "And think she was doing me a favor."

Wes blew out a breath. "And here I was thinking my family was rather—" He shook his head. "Well, never mind. Come on."

Della didn't press him to finish. What did it bother her if his family was colder than hers? She wouldn't be joined to them no matter the name.

"Caroline"—Wes tipped his head to the open door—"Is

down here. Father thought it would be easier for her, no stairs and all."

As they passed her mother's room, Della caught sight of pale pink wallpaper and curtains like a snow-laced breeze, and then Wes was turning her away, facing the empty space across from her mother's room.

"Your room is up here." He motioned his free hand to the blank wall.

"But there's nothing—"

"Ah, but there is." Wes pressed on the white wood, and a seam spread out a moment before a door popped open. He dropped his voice until it was as low as a peal of thunder. "This house knows how to keep a secret." He turned to her and, sliding his arm from hers, motioned to the open doorway. "After you."

A spiral staircase waited in front of Della. "I hope only the kinds of secrets that would bore the gossip columns." She placed one foot on the iron treads.

"Ah, but what fun are those?" The clipped *thunk thunk thunk* of his polished shoes on the metal stairs followed Della up, sounding an awful lot like time ticking away.

A door handle waited for her at the top of the dimly lit stairs, and Della turned it slowly, brass against brass creaking in the small, claustrophobic place.

She pushed on it, and pale, storm-tossed light seeped into the stairwell from a window to the right. It opened up to another hallway with white walls and dark wooden floors.

"Your room is just there." Wes followed her into the hall, pointing to an oak door intricately carved with long stems, pointed leaves, and small flowers that drooped down as if they were bowing. "It was my mother's favorite room." He smiled as he opened the door.

Moody green walls greeted Della. A large bed with four posts, draped in swaths of fabric the color of burnt charcoal, sat in the middle of the room opposite a black-framed fireplace. Windows lined almost an entire wall to the right.

Della walked through the room and over to them, Wes following behind her.

"You can see the whole lake from here." He stepped up beside her, staring out.

"It's breathtaking." Della watched the storm thrash the water. Even in its violence, it was beautiful. The lake churned, stretching on and on, and crowded along its edges were woods, the trees at its far end mere dots.

"As are you." Wes turned from the view to her.

Della forced herself to stare at the water, to not roll her eyes. There had been many words used to describe her. Her father had called her *smart*, *perceptive*. Her mother liked to use words like *stubborn* and *rebellious*. The gossip columns wrote things like *plain* and *nothing special to look at*. Every single one had pierced her heart for different reasons.

But no one had ever used *breathtaking* before.

"You don't have to flatter." Della twisted to face her supposed fiancé.

"I wasn't."

She had no answer to that, but didn't trust the easy words he spoke either. She turned away from him, facing the fireplace.

"And . . . I am sorry." He paused. "For saying you only wanted my name." He took a small breath. "It was rude. Could you forgive me?"

Della wasn't sure what to say. It was true after all. Her mother wanted his name for her, and he wanted her money. There wasn't anything to forgive, but she nodded without turning around.

Wes must've seen it, though. He clapped his hands together once. "Well . . . this is your room for the week." He cleared his throat. "Do you like it?"

Della turned and stared at the black fireplace beside her. "It's lovely." A vase sat at one end of the mantel full of white roses, their petals like velvet and as ruffled as a bird's feathers. A wooden jewelry box painted in creams and golds waited on the other side. And in the middle, perched like a queen on her throne, was an odd glass box. "Wait. Is that . . ." She twisted around to Wes. He stood close to the room's door as if about to leave. "Is that . . . a . . . a heart?" A second glass box nestled close to the first, but empty.

She'd seen antlers scattered along the walls in the hallway downstairs, but a heart? A shiver split down her spine.

Wes nodded. "It was my mother's." He opened the door and stepped out but not before adding, "This *was* her favorite room."

And then he was gone, leaving Della to wonder if that was a human heart preserved beneath glass—his *mother's* heart—and who the empty box was for.

3
The Housemaid

Afternoon
May 9th, 1910

Violet slipped down the hall where the twins' fiancées would be staying, a bundle of linens filling her arms. She'd prepped two rooms, fluffed feather pillows and dusted stone hearths, even set out vases of flowers over stoked fireplaces. All for Eloise Sutcliffe and Della Drewitt, when it should've been for *her.*

At least in regard to the second twin's fiancée.

What did Della Drewitt have that she didn't . . . besides money?

She whispered the heiress' name, the four syllables scraping up her throat like a curse, souring her taste buds.

Violet had known from the moment she stepped into the manor three years ago that Eloise would one day be an Asquith. With her warm smiles and bubbling laugh and a face even more beautiful than Violet's, how could she not be? Especially since Eloise's friendship with the twins went all the way back to their childhood, before Violet had even heard of the Asquith name.

But Della Drewitt . . . she would have to trample over Violet to steal Weston from her.

She'd seen the heiress creeping out from the hidden stairwell with Weston—*her* Weston—on Della's heels.

Violet had almost dropped the bedding she'd so carefully folded when she'd stumbled upon the two of them together. Weston had *smiled* at Della, a girl who had no right to his grins.

Yet, despite the curl of his lips he'd given the heiress, now that Violet had seen Della, she had even more hope that Weston *would* choose her. Della might be rich, but she was plain—ashy-blond hair and eyes so watery blue they bordered on a dull gray, as if the stormy lake outside had gathered in her gaze.

And while Violet wasn't one to boast, she knew how the men in this manor had watched her the moment she'd opened its doors at nineteen. She'd stolen all the attention, from butlers to drivers to Asquiths. Well, not Lachlan's, who still mourned over Roslin—or Easton's. She'd never quite caught his attention, but he was the son set to inherit with a beautiful fiancée tucked into his arms. He'd been too high of an aspiration even for her.

But Weston, oh she'd snagged him with a single flutter of dark lashes, a quick pout of her heart-shaped lips. And honestly, Weston and Easton were so alike, even she couldn't tell the difference between them, so what did one over the other matter?

Except for the money.

Still, being on the arm of the Asquith twin that wouldn't inherit was far better than being their maid—folding their laundry, shining their silver, and setting out the tea trays every afternoon. It's why she'd rejected every other offer. Weston was the best opportunity, and she'd risk turning into a spinster if it meant gaining the Asquith name.

One week. That's all the time Violet had to scare Della Drewitt and her inheritance far away from Weston Asquith. Or convince Weston she was better than an heiress.

Violet opened a small closet and tucked the linen in her arms into it. She'd make the fiancées' beds tomorrow, with fresh sheets and blankets, all the while knowing it should be her in there, sipping rose tea in the afternoons and draping off Weston's arm in silk gowns every evening at dinner, pearls strung along her neck in long lines.

The soft *click* of a door at the other end of the hall snapped Violet's attention back to the fact that Weston was there, in the room that overlooked the lake—with the heiress. She ducked into the small closet, nearly closing herself in, leaving it open just enough for her to turn her head and peer down the hall through the wooden slats.

"This *was* her favorite room." Weston's voice trailed through the air like a wisp of smoke, reaching Violet and curling around her as if she could almost feel its warmth.

She wanted to run to him, fold herself in his arms and hear him say how he most definitely *didn't* want Della now that he'd met her, that he'd defy his father—for *her.*

But she stood still, remembering the first thing he'd told her when he had confessed to liking her.

Don't ever approach me. Wait for me to come to you.

The words had stung, at first. He'd had his arms wrapped around her waist and her lips still remembered the heat of his against them when he'd said it. She'd worried he would toss her aside one day because of those words, that she was something to keep hidden.

But then he'd explained why, and it had made sense. It wasn't because she was nothing more than a maid and he was an Asquith that forced them to stay quiet.

It was Della Drewitt's fault.

Or rather, Lachlan's push for him to marry her. Once Weston convinced his father he didn't need an heiress' money, he'd tell Lachlan. He'd promised.

Or, Violet supposed, if the old man died first, they could be together. And he was rather old. It was a possibility. Not that Violet hoped for his death. But still, he'd lived a long, good life, and wouldn't he be reunited with Roslin? He did still love her after all.

Violet shook her head, her black locks grazing sharp cheeks, and pushed away those thoughts as she watched Weston ease open the hidden stairwell's door once more.

But those small thoughts crept back, because until the old man died or Weston convinced him, she had to stay silent. She couldn't approach him first because—

What if it was my brother that you approached and not me? If he found out . . . he'd ruin us, my bird. He'd ruin this. You know he practically hates me. And she did know that. The twins grew increasingly more hostile toward each other as the years stretched. So she'd nodded, and Weston had leaned in then, set a soft kiss on her cheek, and reminded her it wouldn't be like this always.

And she believed him, so as quietly as he'd reassured her, she'd eased his mind and promised not to approach first, just in case. The twins *were* difficult to tell apart—the only difference between them she'd heard of was a small scar that Easton carried on his shoulder, and how was Violet to know who was who from that? She'd never even seen either of their shoulders.

But . . . surely it had been Weston leaving the Lake Room where Della lodged, so it was Weston heading down the hidden stairwell. Why would Easton be there? He should be downstairs waiting for Eloise or escorting her to her room if she'd made it here already.

Violet pushed open the closet door and stepped out, her

feet eager to run after Weston and let him know she was there, that maybe they could steal a few moments together before dinner started. Perhaps he would tell her that after meeting the heiress he was just as eager to run from her and her money as Violet wished him to be.

But a thought ticked through her brain, one she'd long been familiar with herself.

Money was a strong lure.

Violet worried her lip, her canine tooth popping out to snag soft skin.

She needed to convince him. Now.

Quickly, Violet slipped down the hall, her feet chasing after Weston, running to steal him back from Della Drewitt. She eased down the spiral staircase toward the main floor, expecting him to be there, just on the other side of the wall. She'd only hesitated a moment upstairs. He couldn't have gotten too far, but as she slid out from the hidden stairwell, only Caroline's cracked door greeted her. Had Weston stopped in there? Did he think of Mrs. Drewitt as his mother-in-law already? Would he talk about the engagement, make plans? Or . . . maybe he was breaking apart the relationship before it could even start?

Violet crept closer to Caroline's bedroom, and it was the howl of the wind that had her pushing the door farther, that made her peek inside.

The room was empty except for two large suitcases sitting near the foot of the bed, and though Mrs. Drewitt should've been resting after a full day of traveling before dinner, the old woman wasn't there. But neither was Weston.

A low fire crackled in the hearth. The small flames flickered as a cold breeze blew through the room, billowing white curtains toward an unruffled bed. Staccato raindrops slipped off the manor's roof and dripped down, the last bits of a storm already spent. Their irregular pattering tapped outside the open window and pulled Violet toward it, her curiosity pushing her along.

Night crept close, dragging a strong chill with it after the storm. Why would Caroline open her window to the cold while a low fire already fought to warm the stony walls and brick floors?

Violet peered outside, the curtains sliding across her shoulders as she did. Chickens pecked through the muddy yard with pigs waddling fat bodies behind as the churning lake slowly settled. Violet doubted a handful of farm animals were what caught Caroline's eye.

So what *had* stolen the Drewitt woman's attention in the gray evening when night hovered so close? And where had Caroline gone?

4

The Cook's Assistant

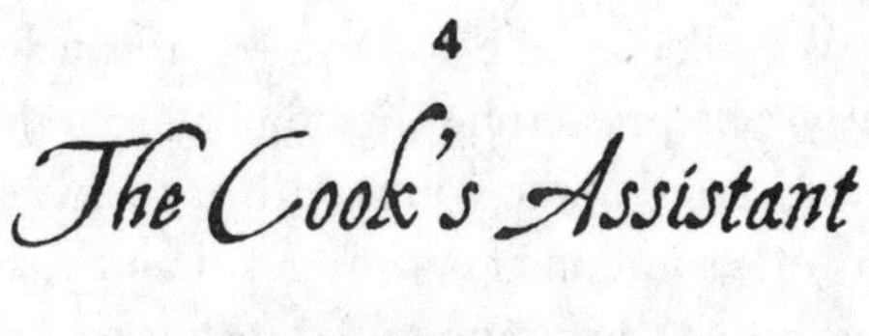

Afternoon
May 9th, 1910

"Know what?" the soft voice repeated again, and Sadie froze with the nightshade berry tucked within her palm.

The kitchen was warm. Too warm, as if the hearth's flames had escaped the oven to crawl across the stone floor and flick its tongues against the edges of her skirts—or maybe it was the fear rising within her chest, flushing her cheeks. She took a deep breath and slipped her closed fist into the folds of her skirt, hiding a berry that could kill a child—and wishing the heat building in her chest could burn away the evidence in her hand that she'd been in a garden filled with death.

Turning slowly, Sadie faced the voice, and found herself opposite a girl in a pale pink dress of flowing layers. Her hands grabbed fistfuls of fabric, balling the silken ruffles at her sides.

Lucy Asquith.

She mirrored the twins except, where Easton and Weston had inherited their father's jet-black hair, Lucy had Roslin's chestnut locks that curled softly at the ends. She had Lachlan's eyes, though, just like the twins—irises like roasted almonds warmed with honey.

"Know. What?" Lucy asked again, and her voice was hard, striking the two syllables like a crack—as if she were used to getting her way. She pressed her lips tightly together.

And, as Sadie stared at the young girl, as she watched Lucy's movements mimic someone far younger than the girl's fifteen years, Sadie supposed the youngest Asquith *was* used to getting whatever she wanted—at least here, in this manor. Elsewhere, well . . . that would be different.

Agnes stepped up to Lucy slowly, a lie slipping off her aunt's lips as easily as air. "That you've run away from your nursemaid, Lucy-dear. Your father won't be happy if he finds out." The older woman bent, her calloused fingers gently resting on Lucy's shoulders. Her aunt would look . . . maternal, concerned—if it weren't for the scarlet flushing Agnes' neck. If it weren't for the cream-colored bowl discarded on the worktable smeared with slashes of berry juice the same shades as ink and bruises.

Sadie had yet to meet Lucy Asquith, but she'd heard enough about the young girl to stay in her aunt's shadow.

"I don't—I don't need her!" Lucy's fists rose to the sides of her face, pressing against her cheeks. "I'm fifteen. I'm fifteen! I'm not a baby!"

Agnes patted her shoulders, pulled her in for a hug. "Yes, dear, but your father is still in charge and he says you need a nursemaid. I think you should go find her before you're both in trouble." Her aunt let go of Lucy and tipped her head down the long hall the girl had come from.

"I'm not . . ." Lucy's shoulders slumped, and her voice deflated in one breath. "I'm not a baby."

Agnes nodded, her copper curls bouncing. "I know."

"I'm not." She looked toward Sadie, staring at her hard with those cinnamon eyes.

"Of . . . of course not." Sadie took a step back, bumping into the worktable where the empty cream bowl tipped, rattling through the room until it settled again. She ignored it, faced the youngest Asquith. "Everyone knows you aren't, even me"—she pointed to herself with her free hand—"And I just got here." Sadie forced a smile, her lips stretching stiffly across her face as she tried to reassure the girl, as she tried to get her to leave. Her mind stayed on the berry hidden in her hand. They needed Lucy to go. They needed to get rid of all traces of the nightshade.

Lucy stared at Sadie's lips, at her too-tight smile. "I don't like you." The girl's eyes narrowed, staying on her a moment longer. "I liked Betty better." Lucy glanced toward Agnes, and then, in a quick movement, she turned without another word and ran down the hall, her pink skirts flapping behind her like kite ribbons.

Sadie sucked in a deep breath, let it out slowly. Her thoughts buzzed around the previous kitchen maid's name on Lucy's tongue. The girl was the first person to not whisper it, and as much as Sadie wanted to ask her aunt why no one but Lucy spoke of Betty, the poison in her hand stopped her. She needed to get rid of it, not worry about a maid that left for a better position or marriage. She discarded Betty, and Lucy, from her thoughts as easily as one throws out kitchen scraps and focused on the nightshade in her hand.

"You'll get used to her. She's . . ." Agnes sighed. "She's just . . . delayed a little, was born that way. She has her tempers, too, but only because Lachlan spoils her so much." Agnes shook her head. "The more he spoils her, the more her outbursts grow. She needs love—a little more than most, but she also needs to hear the word 'no' every once in a while. Shame that Easton wants to—"

"I'm not worried about her right now." Sadie held out her hand, uncurling her fingers slowly. She'd balled her fist carefully, but tightly, and now it felt as if her knuckles were cracking apart as she opened them. The deadly berry stood stark against her pale skin. "It fell."

Agnes' eyes widened, the ambers and olives in them seeming too bright in the storm-darkened kitchen. "Did any others? If Lucy found some . . . Just one could—"

"I know."

Agnes touched a hand to her heart, and as her aunt bent to search beneath the worktable, Sadie stepped over to the hearth, grabbing a towel and wrapping it around the oven's metal handle. She pulled it open, watching the flames move inside the cast iron, and then threw the berry in, let the fire devour it.

"I don't . . . I don't see any more." Agnes groaned as she stood upright again, her hands reaching to hold the small of her back.

"I only saw the one fall." Sadie grabbed the bowl, carrying it to the sink where she first scrubbed it and then her own stained skin until every last hint of dark nightshade was scoured away. She turned to her aunt after she'd finished and dropped her voice to a whisper. "Why do they have a poison garden?"

Agnes shook her head. "The better question is . . ." She glanced around, her eyes shifting to all the doorways to make sure no one was coming. "Who unlocked it?"

Sadie slipped back down the long hallway, treading to the heart of Asquith manor. She left behind the kitchen, her aunt, and their questions. Dinner was fast approaching, and she had huckleberries to gather still, and this time, she was sure to go to the right greenhouse.

The black-framed one, Agnes had sternly warned her. *Not Roslin's golden garden!*

Her aunt had given her instructions, but never did share why Asquith manor grew a greenhouse filled with poison. What if one of the plants in there had killed her with a simple touch? Sadie shuddered. And with Lucy running free, who would unlock such a dreadful place?

A thought slithered through her mind, one she tried to shake away, but it clung to her like too-wet dough sticking to her hands.

Had it been done on purpose? Did someone leave the poison garden unlocked so *she'd* go into it?

Sadie knew how coveted her position was at Asquith manor. She knew that if Betty hadn't left and if it hadn't been for her aunt, she wouldn't be there.

Was someone trying to get rid of her—by getting her fired for trespassing where she shouldn't have been . . . or had they hoped she'd eat the nightshade herself while picking them? Did someone want to be rid of her so badly they didn't even mind if it was by death? Is that what happened to Betty? Is that why the staff only whispered of her?

Anyone who'd seen the menu tonight knew there was to be huckleberry compote over cream-dolloped pastries for dessert. And it was a kitchen maid's job to gather them, not a head cook's.

Sadie gripped the basket in her hands, the old wicker cracking in the silence as she walked. Only the faint drumming of the last of the rain far outside competed with Sadie's soft, slippered steps on the aged brick floors.

As Sadie neared the greenhouses, the sounds of the dying storm rose and a single peal of thunder shuddered her bones. She flinched and tried to push away the thoughts of someone plotting against her.

She met the golden greenhouse first, just like last time, and crept over to it on soft steps. Looking around once, twice, she made sure no one was watching her. Her heart pounded. She should be telling Mr. Lachlan her mistake, not sneaking around, casting furtive glances up and down the halls, covering it up.

No one can know. The words slipped through Sadie's mind as she turned the handle on the thin wooden door that opened up to the golden greenhouse.

It was the right thing to do, she told herself. She wasn't covering up her own mistakes. No, with Lucy running around, Sadie had to make sure the poison garden was locked once more. It was for Lucy really, not herself.

Sadie glanced around the hall, hoping no one slipped out from behind one of the many doors that lined it as she opened the greenhouse. There were too many doors in this manor, and it seemed that at least half of them hid behind what pretended to be a regular wall. Sadie had to be quick. She never knew when someone might pop out.

As she pushed on the poison garden's door, it groaned open on rusty hinges, as if the greenhouse wasn't used to visitors. Had it creaked so loudly when she'd entered it earlier? She slipped her hand into the crack between door and frame, sliding her fingers to the inside knob, the brass cool against her too-flushed skin, and twisted the lock with a soft, small *click*. Quickly—quietly—she closed the door once more, letting out a slip of breath as it latched.

Now only whoever had a key could open it again, but knowing that only made more questions crawl through Sadie's mind. *Who has the key? Who unlocked it?*

And why?

The sound of wood groaning suddenly stole her attention.

Sadie spun around, her back pressed against the old wooden door, and took only two breaths before a deep voice said, "And what's a kitchen mouse doing so far from the hearth?"

5

The Fiancée

Early Evening
May 9th, 1910

Eloise Sutcliffe crouched at the edge of the churning water, her lacy black gown flowing across wet grass and dipping into the brink of Lammore Lake.

The rain had eased from its downpour, softening to a light mist, the thunder chased away with it. Not that she would have minded the storm. The dark weather suited her just fine. She longed to stand under the flood, to dance with the lightning.

A memory shot through her. Cold and gray and nearly at a year's distance, but sharp even at the edges. Another stormy day. The rain drenching her short dark curls. An Asquith twin with soft lips.

Eloise tossed the memory aside, letting it slip beneath the lake where it could drown under the water's weight.

She stepped into her small boat. It was tied to a wooden post at the lake's bank, a suitcase already tucked next to the seat inside it.

The dinghy shifted under her weight, rocking back and

forth on the gray water, the remnants of rain misting around her as she sat, settling on her shoulders like a shawl. Eloise wrapped herself in the fog, welcomed it. She knew the way. Didn't need to see to navigate across Lammore. Her heart was always tugging her to where Easton and Wes lived no matter where she stood. It had for years.

And she knew this lake better than she knew the Asquiths. Eloise belonged to Lammore. And it belonged to her. They'd grown up side by side. Lammore stretching its banks in inches as Eloise grew in feet. It had been there for all of her firsts: first steps and first swim, first picnic and first kiss. She'd shared her first heartbreak with Lammore, had whispered plenty of secrets to the dark water over the years. Eloise Asquith was the deepest hope she'd told the lake, but not the quietest.

Everyone expected she'd shed Sutcliffe for Asquith one day.

But no one, aside from Lammore, knew that it was the wrong brother giving her the name.

Eloise bent over the edge of her boat, dipping her hand into the black water. Her reflection stared back at her in muted colors, and she was surprised to find her eyes looking so hard. Plunging her hand in deeper, she cupped the water, pulling it back up and letting it glide through her fingers, saying hello. And then she whispered one more secret to Lammore. Eloise could trust the lake to keep it safe. She knew the lake would smother her words under its depths as surely as it could a lungful of air, not letting even a single breath of what she said escape.

Lammore was good at keeping secrets.

And Eloise was determined to make this one come true. Because it wasn't Easton with his wide grins and quick eye rolls and all the lies he twisted off the tip of a tongue—one he'd always held too tightly—that she wanted.

She'd known the Asquith twins since girlhood, long enough to know there was only one of them for her.

And that was Wes—the brother that adored his little sister, that had taught Eloise to hunt when no one else would. It was the boy she'd grown up playing cunning little games with, the kind only they'd enjoyed—half snooping, exploring, investigating, the other half a never-ending contest of who was cleverer.

It was the younger twin's small, shy smiles she wanted to keep, his soft, hidden heart she wanted to hold, and his sharp mind she needed to convince to want the same.

So, she whispered her secret and hoped the lake would hold it tight.

It's Wes I want, Lammore. At any cost.

Eloise tied her boat at the end of Asquith manor's long pier while the clouds above hung low and spent and gray. Even in heeled slippers and a dress that trailed behind her like a shadow, she climbed up the ladder easily, the worn wood as familiar to her as the lake.

Not a soul greeted Eloise under the darkened skies. Just the way she liked. She was less guest and more family, and the entire manor knew it. She came and went as she pleased.

Eloise reached down into her dinghy, grabbing the stuffed suitcase and hauling it up onto the old planks. The creak of its worn leather handle was her only hello as she crouched on the pier, the soft sloshing of Lammore's waters against the dock's posts playing in the background like Eloise's favorite song.

She stood upright, gathered herself, and turned to Asquith manor. The little beaten path that snaked its way to the kitchen's back door was long and muddy. Eloise scooped up her dress' train, hanging it over the crook of her elbow, and stepped lightly. Chickens, their inky black and rich brown feathers ruffled after hiding out from the storm, scattered at her feet. They squawked as she interrupted their foraging.

"Hello, Mattie and Flora." Eloise tipped her head to a cream-color hen. "Sophie. I see they haven't eaten you just yet." She squatted, setting her suitcase down in the mud and reached for the pale chicken. "Life is fast, especially for a meat bird, dear Sophie. I hope you're enjoying this beautiful day."

"Life *is* short," a deep voice said above Eloise as a hand reached down beside her. Fingers curled over the handle of her suitcase. "I . . . I hope you're also enjoying it."

"Wes." His name came out more of a whisper than she'd intended. She'd known she'd see him at some point, would have to face his fiancée at his side as well, but she wasn't ready. Not yet.

Though maybe this was her opportunity. Della Drewitt wasn't there, no one but Mattie, Flora, and Sophie to eavesdrop on anything she said to him, and they'd never minded her and Wes together.

A soft sound, like wood sliding against wood, stopped her. She stood up and glanced to the manor, searching for the source of it, making sure Della or Easton weren't around to catch her heart bleeding out before Wes. When she saw nothing but the long shadows of the manor and the pigs rounding the corner toward them, she turned back to him. His eyes snagged on hers, and she said nothing, only watched him. He didn't look happy, not like a fiancé should on the eve of his engagement festivities. And she supposed he saw the same thing in her. He knew her well, after all.

"Wes, it should be us." She took a step toward him, her arms longing to curl around his waist as they'd been so accustomed to. She ached to hug him, rest her cheek against his chest. She tipped her chin up instead, meeting his gaze. "It should be our names paired on the engagement papers."

Wes swallowed hard as if her words choked him. "El . . ." He stepped over to her, stopping only when she could smell him above the remnants of rain—notes of warmed vanilla and freshly cut cedar wood. "We—" He cleared his throat, his voice turning hollow, empty. "We talked about this."

Yes, they had. He'd broken her heart three months prior in the same place he'd first kissed her. And now Lammore held some salt in her fresh water, having gathered Eloise's tears and tucked them away for her.

Ninety days of Della Drewitt's name running through Eloise's thoughts.

"Let Easton marry *her*." She didn't say her name, didn't like how it haunted her. Of course, she didn't need to say it, though. Wes knew who she meant.

He shook his head, his black hair as dark as a nightmare under the gray skies. "He doesn't need an heiress."

"And you do?" Eloise stared at him.

Wes looked down, avoiding her eyes, twisting a polished shoe into the mud. "For now."

Hope—stupid, foolish hope—crawled into Eloise's chest, twisted under her ribs, and gripped the soft flesh of her heart. "*Now?* Are you playing a game, Wes? What does that mean? For *now*?"

His focus whipped to her, and he leaned close, bending down to reach her height, until she could see the flecks of honey in his chestnut eyes. "No, this isn't a game. Not this time, El. You're going to marry Easton Anthony Asquith." He said his brother's full name slowly as if it meant something, as if she'd want to hear it. "It's the only way forward for all of us."

"You don't mean that." Eloise didn't like the way her voice shook, or how, if she paused and listened closely, it almost sounded like another fissure was cracking in her chest—and that maybe that tender flesh under her ribs wasn't as soft as it used to be. "You love me. I know you do."

Wes took a step away, his back rigid. "Of course I do. I'll love you until my death and . . . even after. I'll never deny that."

"Then . . . why?" Eloise glanced around as if an answer might appear among the grass and mud and feathers. "Is it just for her money? I have some too. Nothing like *hers*, but . . . but, Wes, I have money."

He tore a hand through his hair, mussing the black locks. "I don't want to buy you, El."

She smiled—just a small thing that only turned up one corner of her mouth. "Technically, I'd be buying you, and honestly, I've no morals against that."

"You know what I mean." Wes hung his head, his shoulders dropping in the same moment. "This is serious." His voice was low, soft. "It's not a game this time."

Eloise stared at Wes, tried to read what he didn't say in his movements. "But it is *something*." Her words were clipped. "I know it." She took her suitcase from him and raced toward the kitchen door with a heat burning through her as hot and bright as the lightning that had pierced the sky an hour ago. "And, Wes," she tossed over her shoulder, eager, determined. He'd started another game, and she'd puzzle out which rules he was playing by. She'd always been as clever as him. This time she'd prove it. "I'm going to figure it out."

6

The Cook's Assistant

Early Evening
May 9th, 1910

Sadie faced an open stairwell that hid itself within a wall across from the golden greenhouse.

An Asquith twin emerged from it, the shadows leaving the hard planes of his face slowly. "Shouldn't you be by the hearth, kitchen mouse?" He watched her, marking the way her feet shuffled.

"J-just coming to collect some huckleberries for dessert, sir." Sadie held up the empty wicker basket in her hands as if that were enough proof that she wasn't lying, that she hadn't been tampering with the poison garden's door—even if all she'd done was lock it. Would he believe her if she explained? How much had he seen?

"Weston." He smiled, broad and wide, taking a step toward her. "*Sir* belongs to my father, and then I suppose it'll be my brother when he's in charge of this place." His smile shifted, turning more smirk than grin, and Sadie wasn't sure just what history tucked itself in that small movement of his lips.

"Weston," she simply repeated, not knowing what else to say.

"And you are?" He stepped toward her, crossing the short hallway, his eyes staying on her as he neared.

A tremble ran down her spine, and she wanted to shake it off, to stand tall, but worry clung to her bones, making her wonder if he wanted her name to turn her in to his father. Would her aunt also be in trouble for her mistake? Sadie's fingers tightened on the basket's handle, and the wicker creaked under her grip, the only sound besides Weston's measured steps as they echoed off the worn bricks.

"Sadie." She finally relented.

He moved closer, not stopping until he was inches from her. Sadie scooted away until her back pressed against the golden greenhouse's wooden door once more. Her breathing was too erratic for someone who was innocent, and she hoped Weston didn't notice. She pulled in a purposefully long breath, let it out slowly, slowly, slowly.

His attention stayed on her as if he missed nothing.

"You're at the wrong garden for huckleberries, little kitchen mouse." His voice was deep, careful, and his dark eyes never left her. He scanned her—from pale copper curls to gray dress and white apron, then down to her polished black shoes. She wasn't sure what he was looking for. Could he see nightshade stains on her hands? Had she not washed it all away?

"Just—"

"This one is always locked." He reached out, his fingers skimming her arm before he grabbed the handle and twisted it. It clicked, the brass catching brass. "See." And then he let go, placing his hand on her elbow instead. "You can't get in. Here . . ." He guided her down the hall until they faced a second door, and as he opened it, the difference between the two greenhouses was easy to spot. This one was made of hard lines and black metal, thick glass and the fresh scent of life—no hint of cloying poison hanging in the air. But then, no sickly-sweet smell had saturated the golden greenhouse either. Only the soft scents of newly turned dirt and delicate growth had greeted her there. So deceptive. Such a strange blossoming of life in a graveyard garden.

Sadie shook her head, flinging thoughts of Roslin's poisonous plants far from her mind. She still didn't want to believe she'd walked into a waiting cemetery hidden behind velvet petals and tender foliage. *Why do they have a poisoned garden?*

And who unlocked it?

The questions clung to her.

"Huckleberries, you said?" Weston asked, jarring her back to her chore.

He stepped onto a path covered in small rocks. The greenhouse was expansive, stretching out and out, larger than any outdoor garden she'd seen even, but that was the Asquith way it seemed—grand and odd and greater than she could've imagined. No wonder she'd mistaken the poisoned one for the right place. It had looked like a greenhouse should. This . . . this indoor garden sprawled as if it were another wing of the manor. How many different plants must grow here.

Sadie stepped down the path, following Weston. Every few feet new rock-strewn aisles intersected theirs, cutting across. The trees bent over them, crowding with long limbs, fresh fruit, and dew-covered leaves until the pathways narrowed and Weston slowly disappeared from her view, the plants seemingly overtaking him.

"Here they are," his voice called out, and Sadie followed it, finding him standing beside a small shrub with little green leaves and dark fruit that, to her eyes, looked very much like the nightshade she'd picked earlier.

"Are you sure it's huckleberry?" *Are you sure it's not nightshade?* she really wanted to ask.

Weston plucked one of the dark berries, popping it into his mouth. "Of course." He picked a few more, cradling them in his palm before stepping over to Sadie and dropping them into her basket.

She joined him, and they worked in silence for a few moments as her basket slowly filled.

"You're new, aren't you?" Weston asked, letting another handful spill into the fraying wicker. He stayed by her side, not moving to the huckleberry bush for more.

She nodded in response, her pale curls dancing around the sides of her face.

He smiled, a quick smirk that was somehow wide across his face. "You're very pretty."

Sadie's hand stopped over her basket, berries waiting to tumble in. "Sir?" She didn't look up.

He stepped close, the toes of his polished boots only inches from touching her shiny black shoes. "You must know it."

The scent of him surrounded her—hints of aged oak and traces of rich tobacco—drowning out the softer smells of the garden. She shuffled her feet, inching away, and shook her head, keeping her gaze on the rocky path, anywhere but up where she could feel his eyes on her. "You're engaged, sir—"

"Weston. Not sir. I told you my name. Please"—his voice softened—"Use it." And before she could respond, his fingers were on her chin, tipping her head up. "Eyes like honey and jade"—he leaned close, his breath on her cheek—"And lips like cherry blossoms."

Sadie swallowed hard. "You're engaged. You shouldn't be saying such things."

"Engaged to someone who doesn't even want to marry me." He tipped his head, watching her, his black locks smooth and combed down into place, not moving an inch. "Even as a second son, I could have a lot to offer to *you*, though."

Sadie shook her head, and his hand slipped from her chin. "None of this is my business, sir. I'm just a kitchen maid. And"—she held the wicker basket up, placing it between them, and stepped back—"I've enough berries now. I should go."

She twisted around, but Weston's hand caught her elbow, and he spun her back until she faced him once more. Without a word, he pressed his lips to hers, and Sadie froze—her body stiffened, her mind went blank—as if ice had spread its biting touch through her veins, crystallized her nerves, numbed even her thoughts.

He pulled back slowly and whispered, "Think about it."

And as her mind thawed, Sadie thought she heard a door slam in the distance. Weston's head whipped to the sound as he turned to go, but he glanced back once, leaving behind a broad grin for her.

7

The Heiress

Evening
May 9th, 1910

Delicate goblets rimmed in gold and thin dishes the color of snow lined a long table as Della walked into the Asquiths' dining room. The walls were a deep mossy green, which only served to highlight the brass accents scattered throughout. A large electric chandelier hung low over the table, casting warm light across faceted glasses and porcelain dishes. Only the wall behind the head of the table broke the muted green surrounding the place. There, the lake waited behind windows that stretched from floor to ceiling. No matter where Della went in the manor, it seemed the lake followed her, watching through thick panes. There was always a glimpse of the gray water. It had settled since she'd arrived—less choppy and more serene like silvery silk spread out flat.

Rather than make the dark room drab, the view seemed to complement it, letting the gold bits shine, giving Della the feeling that she'd stepped into a gilded forest rather than a dining hall. Everything in there was fragile and exquisite—just like her mother liked. And moody—which Della found herself quite enjoying. But as much as the room stole her attention, her gaze kept drifting back to the Asquith twins walking in front of her. She scanned them, testing each twin against her meeting with Wes earlier, but she couldn't seem to tell which was her fiancé and which was Easton. Both with dark hair parted on the right and brushed over. Both in the same black suits with matching shirts beneath. Both with the same cut of jaw, golden-brown eyes, and slim build. Nothing between the two for Della to differentiate who was who, aside from some specks of mud dotting one of their shoes, she supposed. But little good that did her.

"Wes will be across from you," a soft voice whispered from her left.

"Was it so obvious I couldn't tell?" Della turned as she took her seat to find another woman about her age sitting down on her other side. "Ms. Eloise Sutcliffe?" she guessed.

She nodded, short curls bouncing with the movement. "You must be Della. Call me El." She smiled softly, and it was clear to Della why the Asquith heir was engaged to her. Eloise was beautiful and lovely and everything Della wasn't. Rich, dark brown eyes; smooth skin that looked as if she'd grown up tutored by the sun; lips like rose petals in bloom. As opposite to Della as anyone could be. Not that she'd hold Eloise's looks against her. "Everyone has a hard time telling them apart, but especially at first."

Della glanced across the table as the twins settled into their seats. "I don't know how I'll ever figure it out."

Eloise shrugged and thin black lace stretched across her shoulder. "It's not so hard if you know them. To me, they look nothing alike."

Della softened her voice, not wanting anyone else to hear her. "But I heard not even their father can tell them apart."

Eloise shook her head, a sad smile playing on the corner of

her mouth. "Only because of his eyesight now. Lachlan used to be able to make the distinction more easily than anyone, even me."

Della turned to the twins, studying them. Easton—across from Eloise—watched his fiancée with a smile stretched across his face while Wes's attention was on the doors as if he waited for someone else, as if she—his fiancée—didn't sit opposite him. She turned back to Eloise, ignoring Wes. It didn't matter if he wouldn't look at her like Easton did Eloise—with a softness in his eyes. She didn't want to be tied to Wes any more than he wanted to be tied to her.

The candles lining the center of the long table flickered, a gust of wind shaking the golden flames as the dining room doors opened.

Eloise smiled as a girl swept into the room, her pink dress floating like clouds around her as she moved, settling only when she stopped beside Wes.

"Lucy." He smiled, a small thing that somehow lit up his whole face, reaching all the way to crinkle the corners of his dark eyes. "Here you go." He pulled out the chair beside him, and Lucy dropped into it with a flounce.

"You're late," Easton said, arching around Wes to see her. "As usual."

Eloise tipped her head to Della. "That's their little sister. If no one's warned you, she's—"

"Perfect." Wes stared at Eloise, his gaze harder even than when Della had argued with him at their first meeting. He smoothed his features, turning to his sister. "Perfect timing, I mean, Lucy."

And with that, Mr. Asquith raised a finger, motioning for the servants to step forward. They placed dishes onto the table before everyone—rich squash soup with browned butter, topped with bits of sage, steam rising from it in slow curls.

"What are the plans for tomorrow?" Eloise asked, her voice carrying down the long table as gilded spoons were picked up and the guests dug into the first course.

"A hunting party." Wes kept his head down, not looking at Eloise as he responded, but Della noticed a smile tucked in the corner of his mouth.

"Oh?"

A small twitch of Eloise's lips—not quite a grin—wove its way onto her face as Wes looked at his brother and asked, "How many grouse did you get last time, Easton? I can't remember."

The older twin sighed, his focus on his soup. "Six."

"How many did you get, El?" Lucy sat forward, her bowl pushed aside and forgotten.

Wes put an arm around Lucy. "She got twelve."

Della's mother's head whipped toward Eloise. "You?" Her voice was hard, and then it stretched, rising in pitch with each word. "You hunt? A lady?"

Eloise shrugged with a slight nod as Wes answered, "She's very good at it too. The best of us, I'd say."

"And how many did you get, Weston?" Easton asked as a growl laced itself around his brother's name, hardening the two syllables.

"One," Wes answered with a smile, unbothered by his twin's glare. "El got them all."

"Only because of you, Wes." She dipped her spoon into her soup, taking a small bite, her eyes cast down, away from either Asquith brother. "You . . . taught me well."

Easton rolled his eyes, but Della ignored them all as a thought ticked through her—one of glass and gold and a stone heart that sat within it. She hadn't forgotten the hardened flesh in her room, or the empty glass box waiting beside it, no matter how much she'd tried to push it from her mind. It stuck to her. Clung like a cold sweat, coating her thoughts with questions.

"Did Mrs. Asquith hunt too?" Her voice was light, but the weight of her words lodged in her throat. "Deer perhaps?"

"Roslin . . . hunt?" Mr. Asquith set his spoon down and sat back, his fingers worrying a ring on his right hand. "No, no. She much preferred to see the life in things." He twisted the ring again. "She loved to garden."

Dread threaded through Della's veins like tendrils of ice. Fear like frost laced her warm blood. She tried not to think of the heart in its little glass coffin, but Wes's words wound in her thoughts.

It was my mother's.

Not a hunting trophy like she so very much had hoped.

Not if his mother hadn't hunted.

Servants stepped forward, bearing new plates, but they couldn't distract Della from the box of glass. The gold edges and rigid heart. She stared at Wes, wanting him to turn to her, to say how his mother really did hunt, how she kept a small, calcified heart as a prize like one would antlers. It was odd, but the alternative was far worse.

But he never looked at her as he took two plates, setting one in front of his sister and the other before himself. And as a dish was placed at her spot too, she hardly noticed the cooked bird, the accompanying herbs. Her stomach twisted. Hard, hard flesh that no longer beat consumed her mind.

It was my mother's.

The words hovered in her thoughts.

And the heart waited in her room.

A loud clatter cracked through the dining hall, pulling Della back to the table and away from the nausea curling through her stomach.

Lucy's plate fell, smashing against the floor. Roasted meat and sautéed mushrooms splattered the hardwood as the candles flickered, their flames nearly dying, trying to drench the room in darkness.

And then a high-pitched scream pierced the air. The room chilled as a shiver shot up Della's spine.

8

El

Three Years Earlier
Autumn 1907

"You have to be quiet, okay?" Wes stood still, tilting his head, listening to the breeze while his sharp eyes scanned the forest.

Eloise froze beside him, only letting a small nod slip free as she mimicked his movements.

The air was warm, the gun in her hand cold—as unfamiliar to her as a handshake. The cool metal was cigars and smoke, not the curtsying or teacups or spritzes of perfume she was used to. But she was grown now. Nineteen and nearly a woman. She wouldn't let a bit of brass and metal and an alabaster handle scare her.

"Thank you, Wes." Eloise kept her voice low, not letting the wind carry her words. "For gifting me this." She nodded toward the gun. "For doing this." She glanced to the forest.

"Why wouldn't I?" He toed the ground with a scuffed-up boot. From his head to his feet, he was shades of brown and green—khaki pants and a plaid shirt the exact colors of moss and sage and peppercorn black; a hat like burnt mahogany sat atop his black hair; a long, sleek gun with an oak handle was slung over his arm; and a dark bag stained with deep brown splotches draped his chest.

"Easton wouldn't."

"Easton might not do much of anything unless he gets something out of it, but I think he would consider this"—Wes glanced at her—"To be in his favor, El." His eyes trailed over her.

Eloise straightened under his stare. She wore an old pair of his pants in a dark olive and a loose button-up shirt the pale shade of creamed coffee. Even after a few years of gathering dust in his closet, the smell of Wes permeated the clothing, wrapping her in fresh cedar and aged vanilla.

"Did you ask him?" He arched one dark eyebrow.

Eloise shook her head.

"Hm." Wes glanced past her. "Well, I bet he's out here somewhere anyway, watching to see how you do."

Eloise spun slowly, searching the forest, but everything was the colors of earth—sage and cinnamon and sunlit beams—no sign of Easton lurking in their midst.

"He likes you, you know?" Wes shifted to her, scanning her face, and she wondered what he read in the downward turn of her mouth, in the pinch of her brows and the soft closing of her eyes.

"I know." She sighed, wishing he could hear all the words she wanted to tell him in that small slip of her breath. She looked at him, wondered if maybe he did know.

"You don't feel the same?" Wes stepped forward, avoiding the dead leaves that would crunch beneath his hard boots. "He's not bad. A little selfish sometimes, but—"

"No." Eloise stepped close to Wes, watching him as he watched the forest, unaware of the way she ignored the stout trees, draping vines, and rustling leaves, drinking in only him. "I don't."

Wes focused on the brush gathered around the edges of the

tall oaks and thin pines without glancing her way. "He says he's going to marry you one day."

Eloise's grip tightened on the cold gun in her palm. "That's not going to happen." Could he not see? Like petals blossoming, her heart had unfolded for *him*. And him alone.

"Why not? You're practically family already." He scanned the forest, never looking her way, never seeing how it was him she leaned toward, how it was him she longed for. "Is there someone else?"

Eloise laughed, a bite sharpening it into a hard, barking sound. "Can you not s—" Something staggered from the brush.

"There!" Wes lifted his gun and a loud shot split the forest, sending sulfur and smoke pluming into the air, trailing along the breeze.

Silence hung in the woods, and then Wes lowered his gun and stepped forward. Twigs cracked beneath Eloise's feet as she followed him. He stopped near a bush, reached his hand in and drew it back out with a dead grouse hanging by its feet, its head limp, its brown beak pointed toward the earth.

"See, that's all you have to do." He tucked the bird into the stained bag he wore then held his hand out to her, palm up. "Your turn now. Trade guns with me."

Eloise stepped back. "But . . . I like the small one better." She eyed the long gun nestled in the crook of his elbow, felt the curves of the handgun's alabaster handle in her palm. "And you did give me this one."

He shook his head. "You can't hunt grouse with that."

"Why not?"

"I got you that gun for protection out here." Wes flicked his fingers toward himself twice. "It shoots just a single bullet. This one"—he lifted his arm where the long gun rested—"Is a Winchester. The ammunition breaks apart, spitting pieces across a broader area. You're more likely to hit a bird with it."

Eloise glanced to the metal in her hand, then the Winchester Wes held. "Can't I just start with this small one and work my way up to . . . that?" She took a step away, pulling herself and the handgun out of his reach.

Wes shrugged. "I'm not forcing you here, El. You don't have to use either." He tipped his head to her hand. "But I'm telling you, you're not going to hit anything with that."

Eloise smiled, a quick and sharp thing that always reared itself when he dared her. "I'll take that challenge, Wes." Her lips curled higher. "And win."

She turned from him, and they walked in silence as Eloise scanned the woods for movement.

Minutes slipped by with the sun dappling the forest floor, shading everything in a golden haze. A rustling behind Eloise, just to her right, had her spinning around to find a thicket of trees moving a smidge too harshly to be the breeze. A flash of brown and she raised her gun.

"There," she whispered, her heart beating a fierce rhythm as she aimed, so opposite to the slow chatter of the forest life carrying on around her.

With shaking fingers and adrenaline spiraling through her veins, Eloise pulled the trigger at the exact moment Wes yelled, "Wait!"

And only in the silent heartbeat that followed did she realize she'd shot too low for a grouse.

Wes glanced at her once, his pupils far too big, the black swallowing the dark brown in wild fear. An exhale—that's all it took before he tore the gun from her hand and disappeared, crashing through the forest, his boots leaving a scar on the earth.

Eloise chased after him, Wes's panic swelling around her, spilling off him and drowning her until it seemed as if her lungs couldn't pull in a full breath.

And then his words hit her a moment before he skidded to a stop and curled over the ground.

I bet he's out here somewhere, watching to see how you do.

Wes's body blocked most of her view, but not the legs spread across the grass, one knee bent with a foot pressing hard into the ground—or the way Easton hissed curses between ragged breaths.

"Is he . . . is he okay?" Eloise set a shaking hand on Wes's back and pivoted until red splashed her vision.

Blood soaked Easton's chest, sticky and too much, and Eloise froze, unable to inch closer or help, unable to run away and spill her insides on the forest floor.

Wes's hands moved, ripping fabric and swiping away blood. "It's . . . it's okay. You'll be okay. It hit your shoulder." He took a deep, deep breath, and then, almost to himself, mumbled, "It wasn't . . . it wasn't his heart."

"Did you do it on purpose!" Easton shot the words through clenched teeth, his eyes darting from his brother to the discarded guns beside Wes. They all knew Wes was an excellent shot, couldn't have mistaken a person for a grouse like she had. But the three of them were friends, coconspirators, as close as two women gossiping. Only recently had Eloise looked for opportunities to seek out Wes alone, to leave Easton behind. Wes never would've shot his brother on purpose. It didn't make sense for Easton to think that. Except . . . Wes *was* a perfect shot. And the younger brother. And it had always chafed him to not inherit.

If Easton thought Wes had been the one to shoot . . .

Eloise had to say something before more accusations hit, before Easton's words sidled past Wes's panic and sunk into his bones.

"It wasn't him." Eloise's voice trembled, her confession clinging to her tongue, scraping along her throat.

Easton screamed, rough and low, drowning her out, as Wes took a strip from the end of his shirt and pressed it into the wound.

"Haven't you done enough, taken enough?" Easton clenched his teeth, the words sliding through like a hiss.

Wes stilled, his shaking hands the only movement. "What?" The bloodied cloth trembled in his grip, and he cocked his head as if he were just now hearing all his brother's words and wondered where they'd come from.

Easton's eyes flicked from Wes to her—just for a moment—and in that second, Eloise knew.

Easton meant *her.*

He hadn't been talking about greed, but of her.

She was putting a wedge between them. Not their inheritances.

Her voice shook as she tried again, as she sliced the confession off her tongue. Eloise couldn't help her feelings for Wes or Easton's for her, but she could stop the rift pulling Easton from his brother from ripping further. She let the confession fall from her tongue like a prayer. "It was—"

Me, she tried to say, but Wes cut her off.

"An accident. It was an accident." Wes sat back, his hands covered in his twin's blood. "I didn't mean to." He put out his palm, waiting for his brother to take it, waiting to help him up.

Easton shoved him away. "I don't need you. You've done plenty enough already." His eyes shot to Eloise again, staying too long before he turned back to Wes.

And then his voice dropped, as dark as sin. "I won't forget this."

9

The Housemaid

Evening
May 9th, 1910

Lucy's scream shot through the dining hall, echoing against the clatter of her plate as it crashed to the polished floor.

Violet flinched, nearly dropping the desserts she held. Thin porcelain plates rattled against the thick metal tray in her hands.

Mr. Asquith was on his feet in a moment, the seventy-one-year-old moving faster than Violet had seen in years. "Are you hurt?" His wrinkled hands trembled in the air beside Lucy as if he were searching for an injury. "What's wrong?"

"Mushrooms." Lucy pointed to her food splattered across the ground. "Mushrooms!"

Lachlan turned to Violet and the other staff lining the room's wall, his voice low and angry. "Who put mushrooms on her plate?"

"Sir, if I may." Violet stepped forward. "There's a new kitchen maid. Perhaps she . . ." *Perhaps she shouldn't be here*, is what Violet wanted to say, but she held her tongue, letting her words hover in the air and find their way into Lachlan's thoughts where he could realize it himself. Sadie Fischer had no business being in Asquith manor.

"Call her here at once—"

"Father, wait." Weston lifted his plate, where roasted pheasant dripping in beurre monté sat next to a side of pappardelle and pancetta . . . missing the wild mushrooms sprinkled within. "I grabbed the wrong one. It's my fault." He glanced at his little sister, and his father's gaze followed.

Lucy sat in her chair, rocking back and forth, her hands on the sides of her face and her eyes squeezed tightly shut.

"Next time, let the servants serve, Weston." Easton's voice was dull, bored, as if he were used to Lucy's outbursts. And, Violet supposed, he was. Even she'd noticed that the youngest Asquith's eruptions were more frequent these days. *Just the changes in the household*, Lachlan would say. *What with the boys getting engaged. She's not used to all the fuss.*

"Don't you think it's time, Father?" Easton stared at Lucy for a long moment before he turned to Lachlan. "She needs—"

"How about you have dessert in your room and skip dinner." Weston's voice was sweet, but his eyes were hard—turning the cinnamon shade to a fiery cedar—as he slid them from Lucy to his brother.

Violet stepped forward with her tray, wanting to help Weston, wanting to show him that she would side with him. She would give him her loyalty, even in something so small.

"Wonderful idea, isn't that, Lucy?" Lachlan lifted a finger, motioning for Violet.

She set the dessert tray down on a side table and picked up a single porcelain dish, bringing it to Weston instead of Mr. Asquith. He took it, and she waited a moment, as he held on too, hoping he'd look up at her, smile . . . something. But his attention was split between his little sister and the large grandfather clock tucked into the corner of the room. It was a looming black thing with gold lettering that told Violet it was still too early for dessert, but she would help Weston's idea anyway, and as she reluctantly let go of the plate, she reminded herself that it wouldn't be much longer. She and Weston wouldn't have to hide forever. One day, she'd be on his arm, sitting at the table, not hoping for a single moment of eye contact in a crowded room.

Violet picked up her tray again and walked back to her spot along the wall, barely noticing as Lucy's nursemaid came in and left again with the youngest Asquith in tow. She stood in silence as the family and guests ate, dreaming of the day she'd join them. Their conversations hovered around her, but it was a murmur in the background of her thoughts. Their discussion couldn't compare with the dreams swirling through her head—ones of lace like frost flurrying over her shoulders, of sparkling drinks in thin glasses, of glittering gems like rust and coal scattered along her fingers.

Only when Weston yelled, "You can't!" did Violet gather herself enough to see why the temperature in the room seemed to boil over with those two short words.

"She needs to be in a place that can help her more than we can." Easton dug into his food, his fork stabbing more than necessary.

"We're her family. *We* are who can help her the best." Weston swallowed hard, his teeth clenching, the muscles along his jaw tightening.

"But we can't, can we?" Easton threw an arm out to the doors where Lucy had disappeared. "Look at her. Look what's happening." He turned to Lachlan. "There's a place in the city. I've looked into it—"

Eloise cleared her throat, staring at Easton. He glanced to her and closed his mouth, and before anyone else could say more, Lachlan spoke up.

"Perhaps this conversation would be better had at another time." Lachlan tipped his head to their guests where Della shrunk back, curling in on herself like a flower wilting.

Her mother, though, watched the twins' conversation like a tennis match, her deep blue eyes bouncing between the brothers and looking as if she were tucking their words into her pockets like stolen candies. Violet's thoughts slid back an hour earlier when she'd crept into Caroline's room and the old woman hadn't been there. Had Mrs. Drewitt simply been snooping through the manor for gossip? She certainly looked like she gobbled up secrets like sweets. And Asquith manor had plenty for her to swallow.

"How about dessert?" Lachlan said, turning to Violet and pulling her attention back to the dining room and away from the smirk curling Caroline's thin red lips.

She stepped forward again, the tray in her hands and the plates tinkling against the metal as she walked. It was the only sound in the tense room until Easton—in a quiet, low voice—said, "When I'm in charge, she's getting the help she needs."

Weston—closest to Violet—swiped a porcelain plate off her tray, and she wondered how it didn't shatter in his clenched hand. "Not if I can help it," he murmured so softly she was sure no one else had heard him.

As much as she wanted to linger beside Weston, Violet tugged herself away to pass out the rest of the desserts. One by one, little white plates edged in blue cornflowers disappeared from her tray. Cream-filled puff pastries topped with a huckleberry compote and drizzled in wild honey waited before the guests, and though the dessert was light and sweet, the room was anything but. A heaviness hung in the air after Easton's words. A tension stretched through the room like a growing fire, consuming the guests and suffocating them in an uneasy silence.

And then a second crash of delicate dishes had every single head, including Violet's, whipping to the noise.

Weston hunched over, his breaths slow and labored. Ink-black hair splayed across the table where his head had landed, and midnight pupils nearly swallowed his chestnut eyes as he stared at . . . nothing.

Violet wanted to run over to him, pull him to her, find out what was wrong. But a maid didn't touch an Asquith. And it was already too late. Lachlan stood. Easton joined him.

A crowd gathered beside Weston, dresses and jackets fluttering around him like a flock of ravens.

They blocked Violet's view. The only thing left to see was Weston's lone dessert plate on the floor. Shards of porcelain jutted out between his half-eaten pastry. She stared at the splattered compote as a chill slithered down her back. It was too dark for blood, but as a heeled foot rushed through it, black lace trailing behind and smearing the thick syrup across the floor, it lightened just enough to remind Violet of spilled blood. She kept her focus on it rather than searching for Weston through the bodies.

A chill dripped through her veins, and she stood motionless. And even though she knew he wasn't dead—not when his ragged breathing echoed through the room—the vacant stare when Weston's head had hit the table froze her. She couldn't move, couldn't bring herself to see why he'd collapsed like an old rag doll.

Only when Easton's fiancée whispered three small words—so softly they were nearly a caress—did Violet manage to rip her gaze to where Eloise curled over Weston. Her words traveled the room as slow as smoke.

"No, not again."

10

El

One Year Earlier
May 1909

Eloise crept down one of Asquith manor's hidden hallways, glancing over her shoulder every few steps to make sure Wes wasn't following her. She wouldn't win their game if he were discovering her secrets as quickly as she did his.

And she intended to beat him for once.

The passageway was dark, but she dared not risk a candle drawing Wes to her like a meddlesome little moth. He'd have to flutter around his own gloomy hall. Eloise was good at a lot of things, but sharing wasn't one of them, not when pride wrapped itself around their prize like a bright red ribbon.

She cracked open a door she'd never dared to before, hoping no one else was slinking around Lachlan's study, especially Mr. Asquith himself. He didn't take kindly to snooping.

It was as dark as the hidden hallway in the old stuffy room, except for the last bits of sunlight streaming in through a pair of thick velvet curtains that were as stark as a snowfall. The sun's orange glow gave a warm haze to the place, lightening the somber green walls to a rich moss.

No movement stirred the study aside from Tux, who had followed Eloise through the maze of hidden halls. Wes's cat had taken to shadowing her everywhere she went. He slipped between her feet, his black tail curling along one of her ankles as he waltzed into Lachlan's study like he was lord of the manor himself.

She followed him, stepping lightly into the room and being sure not to disturb the piles of papers Lachlan had strewn across his large oak desk. She glanced at them briefly, flipped a few over. What she was looking for, though, wouldn't be found within ink and words.

But it might be beneath them. Inside the desk. She pulled open one of the smaller drawers, the slow scrape of wood against wood the only sound besides Tux tiptoeing on his padded feet as he crossed the dusty room.

A thin ledger covered in a fine dark leather waited in the drawer. Age creases tucked themselves into the small book as liberally as the wrinkles on Lachlan's face. Eloise pushed it aside, not in the least interested in Asquith manor's monetary affairs. No, what she wanted was shiny and small and solid.

A golden key for a gilded greenhouse.

She rummaged in the drawer—finding no metal, only more papers—and sighed.

"It's not in there." A deep voice curled through the room like a trail of cigarette smoke.

Easton peeled himself from the shadows as if he were a part of the gloom and stepped over to Eloise. He was a storm cloud in that moment—grim—and with dark eyes that never left hers. The room seemed to shrink around him until it was just the two of them standing close, the scent of warm tobacco and freshly cut oak rolling off Easton and enveloping her.

She glanced up at him and smiled, knowing the way his gaze would travel to her lips—how it would soften him to her. She shouldn't be in this room, shouldn't be sneaking around Lachlan's private study.

She knew it.

And so did he.

She'd use whatever wiles she had to if it meant convincing Easton to stay quiet.

Eloise took a soft step closer, let her lips curl higher. "What's not there?"

"You're not dumb, Ellie." Easton took a step away from her. "And neither am I." He pivoted around Eloise, circling her, his eyes fixed on hers the whole time. "I know what you and Weston are up to. Your games aren't as clever as you two think they are."

"I'm just trying to win." Eloise mimicked his movements, stepping with him as if they were partners in a waltz. "I know you want to beat him too. Why not help me?" She looked up at him, reached out and set a hand on his chest, her fingertips brushing soft wool.

Easton grabbed her wrist. "I would have." He dropped her hand and backed away. "Maybe. If you hadn't left me out at the start. But it's always Weston. You and him." He spread his arms out. "And where's that leave me? Am I to befriend the maids while you and Weston conspire together? While you two circle each other like dogs in heat? I'm not a fool. I see what's happening, Ellie." His lips twisted the wrong way, as if the words soured not just the quiet flesh in his chest but his tongue too. "And even though your little club of tricks is juvenile, I still would've helped you." He stepped away, heading for the main door to the study, only glancing back over his shoulder once as he opened it. "I *would have* helped you." And then he was gone in the same way as he'd shown up—with barely a warning, with ire rolling off him as thick as fog.

Eloise stood there unmoving, feeling as though she were an unmoored boat. Easton's words had tossed her to and fro. He saw too much. Wes hadn't caught on to the way her heart leaned toward him. She thought she'd been more subtle in the last couple years, not wanting to break the brothers apart any further than she already had. The twins hadn't been the same since Wes had tried to teach her to hunt, since she'd shot Easton and he'd taken the blame. They'd turned into wet cats thrown together in an old sack—Easton clawing at Wes and Wes hissing back.

She had changed them. With an accident and a wayward heart, she'd altered the twins' relationship.

And now, Easton saw right into her, had always been able to.

It's always Weston. You and him.

He'd looked straight into her heart and plucked his brother's name from its depths.

And he wasn't happy about it.

A pounding slithered through her bones, slowly at first, and then quicker, like a summer rain turned thunderstorm. The rhythm increasing in moments, almost unnoticed, until lightning seared her veins. It took only an inhale for her to realize she was scared, that her heart beat too fiercely beneath her thin ribs.

Easton wasn't someone used to not getting his way.

She took a deep breath, let it out gently, waited for the thumping under her lungs to ease.

Easton was spoiled, but he wasn't cruel. He wouldn't do anything to his brother just because she'd chosen Wes instead of him.

Would he?

Eloise quickly stepped over to the study's hidden door, going in the opposite direction of Easton. "Come on, Tux." She scooped up the cat and stepped into the secret hallway as the shadows nestled close. "Let's find Wes."

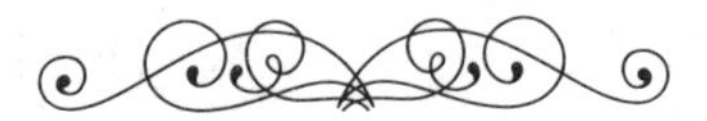

Eloise had an idea where Wes might be, and it was in the direction opposite of where Easton had stormed off to. The older twin had the inclination to sulk in the woods, only coming back when he had a handful of bloody stripes adorning his arm, marking his kills.

It's the quiet of the woods, he'd once said. *It lets me think*. But all Eloise could focus on when he'd come back was each line of crimson he'd painted along his skin like a tally.

She rubbed her own forearm, remembering all the times she'd hunted with the brothers, when thick blood would slash lines across her warm skin too.

She pushed the thoughts aside. Let him sulk. She could no more control his feelings than Wes's or her own. All of them forever looking at the other. Easton glancing at Eloise for her hand. Eloise peeking at Wes for his name. And Wes watching Easton for his inheritance.

None of them happy with what sat before them.

She snuck down the hidden hallway, aiming for a sturdy wooden ladder at its end while her skirts swished behind her like a trailing ghost. Tux meowed once, but as Eloise climbed the ladder, he resigned himself to being left behind and curled up in a tight ball on a small ledge beneath the window at the hall's end. She'd leave him to sleep with the view of Lammore Lake lapping gently against the brink below while she searched for Wes in the attic.

The trapdoor in the ceiling groaned like an old man rising as she pushed it open above her head. The attic was dusty with only a single round window to let in a meager light. Motes floated in the pale beams of the dying sun, and there, staring out the window, watching the lake from the bench seat beneath just like his cat, lounged Wes.

He watched the water as she climbed up. She knew she'd find him there. The small, angled room was their own little space. A fort in earlier days, a haven to get away from the manor's bustle and demands lately. Wes and El had carved their own nook in the dust and gloom and cedar walls.

She climbed onto the bench seat, opposite him, their legs entwining, fitting as comfortably together as a patchwork quilt. How many hours had they sat there just like that, sharing secrets and games, pouring out their souls to one another?

Wes turned to her as she settled in. "How long?"

Eloise cocked her head, her short curls brushing her chin. "How long what?"

He sat up, leaning toward her, and held up a flattened bullet—the one carved out of his twin brother's shoulder. "You won." He grabbed her hand, uncurling her fingers slowly, his touch light and warm and welcomed. "How long did it take you?"

She stared at the broken brass in her palm—the first lie he'd told for her, one they'd kept ever since. And now they passed the bullet back and forth to whoever won their current game. Eloise hadn't wanted to use the mangled metal as their trophy at first, but it was small and hidden and held more than just pride. It held their secrets. It tied them together. And she welcomed anything that wove her to Wes.

Even a bloody bullet she'd shot into Easton's shoulder. Even crushed brass that hid the truth.

"Where was it?" Wes stared at her, his golden-brown eyes bright in the dim room as if a fire burned in him. "Where does Father keep it?"

"Where was what?" Eloise slipped the mangled bullet into one of her skirt pockets. "Do you think I found the key?"

Wes nodded. "Of course. Where was it? Can I see it?" He tilted his chin. "Oh! And the slice of cake." He lifted his dark brows. "Interesting touch, El. I didn't think you were one to gloat, but . . . a consolatory cake?" He shrugged. "What flavor was that anyway? It wasn't blueberry. Gooseberry? Please don't tell me you made it *after* finding the key and slipped pokeweed berries into it." Wes laughed and glanced out the window where the ends of the greenhouses jutted from the manor and melted into the grass. "If you did poison me, it was delicious, at least."

"What are you talking about?" Eloise leaned toward him, set one hand on his until he glanced to her, his eyes dark pools in that moment. Too dark. Wes's pupils drank his irises down, swallowed them whole. The rich brown was too thin, the stark black too large. "Are you okay?" Eloise bent closer to him, letting her gaze travel over the rest of his face. "I didn't find the key or leave you a cake."

Wes swallowed, took a deep breath, and then swallowed again. "Yeah, I'm fine . . . You didn't? You—" He lurched forward, nearly falling across her on the small bench seat. "Maybe—"

"Wes!"

He careened to the side, and Eloise reached out, grabbing for him.

"Maybe I'm n-not." He put up a hand but grasped only air. "I don't—I don't . . . You didn't really poi—" And then he was tumbling, spilling off the bench.

Eloise stretched, taking hold of one of Wes's arms, slowing his descent, but he was dead weight in her grip, and he took her with him.

They crashed to the worn floor in a heap of skirts and tangled limbs. Wes's head snapped against the wooden planks, and the *thump* of his skull reverberated through her veins. His breaths hitched in shallow gulps, speeding from his lungs too quickly. Eloise's own inhales stuttered to match his. Fear constricted her chest tighter than a corset. "Wes . . ." Her voice strangled her throat.

"He'll be fine." Easton stood beside the open hatch in the dim attic. "Eventually."

How long had he been there?

"Easton, help!" Eloise shuffled under Wes's weight until she sat up. His head lolled in her lap, and she skimmed her fingers along him, unsure what to do. "I don't . . . I don't know what's wrong."

Easton stepped over, his movements slow, languid. He stared down at his brother. "You shouldn't mess with the poisoned greenhouse." His eyes flicked to her. "It might bite back."

"What . . . what do you mean?" Eloise set a hand on Wes's chest. His heart was a hummingbird's wings in a cage of bones. She pressed on his ribs, wanting to slow the rhythm below. "Wh—" And then realization hit her like a brass bullet to a shoulder. She cranked her neck toward the Asquith heir, her gaze landing on him slowly. "What have you done?"

"Nothing worse than he's done." Easton shrugged, the gesture falling off his shoulder like water. "He gave me a scar and stole your whole heart." He stood staring out the attic window as if his brother didn't lie slumped on the floor. "I took a secret and gave him half a berry." He turned to her, his dark eyes sharp. "We aren't nearly even."

And then he stepped away, heading to the trapdoor as if he were leaving for afternoon tea.

"Anger isn't control, Easton," Eloise called out, and he stopped. "It only thinks it is. You're going to spiral into chaos one day." She glanced at Wes. "I think you already have."

"Maybe so," Easton whispered back, the words stretching through the thin air, barely reaching her.

"Wh-what did you give him?" Plants raced through her thoughts as Wes's eyes darted behind his closed lids, but she didn't know enough, not of poisoned fruit and antidotes.

"Nightshade," was his slow response, and then he was gone, leaving her with only fear in her fists.

11

The Cook's Assistant

Night
May 9th, 1910

Sadie's hands shook as she sprinkled dried lavender buds—*to help him sleep*, her aunt had said—and chamomile petals—*to calm the hallucinations*—into a teacup for Weston.

Rumors had spread through Asquith manor faster than the evening's dinner had ended, and all the gossip whispered the same word.

Nightshade.

"Aunt, did we . . ." The teapot in Sadie's grip lingered over its cup. "Did I . . . Was it . . . was it us—me?"

"No." Agnes didn't turn from the kitchen stove, didn't look at Sadie. "Not another word about it." She kept her back to her niece, working quickly, keeping her hands busy.

"But—"

Her aunt whipped around, wooden spoon in hand and pointed at Sadie. "No. You hear me?" Her hard gaze flitted around the kitchen, down the hall. "It wasn't you. It wasn't us.

We didn't . . ." She let out a deep, deep breath, the weight of it settling on her shoulders, pulling them down. "It would've been everyone." Agnes nodded, but her attention was far from Sadie, as if it were herself she was talking to. "It would've been everyone if it'd been our desserts. Not just poor Wes, you understand?" She turned to Sadie, staring at her with fear lingering in her hazel eyes, widening the pupils too much. "So not another word."

"How else, Aunt?" Sadie set the teapot down and reached for something, for anything, for proof it hadn't been them. Her hands hovered in the air, empty.

Agnes circled the table, coming close to Sadie, near enough for her to see every single freckle and age spot dotting her aunt's wrinkled face. "Someone unlocked that poisoned garden." She lowered her voice. "And it wasn't you. So it wasn't us." Agnes nodded to the tray in front of Sadie. "Now pour the tea and take it to him. He needs it."

Sadie let the boiling water fill the cup, swirling the lavender and chamomile until a little whirlpool of pale purple and snowy white took her thoughts away from berries like ink. She checked the sugar bowl, straightened the spoon, whatever it took to tear her mind from a plant with long stems, pointed leaves, and small flowers that drooped down as if they were bowing. There was no way she'd mistake any part of the nightshade now. It was seared into her.

Sadie lifted the tray, and as she turned to go, Agnes whispered, "Remember"—her aunt waited for Sadie to stop, to crank her neck and look back—"Not a word."

Sadie nodded even as the tilt of her head tore a chasm between her heart and her stomach. How could she keep this secret inside her from worming its way through her ribs, curling up under her lungs, and lodging there until it fought a path up her throat? Keeping the truth tucked away was as good as lying, and it soured her stomach to stop her shaking voice from spilling what she'd done.

Only Agnes and what would happen to her aunt kept Sadie from running through Asquith's long halls and vomiting the truth at Lachlan's feet.

She swallowed, pushing the words down as she slipped along the manor's halls, up the stairwell, and to Weston's room.

A feminine "Come in" quickly answered Sadie's soft knock, and she pushed the door open to find Eloise Sutcliffe perched on a chair nestled close to Weston's bed. His room was shades of rich brown and muted green and hints of tawny sand, as if the forest outside had crept in and decided it liked it there. A large oak desk sat to the right beneath a window that stretched the wall and showed off the lake, a sitting area with two velvet chairs the color of wilted ivy waited before a dark fireplace, and in the middle of the room was a bed three times the size of Sadie's with posts that reached for the ceiling. Weston lay above the sage covers, eyes closed, breathing deeply from a mouth slightly parted.

Sadie stared at his lips—the broad shape, the hint of brown in them as if they were tea-stained long ago—and a new fear slithered through her chest. He'd kissed her mere hours ago. Unwanted.

And then he'd been poisoned.

After he'd found her outside the golden greenhouse.

What if he woke up and accused her?

She felt, in the marrow hidden deep within her bones, that this *was* her fault. It didn't matter to her who'd unlocked the poisoned garden—*she'd* been the one to pluck nightshade and make a dessert with a berry she must've missed. Perhaps only Weston had been unfortunate enough to react to it. Or was her aunt right? Would it have been everyone if the nightshade had been in the compote?

If it had been her, it'd been a mistake. Not an attempt of murder.

Sadie tore her eyes—and thoughts—away from lips that looked like a prison sentence to find Eloise staring at her.

"You can set the tea down right there." Eloise nodded to a small table by the bed with a clipped tone in her voice, letting each single syllable hit like a knife on a chopping board.

"Yes, ma'am." Porcelain clinked gently as Sadie left the tray beside Weston.

Eloise cleared her throat, and only then did Sadie realize she'd been staring at Weston's mouth again. And long enough for Easton's fiancée to cross the room, open the door, and wait with one dark brow arched.

"You can go now. Thank you."

Sadie said nothing as she slipped out of Weston's bedroom with a tip of her head, fear curdled in her stomach, and his kiss refusing to leave her thoughts.

Eloise pushed the door closed behind Sadie with a hard snap.

And in that moment, the sound of wood hitting wood jostled Sadie back to a black greenhouse and brisk lips that took what wasn't theirs.

Because, in that quick slam, Sadie heard another door shutting in anger, one her memory almost hadn't registered. But it rushed back to her now, tugging an alarm with it until a persistent anxiety constricted her chest.

She sucked in a too-shallow breath, but it escaped just as quickly as she realized what that sound meant.

Weston hadn't been the only one in the garden when he'd kissed her.

Someone in Asquith manor had slammed the greenhouse door after Weston's lips had met hers.

Two witnesses to give her a motive—Weston and . . . *someone.*

Sadie stopped outside Weston's room, names and faces spinning through her thoughts. And then she forced herself to relax, to think. She was always freezing when she should've been moving.

She stepped down the hall quickly—the tails of her apron swishing like pale streamers behind her—heading for her room and solitude, a place to breathe. In the chaos of Weston's poisoning, Sadie was sure her aunt would give her some grace, let her skip the rest of her work. She needed time to think, and she'd get no peace in the kitchen or halls or any of the rooms in Asquith manor where guests and servants bustled about.

Sadie rushed up the stairwell, and as fast as her polished shoes would take her, she hurried through the halls until she stood before a wooden door marked with age. She unlocked it, and only when the soft *snick* of brass clicked behind her did Sadie breathe fully since seeing Weston and his cold, cold lips.

She leaned against the door, her back pressing into the gaps in the wood.

But something small on her bed caught her eye, and she stepped over to it.

There, on her pillow, propped like an invitation with her name on it, lay a piece of paper.

Sadie stared it.

Her name was flourished across its front in bold black handwriting.

She picked up the note. Unfolded the thick paper.

And read five small words that emptied her lungs completely.

I know what you did.

12

El

Four Years Earlier
Summer 1906

Eloise sat on the old wooden dock with her feet bare and her toes skimming the lake's surface. Her pale blue skirt matched the summer lake as it spread across the planks while the sun beat down, drenching the day in warmth and laughter. She kicked droplets into the air, watching them sparkle in the light.

"Come on, Easton!" Eloise peered down at the lake. "You've almost got him. Pull harder!"

Easton leaned back, tugging on his fishing pole as the line went tight.

"It looks like a big one." Wes sat on the edge of the dock with Easton between him and Eloise. He peeked over, staring at the glittering water. "Its eye is as big as a tea saucer."

Eloise glanced to her left, catching Wes's gaze. "He might beat you with this one." She lifted one dark brow.

Wes smiled. "I wouldn't be so sure." He patted a wicker basket beside him with the lid latched closed, its brass catch glinting under the bright sun. "A tie . . . maybe." His eyes creased as he closed them, tipping his head up to bathe in the warm sunshine.

"Come on." Eloise nudged Easton with an elbow. "You have to beat him."

Easton pulled on his line, fighting with the fish on the other end. Sweat beaded along his brow, and Eloise was sure he'd dive into Lammore's cool waters before the day was spent. He yanked his line, finally breaking the fish free of the lake. Wes bent forward, scooping it into a net and pulling it to the dock.

"So?" Eloise stared at green scales and an open eye, the way the water splashed off the fin as it flipped around. "Who won?"

They waited for the life to leave the fish, for it to still, and then laid each brother's catch out side by side.

"Easton!" Eloise clapped her hands. "You won! Oh, won't Cook and Betty be so happy with you boys? It'll be a grand dinner they prepare tonight!" She bent and scooped up the fish, tossing them into the wicker basket and closing its lid.

Wes clapped Easton on the back as broad smiles spread across both their faces. "And here's your prize!" Wes dug one heel down and spread his hands on his brother's back, pushing him into the cool lake as a laugh started to burble from Easton's mouth.

"Weston! I'll get you—" Easton's words were drowned under the lake.

But as his head popped back up—Wes watching him with a smug grin plastered across his cheeks—Eloise rushed forward.

"I've got him for you, Easton!"

"Wait . . . wait!" Wes glanced at Eloise only in time to see her shove him off the dock.

He tumbled to the side, landing in the water with an elbow first and the rest of him quickly following.

Easton's mouth opened, laughter dripping off his lips,

water falling from his face. "Come on, Ellie!" He held his hands out. "I'll catch you."

She shook her head, her long curls brushing her elbows. "No." Eloise turned away from the Asquith brothers as they treaded the water. "Lammore will catch me." She raised her arms up. "Like she always does." And then Eloise fell backward, letting the cool lake envelop her, hold her.

She stayed under long enough for her lungs to burn and Easton to find her. He wrapped his arms around her, kicking them upward. They broke the surface, and when his eyes opened, they found hers.

His voice was husky when he spoke, as if his breath had been smoldering under his ribs. Embers curled around his words. "Don't . . ." He swallowed and took a deep breath. "Don't stay under so long, Ellie." Easton stared at her, and for a moment, she swore she saw a heat in his eyes—the brown warming to fired amber.

Eloise blinked, and then, ever so slowly, Easton unwound his arms from around her, and Lammore's cool water flooded against her skin, replacing his heated touch. They treaded water, both silent and watching the other, trying to read the words left unsaid—until a small, soft voice broke the quiet.

"What did Cook make for lunch?"

Eloise turned to the dock first, catching sight of Lucy. She wore a sunshine-yellow dress made for the summer day.

Eloise waved with a smile turning her lips up. "Luce!"

But as the eleven-year-old girl bent, Wes yelled out, "Stop!"

"It's not lunch," Easton said quietly at the same moment Lucy flipped open the wicker lid.

The youngest Asquith screamed when she saw the basket didn't hold sandwiches but instead two dead fish.

Lucy scrambled back as Wes grabbed onto the dock, pulling himself up. Easton's hand found Eloise's under the water, and he stayed by her, holding on to the dock's post with his other hand.

Wes stepped over to their little sister as she fell to the worn planks.

Lucy kicked out, and the basket tipped, spilling scales and fins and spines across aged wood. She sat down, knees to her chest. Her hands balled into fists, one cradled on either side of her face. Their little sister rocked back and forth on the dock, mumbling words and staring at a pair of dead fish that stared back.

Wes crouched down. He picked Lucy up and cradled her in his arms, and then he sat, rocking with her gently, whispering in her ears, waiting and waiting and waiting as she slowly calmed down. He was quiet for a time. Eloise let go of Easton and climbed up the dock's ladder with the older Asquith twin following closely behind.

They watched as Lucy nestled into Wes's hold, as he sat patiently. He wrapped one arm around her tightly and brushed his other hand over her hair, letting her rock, letting her ease herself down in her own way, not fighting against her outburst, but holding her through it.

Eloise stared at him—at his gentle movements and quiet help, his calm demeanor and soft love for his sister—and something deep under her ribs stirred.

And as Wes breathed tender reassurances to his little sister, Easton whispered two sentences that chilled Eloise's skin, and not even the summer sun could warm his words.

"She can't stay here much longer. Father has to see that."

13

The Fiancée

May 10th, 1910

"You're not going to postpone the hunt?" Eloise stormed down a tight passage, the walls as close as a secret and as dark as her mood. Bare electric bulbs dangled too far apart for their warm light to brighten the hidden hallway, and as she chased after her fiancé, Easton was little more than a black shadow with two long guns slung over his arm. "Wes is lying in his bed still and you want to go have an afternoon of sport?" She stared at his back, her gaze narrowed and hard.

He cranked his head to her, his dark eyes glossy in the dim light, almost shining. "He'll be fine by evening, I'm sure." He turned away, not waiting to see if she followed or ran back to Wes's room. She'd kept a vigil all night, holding Wes's clammy hand and giving him sips of herb-swirled tea between his hallucinations.

But in the shadow-stained passageway, Wes's mumbled words from last night slithered back, tracing shivers down her spine until she felt as if it were *her* slipping breathless beneath Lammore's surface and not Wes in his poisoned dreams. He'd sputtered at water that hadn't been there all while drowning his sheets in sweat and fear. His panic had bled through the room, making her feel as if she were suffocating alongside him.

It'd been a long night.

One Easton had slept through.

"You would know," she spit at her fiancé, the accusation hitting him like a slap to the face.

Easton froze. Turned around slowly. Watched her with wary eyes. "You think *I* poisoned him?"

Eloise stared at him. "It wouldn't be the first time."

"That was years ago, Ellie."

"One year, Easton." Eloise cut the words from her canines, sharpening the syllables. "One. Year." She stepped forward until the tips of their shoes nearly touched. "How many berries was it this time?"

Easton shook his head. "I had nothing to do with this."

Eloise lifted her hand. She touched his shoulder exactly where her bullet had severed his flesh. She knew the space well. "You've never forgiven him."

Easton shrugged, shaking off her touch. "It's never been the same. It aches in the winter. Did you know that?"

Eloise shook her head. Three years since she'd shot him, and she wanted to let the truth spill from her like blood. Go back before Wes had asked her to stay quiet. Before she'd let him take the blame.

She still wasn't sure why Wes had lied for her.

Had he known then the damage it would cause? So much more than her single bullet had. She'd wanted the truth to leak out ever since.

But she'd never break a promise to Wes.

Easton turned away, stepping down the hall as if Wes's poisoning meant little to him.

"Aren't you worried for him?" Eloise followed Easton.

"Why would I be," he tossed over his shoulder, "when you're worried enough for the both of us?" He cracked open a door at the end of the hall, letting bright afternoon sunlight pour over them and flood the tight space.

Easton slipped out of Asquith manor with Eloise right behind him, the door they'd gone through disappearing into the stonework as it closed, as if it had never been there. He sauntered to an empty clearing at the edge of the forest and looked around. "I guess no one else is joining us." He shrugged and handed her one of the long guns.

"I'm not hunting with you, Easton." She stepped back, but he placed the Winchester in her hands anyway.

"I know your usual hunting partner is incapacitated," he drawled slowly, "but seeing as how *we* are to marry, perhaps you could let me be your partner . . . for once."

He turned away from her, facing the forest, but not before she saw a shift in his eyes, like a dark cloud sliding away from a bright moon.

Hope.

It was hope, she realized.

Easton hid hope behind his clenched jaw and lazy words, his hard gazes and slow shrugs. But there, in that tiny moment, Eloise had seen it.

And she *had* promised him a life together. Not Wes, but Easton.

She held the gun in shaky hands and let Wes slip between her fingers, the cracks of her heart. He'd fissured that soft flesh, after all. It was Wes's own fault if his name fell between the fractures. She had tried to hold her heart together, but he'd ripped it apart and now it didn't quite fit the same.

Eloise glanced at Easton. "All right."

Easton stopped, his back to her, each vertebra stiff. "All right?"

She stepped up beside him, watching the forest, cradling the gun. "All right."

He nodded once and swallowed hard. "Let's see what you can do then, Ellie."

Not much, she thought, but Easton didn't know that. No one but Wes knew that she hadn't fired a gun in three years, had only ever pulled a trigger once. Eloise was far from the perfect shot everyone thought her to be. That was Wes. He never missed. And then he'd give his kills to her just to annoy Easton.

"I don't actually like to hunt," Eloise whispered as they stepped into the forest. "Did *you* know *that*?"

He shook his head. "You've learned to keep secrets well, Ellie."

She nodded. "I've a feeling you have too, Easton."

"I didn't poison him." He waited a breath. "This time." Easton stopped and turned to her, and only when she looked him in the eye, did he add, "But you don't believe me, do you?"

She went as still as the forest after a shot fired. "I don't know what to believe," and as he opened his mouth, she added, "yet."

"I know it's hard for you to think about, but what if . . ." He let his words linger in the air until her full attention was on him. "What if I'm not the only one who doesn't get along with Weston?" He arched a dark brow and then dropped it. "It's not like I want him dead anyway."

"You . . . you think someone was trying to kill him?" The gun slipped from her grasp.

Easton shrugged and bent down, picking up the Winchester. "I don't know what to believe." He handed it back to her. "Yet."

"But—"

"Why else would there be nightshade in his food?"

"Oh, I don't know." Eloise's lips flattened. "Maybe his brother was getting back at him for something."

"Or maybe his fiancée wants a way out." Easton tipped his head back toward the manor. "It's not like she's clinging to him."

"She wouldn't—" Eloise drank the rest of her words down. She didn't know Della well enough to say it hadn't been the heiress. She was no fan of the woman who'd stolen Wes from her, but did that mean Eloise should suspect her of poisoning him?

"Though, with the way Weston's been looking at me," Easton went on, oblivious to the thoughts spinning through her, "I've almost a mind to give him half a berry again." He clicked his tongue. "Too bad someone beat me to it."

Eloise narrowed her eyes at him. "Easton."

His voice flattened. "I'm joking."

"What do you mean 'the way he's been looking at you'?" She thought about the last month, the last *few* months. Wes had treated her differently since Della's name—and money—first popped up, but he'd been the same toward his brother . . . even after she'd run off to Easton. "He looks at you like he always does."

"Yes, he does." He glanced to the thick forest, scanning the trees as they walked farther into the woods.

Eloise stepped beside him, her skirts snagging the brush as she went, and though her footsteps were light, there was a heaviness in her lungs. The night had worn her out and now this conversation was tugging on the last of her strength. "What's wrong with the way he looks at you?"

Easton stopped and turned toward her, his brows crushed together as if he were trying to see if she were joking. "Because he looks at me as if eight minutes mean a lot more to him than they do to me."

"You think he's still mad he was born second?"

Easton nodded and stared at her, his cinnamon eyes focused, serious. "If he were heir, he'd still have you on his arm." His voice darkened, turning a shade deeper. "You don't think that means a lot to both of us?"

Memories flooded her thoughts. Of the three of them growing up together. The tension between the brothers that started before a bullet hit a shoulder, that grew as Eloise leaned toward the younger twin. Wes's first poisoning and Easton's words. Everything jumbled together, knotting up and making a mess. But she'd never quite forgotten what Easton had said a year ago.

He gave me a scar and stole your whole heart.

"But he gave me up." Eloise shook her head, and her curls danced around her chin. Wes *had* stolen her heart and then gave it back as if he had any right to. "I'm marrying you, Easton. Wes gave *you* my heart."

Easton leaned close, tucking her hair behind her ear. "Oh, Ellie." He cupped her face in his palm and rubbed his thumb across her cheek. "No, he didn't."

14

El

Ten Months Earlier
August 1909

The soft creak of the attic door pulled Eloise from her book, and then slowly, the rest of the noises in the room crept over to her—the rain pattering outside the window she sat beneath, Easton's footsteps across the old wooden floor, the way he cleared his throat as if he were unfamiliar with the small space. And, she supposed, he no longer was used to the meager room. Not anymore. It'd be two years since he'd joined her and Wes in the little nook they'd carved out for themselves in Asquith manor.

"Can you—" Easton's voice shook, and he stopped to clear his throat. "Would you . . . would you join me, please?"

Eloise set her book down on the bench seat, the tremble in his words stealing her attention, and watched Easton. He'd look composed to anyone that didn't know him as well as she did, but there, in the tapping of his right index finger against his thigh, she saw that something bothered him.

"Of course." She stood up, her dress draping around her legs like falling petals. "What's wrong?"

He shook his head, his perfectly combed hair not moving. "Nothing." Easton swallowed hard, and only then did Eloise realize he was wearing a tie.

"Do we have guests then?" She glanced down at herself. She wore a black dress with a silk underskirt and lace overlay. The top swept across her collarbone in fine ink-toned Chantilly. It was pretty, but plain. No beadwork. Nothing to adorn it. And she wore no jewelry. "I'm not dressed for com—"

"You look perfect, Ellie." Easton's voice steadied as he added, "But no, we've no guests."

"Then—"

"It's a surprise." He put a hand out, palm up, waiting for her to take it. "Come with me." He smiled, and for once, his broad grin was shy, making him look even more like Wes in that moment. "I'll show you."

Eloise placed her hand in his, and he led her to the trapdoor, letting go before she climbed down its steps.

They walked in a strained silence, Eloise wondering what made Easton's finger tap, tap, tap against his leg as they walked, and him offering no more conversation. Instead, he stared straight ahead with an occasional glance to her from the corner of his eye.

"Lachlan's not throwing another boat party, is he? Last time he started fishing with a shotgun."

"Only the catfish." Easton kept walking, heading to the back of the manor where the lake spread out beyond its stone walls. "Mother never did like them, after all."

Eloise thought of Roslin and how the late Asquith had rarely ever gone near the water. "It was their eyes."

Easton nodded. "They made her flesh creep." He glanced

at her. "But no, Ellie, we aren't headed for the lake in the rain." He smiled again, and it was so small and timid—nothing like the quick cuts that curled the edges of his mouth so sharply.

They rounded a corner, and Easton paused to open the door to the manor's black greenhouse. Mulch crushed beneath his polished shoes and her soft slippered heels as they entered, and only when the center of the garden spread out to Roslin's old sitting area did Easton stop.

Dark jade roses curled over an arbor above them, their soft petals so deep a red, they bordered on black. A sweet fragrance wafted through the air from them, and as Eloise sat beneath Roslin's favorite flower, she could see why Roslin had been so fond of them. Eloise wanted to wrap herself in their thick scent and steal their color for a velvet gown.

Candles were scattered on the edges of the little open area, tucked into the gravel at her feet, their warm light flickering against the gray day. Rain pattered against the rooftop above them, sliding down the glass and making the greenhouse feel so much smaller, more intimate. Cozy, with the dancing flames.

"Ellie . . ."

She turned from the sky to find Easton with a bouquet of flowers. Little purple blooms all crowded together on a single stem. Tiny white buds that grew tall before fanning out in a group. Tubular pink blossoms stacked on top of each other. Cream-colored petals with dark centers. Deep violet florets with curling yellow stamen.

Monkshood.

Hemlock.

Foxglove.

Henbane.

And nightshade.

A handful of flowers from poisoned plants.

Eloise swallowed, knowing what that bouquet meant. "East—"

"I fell for you the day you tied your dinghy to our dock, declared yourself captain of Lammore Lake and demanded to know where my and Weston's allegiances lie—with you or the pirates."

Eloise's heart hammered, throbbing somewhere between her chest and her teeth, stealing the words from her tongue until all she could say was, "Easton, wait . . ."

"It was with you." He knelt. "If you'll have me, I would give you my allegiance always, Ellie." Easton lifted the bouquet to her and there, hanging from a black silk ribbon tying the stems together sparkled a gold ring with a round diamond in the center, surrounded by smaller diamonds, making it look as if a jeweled flower glinted at her in the candlelight. "Eloise Martiná Sutcliffe, will you have me?"

Time held its breath, and Eloise noticed every detail unraveling. The way Easton looked at her with eyes the exact shade of fired cedar. How anticipation hung in his stare and apprehension hid in the way he swallowed hard. Even his chest seemed to pause its labor, lingering a moment too long. Everything waiting for her.

A dark petal fell from the arbor, drifting down softly, tumbling over itself. She focused on it rather than the way Easton held the bouquet out for her.

The petal dropped halfway between her and him.

And as it hit the ground, time chased after itself, making up for its slow arrival, blurring everything, until as if just risen from a sleepwalk, Eloise found herself outside in the rain, running toward her oldest friend, chasing the tide, rushing for Lammore with two words echoing in her mind.

I can't.

Had she said them? Spoken those small syllables out loud to Easton? Or had she simply sprinted off, leaving him with nothing but a dying bouquet and a broken heart?

She stood at the edge of the lake and crumpled to the ground.

He'd ruined everything.

Eloise pulled her knees up to her chest. They were to be friends, his feelings a background thing, something they both ignored just as Wes pretended he didn't know of hers. She let the rain pour down on her, wishing it could wash away the last hour. She stared at the gray lake, watched the choppy water stretch for the sand.

How were they to come back from this?

She should go home, to her own small manor in the woods where the servants would welcome her.

But her parents were gone again.

Only six months this time, Elsie, her dad had said as he'd smiled from across their dining table.

You could always join us, her mother had added. *Twenty-one is a wonderful age to travel and find a spouse.* They'd looked at each other, and Eloise had seen their own pasts flit between them. *Come with us.*

Eloise might look like her mother—with her dark eyes and darker curls—and smile like her dad, love like him too—in a stubborn way, knowing what they wanted—yet adventure wasn't in her blood like theirs.

A little over two decades ago, her dad had been searching for pale pink salt, not a wife, but between the white beaches, brilliant blue water, and rainbowed houses of Curaçao, that heart of his had been stolen. And her parents had been chasing the world together ever since.

Eloise didn't begrudge them that, but she had never longed to see other places like them. All she craved was a little space she could carve out and call home.

And her house had always been nannies and runaway parents and unlit rooms. Empty. Quiet. Lonely.

Home was a gray lake and twin brothers. An attic that felt like a secret and a manor that bustled with life.

If her parents could steal each other away and not let go, Eloise didn't see why she couldn't do the same. Only, it was a family she'd plucked up, nestled into, and called her own.

And now Easton had broken that.

How could she see him again when his feelings were so exposed? So tangible. Embodied.

Real.

She dropped her head, resting the bridge of her nose on her knees.

"El?"

Wes's voice rose above the heavy rain, and Eloise looked up to find him bending down.

He knelt beside her, his shins in the wet sand. "I saw you run out here." Wes glanced around, his eyes as warm as honey under the cool rain, his lashes dark and wet and catching droplets that he ignored. ". . . in the middle of a storm." He placed a hand on her shoulder, and she wanted to curl into him, wishing it had been him with a ring reaching for her finger. "What's wrong?"

"Your brother," she whispered, tucking her feelings into her chest—just like Easton should've done.

Wes sat beside her as if the rain weren't drenching his fine wool sweater and wrapped his arm around her. "What did he do now?"

Eloise thought about trapping the last hour in her chest, winding it up tight and pretending nothing had happened, but the truth would leak out. Five deadly flowers wrapped up in sable silk would tell the entire manor the whole story, so she let the words spill from her tongue, wishing they didn't taste so sharp. "He proposed."

Wes's body stiffened beside her. His fingers curled over her shoulder. "He . . . he did?"

Eloise only nodded. The words rolling across the tip of her tongue weren't ones she should say. *Why wasn't it you?* So she emptied her mouth and shoved her thoughts back into the dark corners of her chest where they couldn't alter this family she'd stolen any more. She wasn't sure she could bear it if they all turned into broken-hearted strangers because of a few honest words.

"For all his talk, I never . . ." Wes shook his head. "I just never thought he actually would." And then he went as still as a graveyard at gloaming. "What . . ." He took a deep breath and pulled a hand through his wet hair, shoving it out of his face. "What did you say?"

Eloise shrugged, her drenched dress pulling on her shoulders. "What else could I say, Wes, but that I can't?"

He turned his body toward her until he faced her completely, his dark eyes staring into her darker ones. "Why not?"

"Wes." His name slid from her mouth, sounding as sad as broken hope. She slipped her hands beneath her folded knees to keep from reaching for him, from skimming her fingers across his cheek. "You can't possibly be that stupid." She looked up at him, let her face say what her mouth wouldn't and wondered if he spoke its language.

It wasn't until his gaze went to her lips that she realized she was leaning close enough to smell the cologne on his skin—cedarwood and warmed vanilla fighting the fresh rain and autumn wind—or that she stared up at him with eyes that asked one thing.

He answered slowly, taking his time as if he were swimming in new waters and didn't know the depth.

And then it only took a slight shift of his chin for his lips to meet hers.

His kiss wasn't soft, or slow, but desperate. It made hers bold. But he pulled away before she would've liked, with two words clinging to the corners of his mouth. "I'm sorry."

"I'm not." She stared at him, only inches away, and looked for an apology lingering on his face, matching his words. She didn't find one. "What took you so long?" She slipped her hand into his, the familiar gesture turning foreign and new.

"Easton," was all Wes said. He stared at their twined hands. "For . . . for all our fighting . . . I just couldn't. Not until it was—"

"Real." Eloise nodded, her wet curls skimming her jawline.

The rain slowed, dying down, and only when it quieted did Wes whisper, "He moved his chess piece." He glanced back to the manor, then at the lake in front of them. "And I . . . I couldn't let him take the queen."

Eloise leaned back, watching him. "It's not a game this time, Wes."

He shook his head. "It—you—never were."

They were quiet a moment, both watching the water slosh the shore under a gray sky spent of its rain. The only sound was a nearby bird tiptoeing out of its hiding place, and Eloise felt that same, tentative apprehension in the tender muscle under her ribs—as if at any moment the storm might start again and, rather than wash away Easton's proposal, the deluge would drown Wes's kiss, raising the tide until it rushed up and pulled him from her.

"Did he give you my mother's bouquet?" Wes asked, breaking the silence lingering between them.

"Of course." Eloise couldn't help but turn away from the lake and toward the golden greenhouse, where, in the very center, surrounded by all the plants she loved, Roslin lay buried deep in the earth where all their roots could twist around hers. "Til death, right?"

Wes's gaze followed Eloise's. "When she died, Father decided love can cross death." He squeezed her hand. "He doesn't even like those bouquets now. It's not just because of Lucy that he bolts Mother's greenhouse. He doesn't like the reminder, so he locks up all those—" Wes stopped and turned to Eloise, his mouth parted and his brows crushed together, the faraway look on his face telling her his thoughts were spinning.

"What?" She tugged on his hand until his eyes met hers.

"How?" Wes's attention flitted to the golden greenhouse, then back to her. "How does Easton keep doing it?"

She shook her head. "Do what?"

His voice sunk low. "Get into Mother's poisoned garden."

15
The Heiress

May 10th, 1910

Della Drewitt threw an emerald scarf over the little glass boxes on the fireplace, hiding the heart from staring at her any longer.

"We should go." Della turned to her mother. "We should leave."

"Nonsense." Her mother sat on a dark green velvet chair overlooking the lake with the black fireplace to her right. She stared out the window, never noticing—or caring—about the hardened flesh on the mantel beside her.

"Someone poisoned Wes." Della took a step toward her mother. "And you want to stay here?"

"It was an accident. Even Lachlan said it must've been."

Della pursed her lips. "And if it wasn't?"

"Then you should be at his bedside." Her mother leaned over, picking up a delicate teacup from the tray that the maid had stocked this morning. She lowered her voice before adding, "Rumor has it, *Easton's* fiancée stayed up all night watching over Weston." She clicked her tongue. "It's not right. Something odd about that girl. And not just that she hunts with them." Her mother shook her head, her blond locks loose and brushing her shoulders. "I don't like it. If you don't watch out"—her mother lowered her voice—"She might pluck *your* fiancé right out of your hand."

"She's engaged to his *brother.* You don't think—"

"I think plenty, and I listen even more." Her mother tipped her chin up. "And I *don't* like what I hear. I don't like that girl."

"You . . . don't like Eloise?" Della grabbed her suitcase from the end of the bed, placed it on the soft linen covers, and opened its smooth leather top. "That's what you're concerned about this morning? Not that someone poisoned Wes?"

"Ac-ci-dent." Her mother said the word slowly, drawing out each syllable until it sounded like she'd sliced them from sharp teeth.

"Why do they even have nightshade growing here?" Della grabbed a dress hanging in the closet, folded it in half, and then placed it in her suitcase as her mother watched with a scowl sweeping across her mouth. Her mother could pucker her lips all she wanted, but Della would be ready to leave behind this manor for good, never to hear the Asquith name again. They could keep their carved-out hearts, their berries that could kill. Wes had been lucky he'd only had enough for hallucinations, but she'd not stay and be the next one to swallow a sugar-dusted death.

"Oh, they have a whole greenhouse full of poisonous plants, Della." Her mother flapped a hand before pouring hot water over the leaves in her cup. "But that's what people who've had money for too long do." She scooped up a spoonful of honey and plunked it into her tea.

"They grow poison?" Della grabbed another dress, not even bothering to fold it. She shoved it into her suitcase and stepped over to get more as her mother watched, saying nothing about her hasty packing, knowing Della couldn't leave without her. "That's what they do? Grow poison?"

The older woman nodded. "And any number of things. When you're bored and have means"—she shrugged—"You grow eccentric." Her mother stirred her tea with a thin golden spoon, its top fanning out like a flower.

"Eccentric is a favored pup having his own seat at the dining table." Della dropped her jewelry into the suitcase. "Or . . . or Eloise joining their hunts." She raised an ashy-blond eyebrow at her mother.

"Oh Della, my dear. How naïve you are, even for your age." The older woman took a slow sip of her tea. "This is exactly why you need me."

"Things are not right here. If I am naïve"—Della took a deep breath, let the air filling her lungs bolster the words climbing up her throat—"Then you are blind, Mother." She straightened her spine. "Eccentric is *not* nightshade and . . . and"—Della turned to the fireplace, pulling off her scarf and unveiling the glass boxes—"And calcified hearts!"

Her mother glanced slowly over to the mantel, never bothering to even turn her neck, then, just as lazily, she drew her eyes back to her daughter. "You think that's a real heart?" She shook her head, her hair brushing over the silk on her shoulders. "It's carved stone." She leveled a flat look at Della. "An *eccentric* paperweight." Her mother pulled a small leather-bound notebook from the pocket of her plum-colored skirts, a short pencil quickly following. She jotted something in its pages, ignoring Della's narrowed eyes.

"What are you doing?" Della flipped a hand toward the fireplace. "I just showed you a hardened heart in my room and—"

"A paperweight." Her mother glanced up, setting her pencil across the open notebook, but Della only caught sight of several small words scribbled across the fine, thick page. "Don't you think that heart could be so fashionable back in the city?" She cocked her head. "Or those dark berries with their little drooping flowers?"

Della's mouth hung open, but her mother continued without noticing.

"Imagine a small heart carved from white marble and hanging around your neck." She touched her collarbone. "A gold chain with black diamonds dotting it." Her mother sighed before reaching for her ear and tugging on it, her forefinger and thumb snagging the lobe. "Or a polished stone the exact color of a nightshade berry, smoothed out and rounded like one too, dangling from your ears. Everyone would be talking about them. What the papers might say!" She glanced back at Della, the faraway look filled with longing leaving her wrinkled face slowly. "I find all you need to set a trend is a pretty face or a good story."

Della bit the inside of her cheek—hard—before releasing it and saying, "Well, I'm neither of those." She turned back to her suitcase, ignoring her mother.

"You aren't half as ugly as the gossip papers print, you know."

Della's spine locked up. "Oh? So I'm *more* so?"

"What?" Her mother's voice was a sharp sound in the silence that followed Della's question. "How did you hear that in what I said? I swear, Della, you always look for the worst in my words and intentions." Her mother pursed her lips.

Della let out a heavy breath. Maybe she did. Maybe her mother was right, but it wasn't something she wanted to look closely at just then. She didn't want to argue with her mother or delve into their relationship. She just wanted the older woman to see that they should leave this manor and forget the Asquith name. That was what was important. Not jewelry or feelings or old, raw wounds. "Wes said it was his mother's heart," she said softly, and then lifted her scarf again, placing it back over the glass like a shroud.

"Oh, nonsense. He was teasing you," her mother said, but she paused before taking another sip of her tea, and Della wondered if a poisoned plant was running through the older woman's thoughts as she stared at the small leaves swirling in the cup.

"I don't think so."

Della turned to leave her room, but not before hearing her mother whisper, "It's . . . mint. It's just mint." And as Della closed the door behind her, she caught her mother setting the drink down where it could grow cold. The older woman's gaze went to the fireplace, to the hidden heart above it.

Della wandered the halls, unsure where to go now that her room offered no refuge. Should she go to Wes? If her mother was right and Eloise was watching him, Della was glad to leave the nursing to her. She didn't care for gossip like her mother did, and she didn't want to marry Wes either, but questions did tug at her. Why was Easton's fiancée in Wes's room? Surely there should be someone else caring for him.

Della threw those thoughts aside. She'd not let rumors dig their hooks into her like they did her mother. She'd seen how words could cut, and she'd no desire to be the one slicing.

She stepped lightly through the manor, avoiding the turns where she could hear voices at their ends. All of them seemed to say the same quiet word: *nightshade.* It was quickly followed by, *who?* And Della wasn't as naïve as her mother thought. She knew she'd made it clear yesterday that the last thing she wanted was to marry Wes.

And then he'd been poisoned the same night.

Would the murmuring through the halls soon add her name to the whispers?

Della brushed her hand along the wall as she walked and thought about how to convince her mother to leave a manor that held too many secrets. Her fingertips skimmed along the little rivets in the white wood. When her nail caught on a gap, she remembered the hidden door Wes had opened yesterday.

She stopped and pushed on the wall, testing it. A *click* sounded and then the wall's panel was falling inward.

Della's curiosity followed.

Della spent the afternoon far away from her mother, the hardened heart, and all the Asquiths. Instead, she explored the hidden hallway in quiet solitude. So far, she'd mapped the layout of five passages—where they started and where they ended. She never knew if her name would be added to the gossip or when her mother would decide to leave this place, so she studied each crooked turn and every secret door, tucking them into her memory in case she'd need them later.

The hidden hallways were narrower than the manor's regular ones, and there was nothing to adorn them except the scent of aged vanilla and rich musk as if the pages of an old book had been folded into the walls. Bulb light—spaced out too far to provide any real illumination—gave a dim orange glow. Shadows cowered in every corner and stretched down the long, thin walls. Unpainted wooden doors bore the signs of use. And the only sound was the ghosts of conversations tucked behind thick walls.

Della slowly curled her hand around a smooth brass knob, turning it carefully, cracking open the door to see where it led. When a soft, feminine voice floated over to her, she nearly snapped the wood back into place, but one word stopped her, tugged at her.

Weston.

Della pulled the door all but closed and peeked through the slim crack. A maid with long black hair leaned over Wes. He lay on his bed sleeping, and Della wondered why the maid hovered so close to him. Had she been the one to poison him?

Was she there to finish her handiwork?

Della stayed, ready to jump out if it looked like the smaller woman was going to harm him. She'd no reason to wish him ill despite not wanting to marry him.

Della stood on the balls of her feet, waiting. Ready.

The maid bent close. Her straight dark hair draping over him. Her face inches from his.

And while Della stood guard, she watched as the maid's heart-shaped lips meet *her* fiancé's mouth.

16

El

Three Months Earlier
February 1910

The wind whipped across the lake, curling underneath Eloise's wool cardigan. Wes pulled it tight around her but said nothing as they stood beside Lammore. Instead, he turned away from her and watched the gray water slice the shore under a pale winter sky.

Something was bothering him.

Eloise could see trouble hiding in the clench of his jaw, in the hollowed side of his face when he bit his cheek.

She stayed quiet, content to let the crashing waves be the only conversation in the morning air. She'd leave Wes to wrestle his thoughts, knowing he'd spill them to her in time like he always did. Perhaps he was going to ask her to marry him and was just nervous. Though he'd no reason to be. They talked of a life together frequently. But quietly. And only when Easton wasn't near. She knew she'd cleaved Easton's heart and how it still bled. The wound was fresh, raw—but Eloise couldn't seem to let it dampen the feelings she and Wes shared. If anything, they'd grown closer in the seven months since Wes had first kissed her.

A ring wrapped around her finger was bound to happen, and Eloise wondered how they'd tell Easton when it did. In hushed whispers to try to not hurt him much more? Or would she finally be able to smile without guilt?

Wes cleared his throat. "El . . ."

She leaned into him. "Yes?"

"I need to tell you something." His voice was soft, the wind nearly stealing his words. "About you and me."

Eloise slipped her hand into his and squeezed. "And what could that be?" She watched the gray water slosh, glad that if he asked her now, Lammore would be there, watching her as she always had.

Wes took a deep breath. "I don't think you'll like it, El."

Eloise laughed, her thoughts wrapped around four small words that formed one big question. "You could tie a ribbon around my finger and I'd say yes. I don't care what the ring looks like."

Wes shook his head. "El. That's . . . that's just it." He pulled his hand from hers. "I . . . I can't marry you."

Eloise leaned back and stared at him. "What?"

He didn't look at her, but his words tore through her mind. *I can't marry you.* That single sentence twisted under her ribs, cut to her heart, and stole her thoughts.

"It's . . ." Wes took a step forward, his focus still on the lake, the toes of his shoes nearly dipping into the water's edge. "It's not what I want either. It's not . . ." He bent, crouching above the gray sand, and picked up a black rock. He flipped it between his fingers, stared at the smooth stone rather than look at her. "I want you. I do, but—"

"Is this because of Easton?" Eloise kneeled, sitting beside him, and placed a hand over his, forcing him to stop his fidgeting. When Wes finally looked her in the eyes, she added, "He's been upset, but he'll—"

"No. It's—" He dropped the rock. "This is my choice."

"But it's not what you want. I know it's not." Eloise stared into his face, searching for an answer. "So . . . why?"

"There's . . ." He stood up again and turned to the forest, refusing to look at her. "There's an heiress. And she'll take my name."

"Money?" Eloise pivoted until she stood in front of Wes, until he had to look at her. "You want us"—she grabbed the edges of his shirt in each fist and tugged him to her—"To end because of money?" She leaned close, her lips nearly brushing his, and whispered, "Do you really think I care how much money you have? I'd live in a cave with you and bathe in a creek if it meant being together. Nothing could keep me from you." She stood up on the tips of her toes and rested her forehead against his. "Especially something so trivial as money." Eloise let a quick smile tuck itself into the corners of her mouth. "Besides, I'll eventually inherit. It's nothing like Asquith manor, but it's enough. And Lachlan will give you *something.* We'll be all right. I don't need much." She kissed him, gently, quickly. "Just you and this lake."

Wes set his hands over hers and slowly uncurled her fingers, pulling them free of his shirt. "It's not just that." He let go of her. "It's Lucy." Wes stepped away. "Easton wants to send her off. He thinks she's better in a hospital. I can't let him." He took another step away, leaving her on the sandy shore. "I need to take care of her too."

"Wes, wait." Eloise reached for him.

But he shook his head. "I'm sorry." He turned away, facing the manor. His voice was low as he added, "It's not really a choice after all."

And then he was gone, leaving her with only Lammore to catch her warm tears on a cold, gray morning.

Eloise had let herself cry under the pale sky, and then she'd wiped her cheeks and stormed into Asquith manor, heading in the opposite direction to which Wes had slunk. Fury coursed through her veins, but for whom, she didn't know. Wes, for choosing money over her? Or Easton for being heir to begin with?

Though, if she were honest, and she wasn't in the mood to be, she knew Wes was really choosing Lucy over her, not money.

But marrying an heiress didn't explain how Wes would care for his little sister. Not entirely. Not when she would become Easton's ward when Lachlan passed.

Wes might stash away enough money with an heiress to provide for Lucy, but he'd still have to convince Easton to give him charge over their little sister.

And none of that helped Eloise. She didn't want to see Lucy pulled away from her home any more than Wes did.

But she didn't want to lose Wes either.

Her footsteps echoed as she stomped up a hidden staircase and down a narrow passageway, not wanting anyone to see where she was headed.

Especially Wes.

When she stood behind the door that would open up to Easton's room, Eloise stopped and took a deep, deep breath, hoping it would calm the heat spiraling through her blood.

She should've knocked, but there was so much noise in her head that she found herself pushing the hidden door open and spilling into Easton's room without even a tap on the worn wooden frame to warn him.

But he was already staring at her. "What are you doing racing through the walls and making so much noise?" He sat in a wingback chair, his feet kicked up on a stool, and watched her over the pages of an open book. "Did you and Wes have a fight?" His voice was flat, and he glanced back to his novel as if it held more interest than Eloise crashing into his room.

"What could I give you to not send Lucy away?" Eloise stepped over to him.

Easton looked at her and cocked his head. "Why are you asking this?"

"I need to know." She sat on the edge of his stool, her ruby skirts draping over its black velvet.

He moved his feet, taking them off the footrest and giving her room. "Nothing, Ellie." Easton set his book on a small table beside him and splayed his hands out to her, palms up. "Lucy needs more help than we can give her. She isn't learning, progressing, like a fifteen-year-old should."

Eloise grabbed one of his hands. "We can help her here."

He stared at her fingers wrapped around his for a moment before gently pulling free. "Father has done nothing but spoil her here. Weston too. No one pushes her like she needs." He shook his head. "She looks too much like Mother for Father to do anything but spoil her, but Wes . . . he should know better. There are places in the city—"

"How about me?" she whispered. Eloise knew what he would give up his little sister for. Because she was selfish enough to do the same.

He would trade Lucy for her.

As Eloise would for Wes.

She and Easton were the same—both thistles with their thorns out, strangling every delicate flower in their way.

Eloise shook her head, not wanting to admit that even to herself. She held his hand again. "If I married you"—she gently rubbed her thumb across the side of his wrist—"Would you let her stay here?"

Her words sounded sweet, but they tasted sour. A bite in the back of her throat. She ignored their bitter flavor. Eloise Sutcliffe was villain enough in that moment to not care that she played with Easton, that she gambled on toying with Wes, or that she would sacrifice Lucy.

Jealousy was powerful.

And it had already won her Wes once. Perhaps it could again.

"Yes," Easton answered, and Eloise smiled as she moved her chess pieces against each other.

17
The Heiress

Evening
May 10th, 1910

Della stared at the maid over a cup of tea.

Dinner had come and gone without Della. She'd spent the day slinking through hidden hallways and now found herself in the manor's lounge, where a small stock of light foods had been spread out beside a setting of hot drinks. Nothing she'd seen of the Asquiths showed her that they cared for propriety, so—though she was sure to get a lecture from her mother—she doubted anyone else was bothered by her absence.

Especially not Wes if he was feeling better. Not when he had a pretty little maid to keep him company.

Della glared at heart-shaped lips that stole too much as the maid set down a tray of scones beside a teapot. True, she hadn't wanted Wes—still didn't—but she was tired of being pushed aside, sick of being plain, boring Della.

Lightning burned in her veins, and all it had taken to sear her blood was a kiss she shouldn't have cared about.

But oh, how she could hear the gossip now, knew what the columns would print.

Whispers of: *Dull Della Drewitt couldn't even buy a fiancé with all her money.*

Headlines that read: *Weston Asquith Prefers a Penniless Maid to the Drewitt Heiress.*

Della's fingers curled tight around the teacup's handle as she watched the other woman scurrying from one tray to another, tidying up.

The maid was pale and skinny with eyes that flitted to Della only to bounce away when she saw Della staring. Her gaze was a deep, deep blue edged in slate gray like the sky after a summer storm, and her hair was glossy and long as if black silk draped down her back.

Was that the taste Wes had for women? Pretty, dark, and lithe?

The very opposite of Della.

She knew everyone saw her as chubby, short, and plain.

She knew Wes looked at her as gold, jewels, and paper bills.

But Della was smart and clever. And angry.

Perhaps she'd stared too long at a calcified heart, had let it slither under her skin until her own was just as hardened. But pride wasn't an easy thing to let go of, and though they'd tried to slice hers apart with nothing more than a brush of a maid's lips meeting her fiancé's mouth, she closed it in a tight fist, refusing to surrender it.

Della Drewitt would show Weston Asquith she was no fool to play.

"What's your name?" Della set her cup down, letting it clink sharply against the saucer in her other hand. She and the maid were alone with only the lounge's black walls and charred fireplace to keep them company—a room as dark as Della's mood.

"Ma'am?" The maid looked up with doe eyes and long lashes.

Della stared at her. "I asked what your name is."

"V-violet, ma'am." She straightened the sugar dish and turned to Della. "Can I . . . Can I get you anything?"

"How's Wes?" Della said the two words slowly, letting them seep across the room as rolling and heavy as city smog.

Violet nearly choked on them. "What?"

"Have you seen him?" Della set her teacup and saucer on a little table, never looking away from the maid.

"He was at dinner, ma'am." Violet turned away, fidgeted with a teacup.

"Oh?" As much as Della wanted to exact a confession from the maid, she wasn't one to scream or yell. She was patient—restrained—so she softened her voice and, instead of saying *You only saw him then? You didn't kiss him in his room?* she said, "So he's feeling better?"

"Yes, ma'am." Violet edged for the door. "Everyone is awfully glad."

Della smiled, but it didn't reach her eyes, barely touched her lips. "I'm sure you are."

Violet tilted her head, her hair falling over her shoulder like ink. "Ma'am?"

She flapped a hand, just like her mother did when she would dismiss Della's thoughts. "Did he say anything?"

Violet tucked her hands behind her back. "Just that he's upset he missed today's hunt."

Della shook her head. "I meant about how he ended up being poisoned. Does he know who would do such a thing to him?" Della arched a brow. "A jilted lover perhaps? Someone upset we're engaged?"

Violet took a step back, toward the door. "What?"

"I'm just trying to see if I'll be poisoned next." Della picked up her tea, taking a slow sip with a straight face.

"I—I heard it was an accident," Violet said, and then without so much as a *Good evening*, she slipped out the door, leaving Della to figure out what to do with a dark-haired maid and a wayward fiancé.

18

El

Three and a Half Years Earlier
Winter 1906

Eloise slid her oars into the lake, cutting the water quietly. She rowed over to the Asquiths' dock, where only a handful of months ago, on those very planks, she'd fallen in love with a younger brother in a single moment and many years. Her heart had tripped over itself under a bright summer sky as Wes had comforted his little sister on worn planks with fishing poles at his feet.

Eloise edged her boat over to the dock as she had so many times before. The winter sun shone on her, tossing pale light over the day, thawing the bite in the air. She grabbed the wooden ladder running the length of one of the posts. It dipped into the lake, and she tied her dinghy to it, eager to see Wes, wondering where he might be—hoping he'd want to curl up with her in the attic and share a story bound in leather and ink. She'd sit beside him, perhaps rest her head on his shoulder as they read together, warmed by each other and his old quilt. Maybe he'd even wrap an arm across her shoulders as he held the book out for them. They'd delight in a novel and one another. *Today,* she thought as she gripped the ladder's rung and stepped from her small boat, her skirts settling around her ankles. Today could be the day Wes finally turned to her and his heart spilled all the things hers harbored.

Hope bloomed a smile across her face. Her mother had found her father at nineteen—perhaps Wes would find her at the same age.

Today, she thought again as she had for all of summer, autumn, half of winter. *Maybe today.*

She pulled herself up the ladder, her head just popping above the dock as a deep laugh broke the birdsong.

Wes.

His whole chest vibrated when he laughed as if the sound had been buried down beneath his ribs, pouring through his body until it fell from his lips. It was contagious, and she almost returned it without even knowing what had pulled it from his mouth, but a light giggle replied before hers could.

Eloise caught sight of Cora—Lucy's newest nanny—her head tipped back and pale throat curving down to a delicate collarbone. Blond hair—so sleek and shiny it looked as if it were melted gold—cascaded down her back, and her eyes were squeezed tight as if even their corners had to smile for Wes.

But it was the way Wes stared at the girl—who was far too young to be a nanny, twenty-one at most—that stole Eloise's attention.

He stared down at Lucy's nursemaid with eyes that saw only the woman before him. And when Cora opened hers, they responded in like, fixed on him alone.

Eloise ducked down, hiding below the dock, clinging to the ladder, her heart falling to the bottom of the lake.

Cora had arrived one month prior when Lucy's previous nanny had left. They never did stay long. And Lachlan had picked someone young. *Perhaps she needs more of a friend than a guardian*, he'd said as Cora had unpacked.

Eloise had noticed the way Wes's eyes had flitted to the nursemaid ever since she'd shown up at Asquith manor.

But this was the first time she'd seen his gaze *stay*.

She peeked over the dock again, searching for Lucy. She could use one of the girl's outbursts right now. Cora should be watching the youngest Asquith, not her brother.

Eloise found Lucy staring into the forest. She shifted one foot—slowly—and then the other just as softly, moving in small, suspended moments.

And neither Cora nor Wes saw as Lucy slipped into the woods, away from a nursemaid that could be sacked for losing her ward.

Eloise opened her mouth to call out, to tell them that Lucy had disappeared, but then Wes reached out and brushed back golden hair tossed by a breeze.

Her lips closed, smothering Cora's name on her tongue.

And then, just as slowly as Lucy had slipped into the forest, Eloise crept up the dock and down the dirt trail toward the kitchen, her eyes snapping to Wes and the nanny, but they saw only each other.

As Eloise opened the old wooden door, the hearth's heat greeted her before Cook and Betty could. She mumbled a hello and then wound her way through the halls until the south entrance stood before her.

Her fingers grazed the brass knob. It wasn't too late to turn around, to tell Cora where Lucy had gone. Then Lachlan wouldn't fire a nanny that couldn't keep track of her charge.

But Wes's deep laugh, given to a girl that wasn't her, had Eloise twisting the handle and stepping quietly outside.

She skirted the grounds, hiding behind the manor's shadow until she'd made it to the woods. One glance back to the open grass resolved her decision. Wes sat, facing the lake with Cora tucked close to him, and in that moment, Eloise didn't even blame the nursemaid. Wes was warm smiles and generous laughter, a soft side that leaked out for his sister. How could he not be loved? He was sunshine, and Cora was just another flower leaning toward his light. Worry tucked itself into her heart. She might be able to get rid of Cora, but who else—how many others—might she contend with until Wes realized they belonged together? Would a new nanny be any different?

Eloise swallowed. She paused only a moment longer before something shifted under her lungs, sticky and angry, but feeling a lot like justice.

Lucy was missing.

And Cora had let that happen. She didn't deserve to be at Asquith manor.

Eloise was doing Wes a favor.

Eloise slunk through the trees with the sun shifting slowly and fear pinpricking her chest. It felt as if hours had passed, and she hadn't found Lucy yet.

She should've called out to Cora and Wes when she'd seen the girl slip into the woods.

What if Lucy was hurt somewhere?

She circled thick brush with her heart crescendoing with every step she took. Eloise turned around, about to head back to the manor. She'd gather the others and they'd search the woods, even if it meant admitting she'd watched Lucy enter the forest without saying anything.

But as she took her first step back, a quick crunch of twigs snapping stopped her.

"Lucy?"

It was Easton that stepped out from behind a thick trunk. "How long were you going to stay out here?"

Eloise swallowed. "What?"

"I saw you." He took a step forward. "And Lucy." He stared at her. "From the attic."

"What do you mean?" Eloise searched his face for an answer, but it was as grave as a storm cloud.

"You let Lucy sneak away."

Eloise shook her head. "I don't know what—"

Easton looked away from her. "She's already packing her things and blubbering apologies." He picked at a bramble clinging to his sleeve, staring at it rather than her.

"Who?" Eloise said it quietly, lightly, as if it meant nothing to her, as if she didn't know, hadn't hoped for this.

"That new nanny." Easton's eyes flicked to her. "The pretty one." His gaze roamed over her. He was silent, and in that moment, she was sure he saw right *into* her. "The one Weston fancied."

She swallowed and looked away. Then stepped past him, heading for the manor, for Wes.

But a single sentence from Easton stopped her steps and infected her blood with traces of guilt.

"Aren't you going to ask about Lucy?"

19

The Housemaid

Morning
May 11th, 1910

Violet fluffed out a dress the exact shade of dew-covered ivy, glad to shed her black-and-white uniform for the day. She knew the green fabric brought out her eyes, contrasted sharply against her sable hair, even as it would let her blend in with the forest.

Hunt days were her favorite, and she'd missed yesterday's. With Weston sick and the house in an uproar, Lachlan had cancelled it. There'd been no picnic to help with or chase to attend. She'd heard Easton had slipped out—not minding his brother as usual—with only Eloise on his heels.

But Weston had insisted today was the perfect day for a hunt together. He wouldn't hear of not going, and with him feeling well again, no one argued, and Lachlan was eager to see Weston well and happy—the old man would probably give him whatever he wanted after yesterday. Maybe Violet could nudge Weston into asking for *her*, for that sham of an engagement his father wanted called off.

Violet smiled, a soft curl of her lips that grew as she thought of Weston. She was glad he was all right, and more than happy to seize any opportunity to spend the day with him—even if that fiancée of his had to tag along as well. Violet knew the truth. It was only a matter of time before Della Drewitt went running from Asquith manor as fast as she could. Violet was surprised she hadn't left as soon as Weston had crashed to the dining room floor, would've been happy to see her scared away. But then the heiress' words slipped like smoke through a room back to her, and a cold fear wound up her own spine.

A jilted lover perhaps? Someone upset we're engaged?

They bit, her words—serrated little syllables that cut through Violet's thoughts.

I'm just trying to see if I'll be poisoned next.

Had Weston mentioned her? And in the past tense? Jilt*ed*, she'd said. Did Della think that *she* had something to do with the nightshade in Weston's food? Did the heiress suspect her?

Violet's hands trembled as she slipped into her dress. Her fingers shook as she tied a matching ribbon in her hair. She knew how precarious her situation was. A maid versus the Drewitt heiress. Della's word could hold a lot more weight than hers—like a gold bar to Violet's copper coins.

She had to be careful. She wanted to scare Della away, not end up accused of attempted murder.

Besides, hadn't the nightshade been in Weston's food? Perhaps Lachlan should search the kitchen if he did truly think the poisoning was an accident. Violet could point Lachlan to a certain maid that didn't belong in Asquith manor—and it wasn't her.

She slipped down the servants' quarters with too many questions spilling through the halls. Was it an accident like Lachlan insisted? Or had someone poisoned Weston on purpose? He'd collapsed on the dining room floor after a single bite of his dessert, but how long did nightshade take to show symptoms? Violet reached the main area of the house with that question circling through her thoughts, but she was skilled in dusting and scrubbing, and none of her time here had taught her about poisoned plants. Would the berries have been in his evening meal and sped through his body as soon as he ate? Or would he have to have consumed them earlier?

Someone had to know.

And Violet would find out.

It if wasn't an accident—and how could it have been?—she would figure it out and protect him. Her future depended on it. It couldn't happen again.

Perhaps, she thought, rounding the corner and stepping outside as the beginnings of a hunt gathered, Della's own words could be shot back at her with Violet's accusations.

A reluctant fiancée? Someone upset at a forced engagement?

Would she be poisoned next?

Violet could imagine Della as a villain, especially remembering the heiress' cold eyes as she'd stared at her last night while drinking tea, and she wondered if she really should worry. But why would *she* be targeted next? Her relationship with Weston would have to be known. She was sure he wouldn't have actually told Della about them.

And they'd been careful when together so no one knew.

But oh, how she was tired of careful, of secret, of no one knowing how Weston truly felt for her.

If only it had been Lachlan who'd been poisoned.

Violet halted abruptly, mere feet away from Cook and her new kitchen maid as they set picnic baskets on the lawn, waiting for the Asquiths to arrive. Where had that thought come from?

Yes, Violet was upset that a single person stood between her and her dreams of glittering jewels and sparkling drinks and never folding another linen again, but did she want Lachlan—who'd always been so kind to her—dead for her to have that life?

She bit the inside of her cheek, not ready to wrestle those thoughts.

He's had a nice, long life, though, managed to slip into her mind anyway, and she reached out, grabbing a picnic basket and blanket off the grass to distract herself.

"I can help," she said quickly to Cook.

But it was Sadie Fischer who replied with a "Thank you," and that puckered Violet's lips almost as much as the words circling her mind.

"You can spread the blanket out over there, girls," Cook said, pointing to the edge of the lake. "They'll be wanting lunch after the hunt, and Lammore is a beautiful view, don't you think?"

"Better than two days ago when it was gray clouds and churning water." Sadie shrugged as if she could slip off the spring storms that had been visiting the manor every evening. "Don't you agree?" The red-haired kitchen maid turned to her.

But Violet wasn't worried about the lake or the thunder. All she could focus on was Sadie staring at her—her lips the color of ripe berries, skin like fresh cream, and eyes as bright as a field still lush from a rain—another pretty maid at Asquith when Violet already had Della to contend with.

Was that all that it took to snag Weston, though? A nice face or a pocket full of money?

Didn't he like her for more than just her silken hair and ocean eyes, the curves that slid down her body? Or could a kitchen fox sway him just as easily as an heiress' fortune had?

Violet felt her hold on Weston slip like a thread from a needle when she looked at Sadie, and Della had already frayed the yarn too thin.

"Yes, sure," Violet said as she stepped away from the kitchen maid and over to the water's edge. She spread the blanket, covering the dull sand in bright red and soft white, and opened the picnic box, setting out covered plates and sparkly drinks until it looked like a rainbow splashed over the gray beach.

As she'd finished setting the picnic, the Asquiths were making their way out of the manor. Lachlan first with Caroline at his side, the twins next with Eloise's hand wrapped around the crook of Easton's elbow. Della skulked last, her dull gaze scanning the lake, the forest, the picnic. And was it Violet's imagination that Della had narrowed her eyes as they'd skipped over her, taking in her mossy-green gown with her midnight hair spilling down her back—just the way Weston liked it?

Violet straightened her spine and folded her hands in front of her. She'd let Della Drewitt glare all she wanted. She had no known reason not to like Violet, except maybe for her looks. Della *was* awfully plain, and Violet was not unused to being hated for her pretty face. Perhaps the heiress was just jealous.

But Della's face softened when it skipped over to Sadie, whose looks almost rivaled hers. And she'd not seen any animosity between the heiress and Eloise—whose face was more beautiful than the kitchen maid and hers combined. Violet would never admit that to anyone except herself, but . . . it was true.

When Della laughed at something Eloise said as the six of them walked over, an itch traced its way down Violet's spine, because if it was just her looks, why did the heiress only glare at *her*?

Violet tipped her chin up and let that thought slide from

her like water dripping off a swan. It didn't matter that an heiress scowled at her. Not when Della Drewitt wouldn't be there much longer.

Violet would see to it. Even if it she had to pull secrets down like cloth from a painting, revealing all the angles and brushstrokes and lies this manor liked to hide.

20

The Fiancée

Morning
May 11, 1910

Eloise curled her fingers around Easton's arm, her hold fitting as snug as it used to when it was Wes she wound her grip around.

"Are you sure you're well enough to hunt, Wes?" It was Della who asked the question, even though they were the exact words that should've been dripping from Eloise's lips.

She glanced at Wes, turning her head to see him from the corner of her eye as he walked behind her. He was paler than usual, but his eyes were no longer dilated nor flitting around at hallucinations, and his chest took in steady, even breaths. He seemed well for someone who, only two nights ago, had eaten nightshade.

"More than well." Wes smoothed a hand down the front of his sweater.

"I'll admit. You may have missed my favorite hunt yesterday." Easton glanced down to Eloise, a wide smile sweeping across his face, and her thoughts shot back to the day before when it'd only been him and her and the woods.

They'd caught nothing but each other—a tenuous start to a life together. There were no feelings from her for Easton, aside from the friendship they'd always had. But there was hope.

Hope that she could choose him, spending days working together that grew into something that would let her angry heart thaw.

She gave a shy grin back to Easton, and even though Wes walked behind her, Eloise could feel the heat of his stare on them. It flushed a warmth through her body—for longing or anger, she couldn't tell. Those feelings were too entwined for her now, like weeds whose roots had grown around a flower, twisting together until if you pulled one out, they both broke free.

A bud of annoyance burst in her chest. Wes had no right to watch her with Easton as if he still held any claim to her. Not when his wealthy heiress followed him, asked about him.

She leaned into Easton, and he welcomed her, tucking her close and resting his free hand over her fingers curled in the crook of his elbow.

"Oh, did you?" Wes finally answered Easton, his words slow and careful. "And what did you get?"

"A priceless catch." Easton leaned over and gently placed a kiss on the top of Eloise's head.

Wes cleared his throat, and Eloise could imagine the way he'd scratch the back of his neck when he wanted to avoid looking at something, but Eloise focused on Easton's words instead. On one in particular.

Priceless.

Easton called her priceless while Wes had so easily given her up for an heiress' money. It was a deep cut from Easton to his brother, but like thick honey and lemon balm leaves for Eloise, as healing and comforting as a warm cup of tea.

They made their way over to the edge of Lammore, and Eloise nodded at her, wondering what the lake would think of her on Easton's arm rather than Wes's. Would Lammore disapprove? Her waters were still and calm, but Eloise knew that lake better than anyone. She could thrash and pummel and whip against the shore. Lammore could rage. How often had her dark water crashed in torrents? Lammore was not gentle, and she couldn't be tamed. She held strength in her choppy waves and deep secrets in her depths. And Eloise had learned a lot from her old friend—both of them capable of unleashing dark storms and housing buried secrets.

And Wes was about to find out just how wild and untamed Eloise could be.

She glanced at him. Wes wore her favorite shirt of his—a thick wool sweater the color of slightly creamed coffee. The light hue had always darkened the brown of his eyes while brightening the amber flecks until his irises looked like oak burned under a hot fire. A color that always drew her to it—as if she were a moth so willing to be devoured by flames.

Eloise mulled over that. It was far too warm for such a sweater, even after the unseasonable storms eased the heat from the day, pulled the humidity from the air. Had he worn it knowing her gaze would travel to the tailored fit of it over his torso, and how she loved his dark eyes blazing? Or had it merely been the cooler weather and to simply let him blend into the forest?

Eloise shook her head, her short curls grazing her cheeks. It was a sweater. Nothing more. No motive. Didn't Easton wear a button-up the color of chocolate? And she wore slacks the shade of sugared tea, a shirt like dried sage.

Only Della and her mother weren't dressed in tones to match the woods. Caroline wore a slim gown that looked like someone had melted an amethyst and poured it over her in soft folds, her hands tucking themselves into the pockets at her hips. Her blond hair was swept back with an emerald-encrusted gold comb, and her delicate shoes sunk easily into the sand.

The heiress was draped in a long sapphire dress, as if enough blue might erase the gray in her eyes and brighten them. She wore black slippered heels made for sitting, jewels for glinting, and a scowl fit to be received only by the back of someone's head. Eloise followed the heiress' eyes to where they'd landed on the servants setting out their picnic.

Della wiped the expression away quickly, smoothing her pale features, but Eloise had seen it, and like the sweater Wes wore, it crept into her thoughts. She tucked Della's frown in her mind where she could pull on it later and examine it more closely.

"Well, Wes," Lachlan said as they reached the picnic. "Seems you've picked a fine day for a hunt after all." He didn't mention Wes feeling better, the poisoning, how everyone still whispered the word *nightshade* when he left the room. No, Lachlan swept it all away as easily as an old cobweb, and Eloise wondered if it was because he, too, had suspected his other son.

She glanced at Easton, poked soft queries at the tender roots springing up between them. He'd been so adamant it hadn't been him—this time—but . . . could Eloise believe that? Could she trust him? Did he even deserve her trust when he'd already proven himself capable of retribution?

Wes cleared his throat, and when she pulled her attention away from Easton to him, she found him watching her. Instinctively, as if she'd been caught like a thief pilfering silverware, she loosened her hold on Easton. Hurt and longing warred in her chest, pulling at one another every moment when it came to Wes.

She almost hated him for it.

"Shall we picnic first or let the hunt commence?" Lachlan continued.

"Hunt," Wes answered quickly. "Always to the hunt first."

"But . . . won't you come back bloody?" Della asked, delicately stepping away from Wes.

"Only if I succeed very well." Wes winked at her, and envy like smoke curled through Eloise's chest.

She blew it out, snuffed it, let it suffocate beneath a cracked heart.

If anything good could come from Wes rejecting her for an heiress' money, it was the hope that Lucy *would* be well cared for, but also . . . that Della could be happy. They didn't both deserve to be miserable.

"I . . . I . . ." Caroline's hands fumbled with her pockets. "I don't think I want to be here after all." She swallowed hard, looking from the long guns laid out to the woods and then back. "I . . . I'll join you all later, thank you." And then she was gone, rushing back to the manor as quickly as her shoes and bones would let her, before anyone could say a word.

Eloise cast a quick glance to Della, who looked as confused as everyone else, and then dismissed the old woman from her thoughts. Eloise herself didn't like hunting, after all. If she had her way, she'd be chasing after Caroline for the comfort of the manor as well. She turned to Easton instead. "Well . . . shall we then?" She smiled up at him . . . and hoped it looked genuine.

Easton nodded, stepping over to where the long guns lay waiting. He grabbed one for himself and one for her, bringing it back and holding it out to her.

She took the Winchester right as Lachlan said, "Oh no. It's not a couple's hunt today." He glanced between his sons, then to Della and Eloise. "Today, we shall hunt men against women and see who wins."

"But . . ." Della was already shaking her head. "I . . . I—" She gestured to herself, her gloved hands sweeping down her gown. "I've never hunted." She looked to Eloise in her slacks and shirt. "I didn't even dress for it." Della turned back to Lachlan. "Please, if you don't mind. I'd much rather stay here at the lake and cheer Eloise on."

Lachlan nodded as Easton and Wes watched each other with eyes as wary as a cat's. "If you wish. I won't force anything upon you, Della dear." He turned in a small half circle, surveying the picnic. "You." The lord of Asquith manor pointed to a pretty maid standing beside a sprawled-out blanket, her feet dipping gently into the sand. "You seem competent enough. You'll join sweet Eloise while my sons hunt together."

The twins exchanged a glance, and even though Eloise had plucked them up years ago and stolen them for herself, knew them better than anyone else, she couldn't read the words hidden in that quick look.

Wes said nothing as he slung his shotgun over an arm and headed for the woods. Easton bent before leaving Eloise's side with a whispered, "Good luck, but I hope to have more stripes on my arm than you when this is finished, Ellie."

"We'll see," she returned, but once the twins were gone and Della was seated delicately on the picnic blanket, Eloise turned to Lachlan. "What are you playing at?"

Lachlan shook his head, his gray hair shifting in the lake's breeze. "You've always been like another daughter to me, Eloise." He draped his arm around her shoulders as if he were a hen gathering chicks. "But I'm not nearly as blind as my boys think I am." He cocked his head, his eyes squinting after his sons. "Not mentally at least." He turned to her. "Easton and Wes have a lot to work out. Because of you. It's a hard thing when both their hearts are set on you. It's time they hash it out."

"Wes's isn't." Eloise glance to Della. "Not anymore."

"Hmm." Lachlan let go of her. "I'm not entirely sure of that."

21

The Cook's Assistant

Morning
May 11th, 1910

Sadie woke with the sun streaming in through a small window. It splashed pale light across her bed and gave her hope. Weston had recovered after spending the previous day in bed. Her shoulders had shed some weight with every hour that had passed, with each whisper that he was doing well.

Only five small words still pulled her down and sent a shiver through her bones when she thought of them scrawled in tiny little letters on a slight scrap of paper.

I know what you did.

A single sentence and nothing more.

Sadie had jumped at every call of her name since she'd found that note, waiting for someone to scream that she'd poisoned Weston, wondering when strong hands would grab her thin shoulders and throw her into a cell.

But nothing had happened.

And somehow that made things worse.

Sadie dressed, her focus straying to her small desk—to the drawer in its center where she'd tucked away that awful note. After pulling her hair back, she stepped over to the desk and opened the drawer, the old wood creaking like aged bones. She read the letter, not its words, but the clues hidden in the paper—black letters with a *y* that swirled and a *w* that bent at an odd angle, the faint trace of lavender clinging to the folds.

The manor's guests should be at the day's hunt along with a handful of the servants, and Sadie decided she'd use that time to try to find out if one of them had written the note. If she knew who it was, perhaps she could explain, tell them how it had been an accident. At the very least, she'd make sure they didn't think her aunt had been a part of it. She picked up the note and slid it into her apron pocket.

The lake stood calm and still, so opposite to the churning in Sadie's chest. Her aunt waited beside her, and next to her was another maid. But it was Sadie that Lachlan stared at, pointed to, and said, "You."

Sadie swallowed. Was this it? Was Mr. Asquith about to sack her in front of the man she'd accidentally poisoned? Or worse, would she find herself behind iron bars by day's end?

"You seem . . ." he continued as his cloudy eyes struggled to travel over her. "Competent enough." He nodded. "You'll join sweet Eloise." Lachlan nodded to Ms. Sutcliffe, whose dark brows pinched together while her bow lips curved into a frown, and Sadie wondered if that grimace was for her or Mr. Asquith.

They huddled together, the two of them, as Easton and Weston stomped into the woods one after the other.

"I'll go this way," one of the twins said, "and you can go

that way." And then it was Lachlan's turn to frown, his wrinkles piling on top of each other.

Eloise raised a single brow at Lachlan but said nothing to him, only mumbling, "Well, come on then," to Sadie before she turned for the woods without another glance at the picnic.

Sadie looked to her aunt, who only sent a quick shooing motion with her hands, and while they'd all dressed in shades of dun brown and deep green and hints of cream like clouds, Sadie hadn't expected to actually enter the forest.

Her gown was simple, toasted nutmeg in color with a linen apron like newly poured milk. She'd fit right in with the variegated bark along the birch trees, but she'd never hunted, had never even held a scattergun before. A single berry in her hand had been nearly deadly enough, yet Lachlan handed her a shotgun. She held it out before her like a spoiled fish tail and followed Eloise Sutcliffe into a forest whose branches cast long shadows beneath their limbs.

Eloise waited for her under a large oak tree, her slacks not catching on the bramble like Sadie's dress did.

"Sadie, right? You're quite far from the kitchens, aren't you?"

Sadie nodded as Eloise's words circled her thoughts, reminding her of Weston's question only two nights ago—right before he'd kissed her.

What's a kitchen mouse doing so far from the hearth?

And suddenly, Sadie was glad Eloise was engaged to Easton, but poor Della . . . She was set to marry a pig. Should she tell Ms. Drewitt what Weston had done? Was it any of her business really? Even at less than a few weeks' employment, Sadie knew theirs wouldn't be a marriage for love anyway. Perhaps they had an agreement? The thought soured Sadie's stomach, but she'd stay out of it. She had enough to deal with. She'd let those above her station work out their own deals while she stayed far away from Weston Asquith and his greedy lips.

"Have you ever hunted before?" Eloise asked as they stepped through thick briars, picking their way toward a deer trail. "Or had any desire to?"

Sadie shook her head, and Eloise eyed the way she carried the long gun as if it might spring from Sadie's hands and bite them both.

"I'm not really a fan either if I'm honest."

"Oh?" Sadie pulled her apron free of a thorn. "I'd heard you were the best shot in the manor, though."

"That's Wes, actually." Eloise smiled, but it was a sad turning of her mouth, as if her lips didn't quite like the conversation. "But no one knows, so keep that secret." She winked half-heartedly.

But Sadie was drowning in secrets. She didn't want another. Secrets were like a butcher's blade, able to cut deep and leave a bloody mess.

And someone already knew hers. Five little words followed her around like a ghost taking hold of her skirt ends.

I know what you did.

She glanced at Eloise. Could it be her? Had she written the note?

"Ma'am." Sadie hiked the shotgun onto her shoulder, freeing one hand to reach into her pocket where she'd slipped a few sheathes of paper and a pencil beside that horrid note. "Cook wanted to take suggestions from the guests for the boat party's dessert at the end of the week." She dipped her head, the lie tasting like burnt garlic on her tongue—bitter and wrong. If anyone questioned Agnes, her aunt would find out about the note, and Sadie wanted to keep that to herself. Her aunt already risked too much. Because of her.

"Oh?" Eloise's lips pulled to one side of her mouth. "Well, I'm quite fond of a simple spiced cake."

Sadie grabbed the parchment and pencil, making a show

of juggling her shotgun as she handed them to Eloise. "Mind writing it down for me? I'll never remember everyone's if not."

Eloise rested her own gun against a tree and quickly scribbled down her choice then handed it back.

Sadie glanced at it quickly, studying the curves and angles of Eloise's letters, but she'd need to hold it against the note later to truly tell if the writing matched.

"Thank you, ma'am."

Eloise simply tipped her head in response and picked up her scattergun again.

They walked in silence. Eloise seemed to be content in the quiet and Sadie had her own thoughts to contend with.

Only the birds chittering against the rustle of leaves swept through the woods for a time, until a gunshot—closer than Sadie would've liked—ripped through the air like thunder. She jumped and spun toward the sound, but her skirts caught in a branch of wild blackberries, the short thorns digging into the soft linen.

Eloise let out a small chuckle. "It's not my favorite sound eith—" She bit off the rest of her sentence, letting it fall to the forest floor.

Sadie glanced up from her skirts to see the smile vanish from Eloise's lips. Fear sent her pupils into pinpricks as her eyes fixed over Sadie's shoulder.

She twisted, tangling herself in the brambles to follow Eloise's gaze.

Sunlight filtered down between tree branches, lighting a shock of bright red. A scream tore from Eloise's throat at the same moment Sadie realized what she was seeing.

One of the twins—their face too far to see—sat in the brush with thick, sticky blood splashed across his bare torso.

22
The Heiress

Afternoon
May 11, 1910

A high-pitched cry cut across the forest, slicing through the trees to pierce Della as she walked along the lake's shore in solitude.

There was a moment, between a quick inhale and its sharp release, that Della froze, her heels digging into the dark gray sand.

When a second scream choked the air, she ran back to the picnic, to Lachlan and the cook and the maid that stole what wasn't hers.

Eloise stepped out of the forest with the red-haired girl. They huddled close to one of the twins—one woman on each side of him, arms wrapped around him. His shirt was off, and Della would've looked away, should've blushed—but the red slashed across his arm and chest stole her attention. It bled slowly, making its way down his bicep, his forearm, until it dripped from his fingertips. A dark scarlet trail marred the ground he walked.

But it was the hole in his shoulder, its edges raw and broken, that Della stared at.

"Wes is hurt!" Eloise yelled as if everyone didn't stare at him and the gape in his flesh.

Lachlan thawed first, moving over to his son before the others joined in the jostling, and even in the confusion, Della noted how Violet stepped forward as fast as she could, her hands outstretched as if the maid wished to cradle *her* fiancé.

"What happened?" Lachlan scanned the direction of the tree line. "Who . . . who did this?" And beneath the clouds in his eyes, his gaze bore into Eloise.

"I'm fine." Wes shook off the kitchen maid's grip first, then—more gently—Eloise's. "It's . . . it's nothing."

"It's . . ." Eloise's mouth dropped open. "Someone shot you, Wes! That is the very opposite of nothing."

A heavy silence fell across the lake's shore until Lachlan, his voice as worn as a threadbare cloth, sighed and asked, "What's happened between them now?"

Between *them*? Della's attention bounced to Violet then back. Eloise and Wes exchanged their own heavy glances at Lachlan's words.

"We heard a shot." The red-haired maid pulled up the edge of her apron, biting a corner between her canine teeth and tearing it away until a white strip of the fabric ripped free.

Eloise guided Wes down onto the picnic blanket. He dropped his sweater—balled up and bloody—and his long gun beside him, staring at each item as if just now realizing he'd still been holding them. Eloise reached down, picking up the sweater, and set it next to her.

"It was close to us—to Sadie and me." Eloise took the cloth from the maid and lightly pressed it onto Wes's shoulder, and Della wondered if it looked bad that, *twice* now, he'd been hurt and she'd been content to step back, let someone else care for her fiancé. "Then we . . . we saw him sitting there bleeding."

"It . . . it's not that bad," Wes mumbled, but he winced as Eloise tied the long piece of torn apron around his shoulder.

"Who would shoot someone?" the kitchen maid asked, glancing around, and as she did, a softness swept across her face, almost like . . . relief, Della thought, and she slipped that small piece of information into a corner of her mind where she could think on it more closely later.

"She wasn't here." Violet's cold gaze glared at Della, her eyes as blue as ice.

"Me? I was taking a walk along the shore." Della matched Violet's glare. "Didn't you slip into the forest yourself before I left?"

"Cook thought she saw some morels and asked me to collect them!" She gestured to a small basket on the ground beside the picnic, filled with small brown mushrooms with crinkled, honeycomb edges. "You were all alone and at just the right time, not me!" Violet shot a look toward the manor. "Your mother left in a hurry too. Maybe it was her! Or did she help you? Was this planned?"

"Planned?" A fire tore through Della's veins, and she almost spit to the whole picnic how the maid slithered around with Wes in the shadows. She clamped her mouth shut, saving that piece of information for herself. "My mother left because she doesn't like blood." And as a sharp smirk tilted Violet's lips, the maid stared at Wes as if to say, *So she knew there'd be a lot of blood.* "She doesn't like *hunting*," Della added, "But *you*—"

"Then maybe it was Sadie!" Violet said, cutting off Della before she could spill another accusation at her. The dark-haired maid's eyes bounced from Sadie and then to Eloise. "Or Eloise. *They* could be lying for each other."

"No!" Cook gasped, one hand going to her heart as she shook her head so hard her auburn curls slapped her cheeks. "Sadie didn't. Sadie couldn't hurt anyone." Cook crossed herself, and then reached out as if she could cross Sadie as well. "It was Betty. I know! No one else here would do such a thing." She touched her forehead and chest, one shoulder then the other. "She's come back. She'll be after each of us. One by one."

Sadie's head whipped toward the cook, but no one else said a word. Only Wes let out a grunt as he sat on the ground, a hand to his shoulder, holding the bandage. Heavy breaths slipped from his lungs.

Finally, it was Violet who spoke up. "That's . . . nonsense," she said quietly, but she, too, crossed herself, just as the cook had, before turning back to Eloise. She cleared her throat as her fingers dropped from her left shoulder, then, in a voice that rang across the space, she said, "We all know El—"

"Enough." Wes sat up as if waking from a daze, his voice as dark as a trail of thunder, but hollow—worn out as old leather. And then his words sharpened until their serrated teeth could bite. "You forget your place." The small sentence sliced across the picnic like a knife to the ribs, catching even Della's breath with its harsh syllables and quick cuts.

She flinched even as a small tendril of satisfaction wound through her lungs at seeing Wes's angry gaze directed at his secret sweetheart, at watching the pretty, dark-haired maid's face crumple.

And then he turned to the cook and more softly said, "Betty's gone, but she's no ghost haunting us. This had nothing to do with her."

"Who . . . who's Betty?" Della asked in the quiet creeping through the air.

Wes shook his head. "No one." He took a deep, heavy breath.

"The last kitchen help," Cook whispered, reaching out and

tugging the red-haired maid toward her, tucking her in her arms as if she were protecting her. "She had an accident."

"Another *accident*?" Della asked, and in the silence that lingered after her words, she pulled out her mental ledger and checked her notes on what she knew of each person there, weighing who, besides her, would want Wes gone, and after a moment, she noticed several sets of eyes quickly, quietly flit to her . . . as if they were making the same calculations.

"Did you see who shot you?" Lachlan asked, breaking the tension.

Wes shook his head.

"Isn't it obvious?" Eloise pointed to Wes's shoulder as if an answer hid in his wound.

"What's going on?" a deep voice cut through the afternoon air, and all eyes turned to the forest's edge, where Easton stepped out, his gun in the crook of his arm, a bloody bag over his shoulder.

"You!" Eloise stepped toward Easton, kindling in her eyes, fire in her voice.

But Weston grabbed her arm, held her back. "It wasn't Easton."

"What wasn't me?" Easton sauntered toward the group.

But Eloise ignored him, turning to Wes. "You said you didn't see. How do you know he didn't?"

"He wouldn't." Wes shook his head, grimacing as his shoulder moved. "He *wouldn't*."

"This is my fault." Lachlan's voice was heavy, his words falling from his mouth like shame. "I shouldn't have sent them together. I shouldn't have thought they could . . ." He trailed off.

Eloise bent close to Wes, her voice hushed, but not quiet enough that Della and the others couldn't hear. She leaned into Wes with the softness of a new bride. "Even your father has realized it."

"It wasn't Easton." Wes ground the words out between teeth shut tight, his breaths coming in sharply, leaving just as jaggedly.

"What wasn't me?" Easton parted the crowd surrounding his brother. "Where . . . where's your shirt?" His eyes flitted between Wes and Eloise, so close to him, nearly touching.

"That's what you ask?" Eloise threw a hand toward Wes's hastily bandaged shoulder. "Not who shot him?" She stood and stepped up to Easton. "But of course"—pulling herself to her full height, she glared at him with lightning crackling in her dark eyes—"Because you already know."

Easton studied his brother, took in the fabric wrapped about the joint where Wes's muscle met collarbone. Bits of blood had started to seep through its stark white. He touched his own shoulder in the same spot. "I see." His hand dropped, his voice following. "You think I did it. Again." He turned to Eloise. "You don't trust me. Or believe me. First the nightshade and now a bullet biting his shoulder in a patch of flesh I know better than anyone. But it wasn't me." He set his long gun down and crouched beside his brother, turning away from Eloise to him. "I didn't do this."

Wes looked away, refusing to meet Easton's eyes, and Della wondered what words they kept back from each other in missed glances. "I know."

But Eloise was full of words, firing them at the brothers like bullets until they ricocheted around the small gathering. "Who else!" She waited for Easton to stand and face her again, and then pushed on his shoulder, her hand pressing into the same spot where Wes bled from. "This can't be coincidence. Who else would know, Easton?" She chewed on his name, grinding the syllables slowly, and then she was storming away like an eastern wind.

"Ellie!" Easton called after her. "Where are you going?"

She paused for only a moment, not even bothering to turn around and face her fiancé. "To get him help."

Della watched as Eloise's silhouette shrunk against Asquith manor, and then turned to Wes where he sat upon the picnic's quilt. She should move closer. Offer to help him. She was angry with him and the dark-haired maid, but she didn't want him dead—and didn't want suspicion thrown onto her. Violet's words still hung in the air between them.

She wasn't here.

Would the others question *her* if she didn't start showing some care or affection for Wes?

She'd simply taken a short walk while the others had hunted. She hadn't—

"It really wasn't me." Easton bent down, crouching bedside Wes. "It wasn't."

Wes nodded. "I know—"

"Why?" Lachlan interrupted. "Why can't you two just get along?"

"Father . . ." Easton looked up, his black brows pinched. "I didn't do this. You should be looking for who did." His gaze darted around the group, and was it Della's imagination that it lingered on her the longest? He turned back to his father with his hands up, palms empty. "I don't even have a pistol."

"What?" Lachlan tilted his head, his cloudy eyes roaming the small collection of people surrounding him. "You don't . . ."

And then Della's focus shifted to at all the discarded guns. Long and sleek and ones that sprayed fragments. She didn't know much about hunting, but she knew those didn't leave a single hole.

"We had shotguns, Father." Easton stood again, stretching to his full height. He took off his bag, opened it to reveal a dead pheasant, and then dropped it, tossing it next to the picnic blanket. He turned out his pockets next, lifted his shirt. Tearing it off, he threw it to the ground in one hard movement before spinning in a circle with his arms outstretched.

Again, Della should've looked away. The Asquiths had no sense of decency. But all she saw was truth painted along his flesh.

He had no weapon tucked away, but there, on his left shoulder in the same spot his brother bled, was mangled skin shaped like a star—a clump of tight scar tissue in the center with little tendrils that stretched out.

Wes stood slowly, and side by side, the brothers were more alike than a mirror's reflection if Della ignored the blood leaking through Wes's bandage.

But he wasn't the only one with scarlet on him. There, on Easton's forearm, was a slash of red—a single line of sticky crimson. "What's that?" She pointed to it.

Easton shrugged. "My kill." He tipped his head to his bag.

"Your . . . kill?" Della glanced around the group.

Lachlan spoke first. "They've done it since they could first hunt."

"It . . ." Wes took a deep breath, wincing as he did. "It makes it easy to see who won—who has the most. It's the bird's blood on him. Not mine." He touched his right hand to his wound. "I . . . I should go, I think . . . and lie down."

"Of course." Lachlan tipped his head to the manor as Eloise hurried back with two butlers by her side. "Have John fix you up." He turned to Della and Easton, to the cook and the two maids left before adding, "But tell Henry to come to me." His dim eyes traveled the group, landing on Della last. "He and I are going to find out who had a pistol."

23

El

Two Months Earlier
March 1910

A cool breeze swept past Eloise, bouncing off Lammore and seeping through her clothes. She sat in her dinghy, watching as the Asquiths' steamboat loomed closer. She'd never be able to outrun it with only oars, so she waited, wondering if it was Wes or Easton coming out to meet her in the middle of a lake that churned with the beginnings of a spring storm.

A head popped over the front of the bow, and even from the distance between her small skiff and their taller ship, Eloise recognized Wes.

He leaned over the golden rail. "You can't avoid us forever, El."

She shifted on the small wooden seat, turning her back to him. "I'm in the middle of a sprawling lake whose shores you can't even see from here." She looked back only to toss a glare over her shoulder at him. "Do I look like I want your company?"

Wes climbed over the edge of the boat as the back of it neared hers, his feet landing on a metal ladder running along the hull. He scurried down it until his polished shoes nearly touched the water. "Come on, El, come closer." He bent, holding on with one hand and reaching the other out toward her. "Please."

Eloise said nothing as she lifted her paddles. It wasn't until she rowed over to him and he grabbed the lip of her small boat, tugging it close and tying its rope to the end of the ladder, that she asked, "What do you want from me, Wes?" Her words felt like a snuffed candle—no hope warming them.

"Join me." He waited with his palm out, ignoring the way her question had sighed over the deep water.

She lingered a moment and then placed her left hand in his, and even she noticed how his eyes strayed to the diamond on her finger, how its faceted stones bit into the soft pad of his thumb when his grip curled around hers.

"It's lovely, isn't it?" Her voice was as smooth as silk and as sharp as a hat pin to the ribs, piercing Wes right where she wanted it to. She saw it in his flinch, felt it in the way his grip tightened.

"He's here too."

He said it quietly, but his words hit her hard—not a swift, clean stab like hers, but a blow to the stomach, stealing the air from her lungs until all she could think to say was, "Why?"

But Wes didn't answer. He merely turned around, climbed back up the ladder, and only faced her again to help her over the boat's railing.

Clouds gathered in the sky, blotting out the morning sun, turning the day to a dreary gray that she felt in her chest, in the soft marrow of her bones. It wouldn't be long until a storm grumbled, and Eloise welcomed the gloomy weather.

"Wes," she whispered before Easton showed up and heard her. "Can we just—"

"Don't, El." He turned to her slowly, his eyes avoiding hers.

"You came here." Eloise pulled on his hand, and Wes glanced at it as if he just realized he still held her. "You came to *me*." He finally looked at her. "I didn't chase after you."

Wes scratched the back of his neck. "Can't things just go back to when we were friends?"

"No." The single word sliced through the air, cutting apart his question. He had belonged to her, and there was no undoing that. "We can't." She stepped close to him, pulling her hand from his and setting it on his arm, forcing him to look at her. "Did you love me at all?" She thought of his gentle kisses and soft smiles, of afternoons together spent talking and laughing, of evenings sharing quick contests and good books. "Or was it a game? Was I another competition between you and Easton?" But her words curdled on her tongue, soured the wrong way. The riddles, the rivalry—it had always been between Wes and *her*.

"You were never . . ." He swallowed. "No, El. No games."

Eloise moved closer, letting their arms brush, and it would take just a small twitch of her wrists to hold him, to encircle him in an embrace. "What can I do to change your mind then? Can we go back a month—before an heiress took your heart from me?"

"She . . . she doesn't have my heart." He set a hand on her cheek, and even though she should've turned away, Eloise leaned into his touch, soaked up his words and let them flood her chest. "There are only two people who own that: You. And Lucy."

"Then why?" Eloise hated the way the words sounded like a plea, hated that she couldn't stop herself from asking them. "Why would you—"

"Do you ever think the whole world is against you?" Wes set his free hand along the other side of her jaw, cradling her face in both of his palms. "That maybe it has been since the minute you were born?"

"What do you mean?" Eloise stared into his dark eyes. If he wouldn't voice the answer to her question, maybe she could find it in his gaze. They'd always been able to read each other like a favorite novel, but in that moment, his expression was a foreign language, and she couldn't discern its syllables.

"I think I'm cursed, El." Wes set his forehead against hers and whispered, "I think . . . I think I always have b—"

His hands jerked from her skin, and Eloise realized a moment too late that Easton was there, had been for long enough to hear them, to see them in each other's arms.

He pushed Wes then. "She's not yours anymore." His hand pressed against his brother's chest, shoving him into the railing. "Stop playing with her." Easton's jaw was clenched, and between his teeth, he added in a low whisper, "And me."

"Easton, wait!" Eloise reached out to her fiancé, let him see his ring glinting on her finger. "It's not what you think—" But it was, and her lips closed around the lie.

Easton wasn't listening anyway, and with one last thrust, Wes not even fighting back against him, Easton pushed his brother overboard.

"Wes!" Eloise tore her attention from the churning water where Wes had sunk, and beside her, Easton took a deep breath.

He popped a hip against the railing as if he hadn't just shoved his brother over it. She expected fire in his eyes, but they were dull as he watched her, and his words were slow when he spoke. "Will you always be his, even when you're mine?" Easton closed his eyes, his shoulders falling as a sigh heaved out from deep within his chest. "Do I have to get rid of him for you to notice me?"

But Eloise ignored him and instead listened to Lammore, waiting for a break in the water to cut through the air. She turned to the lake, watching for Wes, her feelings and thoughts a tangle. She had no answer for Easton. She'd regretted the weight of his ring on her finger as soon as she'd realized it hadn't been enough to lure Wes back to her.

"I really thought, when you said yes, that maybe—"

"Where is he?" Eloise stared at the gray water. "He's . . . he's not coming up."

"He'll be fine," Easton answered. "He's a strong swimmer." But he leaned over the railing also, watching the lake. "It's just another prank."

"It's not." Eloise gripped the rail, the water below too still, too calm.

"Ellie, don't."

Before he could stop her, Eloise climbed onto the smooth golden metal, and with his fingertips brushing her arm, she dove into the water.

The lake was frigid, still cold from winter's strong hold on it. It enveloped her in a single pull and nearly tore the air from her lungs with one exhale. But Eloise belonged to this lake, and it belonged to her. Lammore wouldn't steal from Eloise—not her breath.

Or Wes.

The water was black below the surface, but she had never needed to see to navigate the lake. She could always cross Lammore's waters even in murky storms to Asquith manor, her heart tugging her to *Wes.* And it was that compass inside her that brought Eloise to him in the deep, icy lake. She wrapped her hand around his arm and kicked with all her strength, her skirts tangling around her legs as she fought her oldest friend for the man she loved.

But he was too heavy for her.

And her grip wasn't strong enough.

You can't have him.

The thought tore through Eloise's mind, and she was sure tears were spilling from her eyes, slipping salt into the lake's waters.

Her lungs burned.

Her breath was almost spent.

Wes was still sinking.

Something wrapped around her waist, pressed against her back, pulled her from Wes. Her fingers slipped off his arm in one quick jerk, and then she was pushed upward. Only when she was released did she realize it had been Easton.

He'd come for her.

And then the dark shape of him dove into Lammore's depths.

Down.

And down.

And down.

For Wes.

And as the black water swallowed Easton, Wes's words crept through Eloise's thoughts.

I think I'm cursed.

If he were, then she and Easton were doomed right alongside him. The three of them had been woven together tighter than roots sharing the same soil. If one of them were blighted, how could it not spread until all three of them were withered and rotted through?

24

The Fiancée

Early Evening
May 11th, 1910

Eloise waited beside Wes. He lay on his bed, sucking in sharp breaths between his teeth as Lachlan's butler tried to dig out a brass bullet from his shoulder. A long silver tool pressed into his skin as John attempted to clamp it around the mangled metal, and Eloise watched, feeling as though she'd been pulled through time and now sat three years younger, seeing her bullet carved from an Asquith's shoulder all over again.

Only, it hadn't been her to shoot this time.

Wes screamed, and as John dug the tool deeper, he yelled, "Just leave it!"

John shook his head, "I can't. It . . . it would close around it." He pressed farther, gouging more flesh. "It wouldn't heal right."

"It's just a shoulder!" Wes clenched his teeth. "Not a heart. Leave it!"

Eloise's fingers curled around the armrests of the chair she sat in, her nails pressing into the soft velvet. Easton had what he'd always wanted. She had pulled on the first thread of a life together with him, and yet still he'd sought revenge on Wes for a bullet that had always been hers. What more could Easton hope for? Anger burned in her belly as she stared at the blood-soaked bandages. Did Wes have to have the same wound for Easton to be happy? Would he shoot her next if he found out the truth? She should tell him. She would watch his face as he found out she'd been the one to pull the trigger all those years ago, and then she'd know if forgiveness was only kept from Wes, or if he'd keep it from her too.

"Leave it, John, please." Wes took a deep breath, exhaling slowly as John dropped the tool onto his tray. Sweat beaded along Wes's forehead, his upper lip. A grimace marred his mouth.

"Thank you for trying, John." Eloise's words were calm, quiet, though she felt anything but that. "Please tell Cook to send up a chamomile tea."

John said nothing, only tipped his head and slipped out Wes's bedroom door without a sound, a tray in his grasp full of blood and bandages and unanswered questions.

Silence lingered between Wes and her as the door snicked shut, until finally, softly, Eloise broke it. "Why are you making me marry him? Look what he's capable of." She gestured to his shoulder where a bullet still burrowed in his skin.

"Easton didn't do this. He . . . he wouldn't." Wes laid his head back and stared at the ceiling. "And I'm not making you marry him."

Eloise dropped her voice, mimicking him as best she could. "'You're going to marry Easton Anthony Asquith.'" She stared at him, remembering his words from only two nights ago. "'It's the only way forward for all of us.'" She let her words lift, leaving behind her impression of him. "Did you not say that?"

He nodded and watched the ceiling rather than look at her.

"You smile at that heiress and tell me to marry Easton and

think my heart hasn't turned to stone." She chewed her words until they were as broken as she was.

"And I saw the way you looked at him," he shot back. "'Priceless,' he called you, and you smiled at him." His eyes flicked to her. "One word was all it took to turn you to him." He stared at the ceiling again, his brows furrowed. "Yours isn't the only heart being torn apart."

"If you think it was one word from Easton and not the many from *you*, you're as blind as your father!" Eloise stood and paced his room. This wasn't the conversation she'd wanted to have. She had followed him to offer comfort—not fight about a future they no longer looked toward. "Am I still to marry him after he shot you . . . and even though you love me?" She clenched her teeth, needing to hear him say it, wanting to know if, after everything, his mind was still set.

His answer came too quickly for her liking. "Yes." He sat up, slowly. "Easton didn't shoot me. We've had our issues, but . . . he wouldn't." Wes shook his head. "And I can't marry you even though I want to." His chin dropped. "I'm just . . . I've been cursed from the minute I was born, El. And I . . . I can't—"

"Three months ago, you chose an heiress—and all her wealth—and threw me aside like scraps for a dog . . . and you think *you're* the cursed one?" Eloise shook her head. "If you're cursed, Wes, then it's infected me." She pointed to herself, to her chest, where beneath thin ribs, her tender flesh still beat to the sound of his name. And somehow that was worse than if it had forgotten him. It was no wonder his brother had shot him.

Easton's words from only two months past swept back to her.

Will you always be Wes's, even when you're mine?

Do I have to get rid of him for you to notice me?

He might. And that's what scared Eloise, what made her think that it was Easton after Wes, and that maybe . . . just maybe, petty revenge wasn't all he wanted.

"I know." Wes looked away. "You, me, Easton . . . it's poisoned us all. How can the three of us be happy like this?"

She stared at him, letting silence linger until he turned to her, and when his eyes met hers, she whispered, "We can't."

Eloise left Wes to rest and mull over the mess he'd made, not just with his life, but hers and Easton's too, and searched for his brother. She had her own future to wrestle with in the form of a twin bent on revenge.

She found Easton in the library, plucking a book from the shelf as if he hadn't spent the afternoon spilling his brother's blood.

"Find what you're looking for?" Eloise arched a brow and leaned against the doorframe.

Easton shook his head. "Not unless one of these pages tells me who's framing me."

She said nothing, unsure what to believe, and instead watched him. He tucked his book under his arm and walked across the room, settling into a tall-backed chair.

As he opened the novel, holding it up, he glanced over its rim at her. "But you still don't believe it wasn't me that poisoned or shot him."

"He was shot in the exact same place as you." *By me.* The truth was there, right on the edge of her tongue. But even now, she couldn't break her promise to Wes, and what did it really matter after all, especially if Easton wasn't lying? The truth of his scar would just jumble up the present all the more. Her secret was only a single thread in a cobweb of lies being woven in the corners of Asquith manor. And Eloise intended to find the little spider spinning them all. "There's only so many people who know about that."

Easton's gaze was flat as he watched her. "Maybe Wes is doing it to himself to get your sympathy—to turn you against me right when . . ." He exhaled, measured and restrained, but a touch too much, as if it took all his concentration not to let the anger simmering under his skin spill to the surface. That was Easton, calm and quiet on the outside, boiling underneath—someone who could give his brother half of a nightshade berry, at least once—and not let the sweat seep over his skin, not have guilt slither into his thoughts.

"Right when what?" Eloise crossed her arms, watching him.

He stared at his book, avoiding looking at her. "Right when you'd said, 'All right.'" He spoke the last two words softly. "Right when you'd given me hope."

Eloise sucked in a quick breath but said nothing. She *had* given him hope, and how quickly she'd taken it back.

Easton cleared his throat. "*I* think he did it himself just so you'd go crawling back to him."

Eloise took a step toward Easton, her voice careful, but sharp. "You and I both know I went *crawling*, as you put it"—she seared her words with heat, letting them burn—"Back to him several times in the last few months—"

"Since you agreed to marry me, you mean?" He kept his eyes on his book. "Yes, you have."

"And you know what?" She waited till his eyes flicked to her. "He's chosen that heiress and all her money over me. Every. Single. Time."

"He's a fool." Easton stared back at the pages before him, but she knew he was watching her too.

"A fool with money." Eloise shook her head. "But that ruins your argument." She closed her eyes before letting the rest of her thoughts drip from her lips. "He doesn't want my sympathy. He doesn't want *me*."

When she opened her eyes, she found Easton with one

black brow arched. "So that brings your suspicions back to me?" His focus was still on his book, but the rigid way he held himself told her his attention was fixed on her, not the words before him.

She didn't need to answer. For once, the truth sat between them, read as easily at the novel in his lap.

He shut his book with a *snap* and stood, storming past her and out the library like a thundercloud.

"Where are you going?"

He only turned halfway to her. "This was supposed to be a week of celebrating our engagement. A week of enjoyment. And it's been anything but." He glanced over his shoulder, his gaze level. "I'd like a distraction. From you. From *him*." He let his words roll off his tongue slowly as he added, "From this whole mess that I'm not even a part of." And then he was gone, rounding the corner, and leaving Eloise standing there with none of her questions answered and no closer to finding Wes's would-be murderer.

25

The Cook's Assistant

Evening
May 11th, 1910

Sadie had never been so glad to see someone shot.

The thought should've left a sickness in her chest, like tar clinging to her ribs, but instead, a lightness had flooded her lungs when she'd seen Wes's wound. The ragged red flesh had let her breathe again. If someone else had pierced him with a brass bullet, maybe it meant that she hadn't been the one to poison him too. Maybe she was innocent after all and hadn't dragged her aunt into any deadly secrets either.

Sadie picked up a large pot crusted with an aftermath of the evening's soup and thought of a small silver gun as she cleaned it. Lachlan hadn't found any pistols hidden away on anyone at the picnic, and that left Sadie wondering who else might wish to harm Weston the week of his engagement party.

Accusations had flown through the small group on the lake's edge. Della Drewitt had blamed Violet, and the housemaid had thrown suspicion on Eloise and Sadie as easily as she tossed out kitchen scraps, and yet, as Lachlan and his butler had searched first Violet, then Sadie and her aunt, and finally Della—with a grimace on Lachlan's face as Henry searched their guest—they'd found nothing but the shotguns set out for the hunt. Had someone stashed a pistol elsewhere? Left it in the woods? Or had there been another soul slinking through the forest that no one had seen?

It wasn't Sadie's business, she decided as she scrubbed. She had enough to figure out with that note tucked away in her room. Even if she hadn't been the one to poison Wes, someone in this manor still thought it had been her. She wouldn't concern herself with the missing pistol when she had that to fret over. Lachlan was capable enough to discover who was toying with Weston like a barn cat playing with a rat. And a rat he was, she thought. Perhaps there was another maid upset with him. Perhaps he'd stolen more kisses that weren't his to take.

Or perhaps . . . his fiancée had discovered his wayward endeavors. The memory of a door slamming moments after Weston had kissed her in the garden still rang through her thoughts. Della hadn't been found with a pistol on her, but . . . her mother hadn't been at the hunt. Had she—

Sadie shook her head. The notion was ridiculous. Caroline Drewitt was nearing seventy. Surely, she wouldn't hold such a grudge against Weston just over a kiss. But a shiver slowly snaked down her back, itching each vertebra. It was clear to the whole manor that Caroline favored gossip, that she tucked other people's secrets in her palms like pilfered confections, but . . . what if *she* became the talk?

Sadie took a guess she wouldn't like *that* very much. But would that be enough to shoot Weston?

Della couldn't have an embarrassing, cheating fiancé if he were no longer breathing. Was Caroline trying to stop the chatter before it could start? What price would the Drewitts pay to preserve their reputation? But if it *was* Della or her mother, would she be next since Weston had kissed *her*?

Dread laced through her veins, and she thought of the hunt—of Weston hidden away between the brush and trees, barely visible. She'd only seen him in the thick foliage because of the bright red blood. But she and Eloise . . . they'd been standing around, talking, wandering about, and not even trying to be quiet. Had one of them been the actual target? If Sadie weren't around—wasn't alive—that, too, would stop the gossip.

She chewed on that thought and then shook her head. No, Weston had been poisoned also. It didn't make sense for someone to be after *her*. Unless . . . unless Aunt Agnes had been wrong, and they *had* been the ones to poison him.

I know what you did.

Someone had left her that note. *Someone* was after her.

What did they know? Nightshade in a dessert? Or a kiss they thought was wanted?

Sadie still didn't know who had slammed the greenhouse door. Had it been Caroline or Della? Had they seen Weston's lips against hers?

"And what are you doing here all alone?" a deep voice cut through the noise of her worried thoughts and the sounds of her washing.

Sadie stilled as a chill seeped over her skin. If the devil could be called by speaking of him, what was Weston that thinking of him brought him to her?

"Will you not look at me, kitchen mouse?"

She shook her head. "How's your shoulder?" Sadie kept her attention on the full sink instead of looking at Weston, and in short, sharp syllables, she added, "And your fiancée?"

His voice dropped as he answered her. "I don't want to talk about her."

"Then we have nothing to say to each other." She plunged her hands into the hot water. "And I have work to do." She swallowed hard. "Or are you going to try to kiss me again, *sir*?"

"I told you it's *not* sir. It's Weston."

Sadie paused, took a deep breath, and then faced him, the pot still in her grasp and spilling water as she turned. "Weston," she ground out, the name tasting like bitter tea on her tongue.

"How pretty it sounds coming from those cherry blossom lips of yours." He smiled, a wide, sharp spread of his mouth with white teeth flashing.

Her heart sped as she answered. "My lips aren't your concern." Sadie's grip tightened on the pot. She held it between her and him while water dripped from it, landing in the small space between them.

"Kitchen mouse," Weston said, unfazed by the sting in her words. "Wouldn't you like to get away from the heat of this hearth?" He grabbed her free hand, his thumb rubbing across her skin. "You're far too pretty for water-wrinkled fingers, for burn-marked hands and calloused palms. I could—"

"I'm smart enough to stay in the kitchen." *Away from an engaged man and empty promises.* She let her unspoken words circle between them in the silence and then pulled out of his grip. "And be happy about it."

She turned from him with her heartbeat lodged somewhere between the back of her tongue and the top of her sternum. She swallowed it down, breathing in slowly, exhaling just as deeply, easing the racing in her veins. She'd never stood her ground before, had always shied from confrontation, endlessly freezing at the wrong times.

But she was tired of being frozen, of never fighting, never fleeing. Fear forever turning her to ice.

Weston stepped close, the heat of him seeping through the fabric of her dress, sliding down her spine.

She thawed herself in inches, the muscles in her back relaxing one small bone at a time.

She wouldn't let his mouth touch hers again.

And it had only been hours since she'd seen the raw flesh of his wound. She knew exactly where that bullet hole was.

So, when he placed a hand on her hip, she spun around and faced him. Stared into his eyes. Reached up. And pressed her thumb into the soft tissue of his injury, digging her nail into the same spot a bullet had burrowed. And with her heart rearing like an untamed mare, she said, "Leave me alone or I'll tell your fiancée."

But he didn't flinch. Didn't move. And when a smile as crooked as a thief's swept across his cheeks, a single word slipped from her lips.

"Easton."

26

The Heiress

Evening
May 11th, 1910

Della slipped down the narrow passageways, prepared to uncover all the secrets Asquith manor had buried. Whoever had poisoned and shot her fiancé could come for her next. After *she* had been searched like a common criminal at the hunt, she'd memorized the second level's hidden halls.

Embarrassment flooded her cheeks at the memory of a butler's hands on her, searching for a pistol she'd never had. As if she could've hidden even a small gun beneath the form-fitted silk gowns her mother insisted on buying for her anyway. They could've just looked at her and seen all her curves instead, rather than the hard outline of a sleek gun. She'd hoped it would've been Violet found with a pistol, would've been happy to have seen her dragged away, but she'd been found with nothing besides her basket of morels.

Della crept down to the main floor's hall, tucking away the second story's layout. She'd changed out of her sapphire dress from the picnic and into a black gown to match the dark walkways, allowing her to be little more than a smudge of gloom herself.

Soft clinks from the beadwork on her skirt and the groans of the old wooden floorboards followed her like shadows until a familiar voice stopped her.

"Oh, well isn't *that* interesting," seeped through the wall in her mother's voice.

Della pressed an ear to the wood, but no more words slithered through. There was no door to peek into and see where her mother was or *what* she was doing. Della was about to continue on—her mother had probably found an old newspaper and was gladly gobbling up gossip from columns with names she didn't even know—but a tiny, odd square on the wall caught Della's eye. It was as small as a sugar cube, the wood not nearly as aged as the hallway and a brass latch still with its shine, as if it'd been added years after the manor had been built. Della brushed her fingers across the gilded metal, unlatching it slowly, and then quietly, she leaned forward and pressed an eye to the opening, holding her breath, stealing glimpses into a room the color of old, old rust.

Her mother hovered over a desk—a pencil in one hand and a little notebook in the other. Her back was to Della, and she mumbled words so softly they didn't even reach through the small peephole. After her mother scribbled on the paper, she tucked her book and pencil into a skirt pocket and rummaged through the desk's drawers. Della's view was limited, but the way her mother cast quick glances around the room before digging in another drawer had Della believing no one else was there, that her mother shouldn't be either.

The hunt's accusations slunk back to her mind as she watched.

Your mother left in a hurry. Maybe it was her! Or did she help you? Was this planned?

Her mother *had* left in a hurry, but Della hadn't lied at the picnic. It was true the older woman didn't like hunts, didn't enjoy seeing the spilled blood or dead, limp animals.

Her mother stepped away from the desk. "Perfect." She glanced at her pocket watch, the thin gold chain catching the low lamp light. "Now what to do about that girl?" And as her mother's small, short words drifted over to her, Della wondered who she meant.

Was it *her*? Was she the girl her mother spoke of? Della knew she wasn't happy about her attitude toward this engagement.

She stepped away, latching the peephole closed once more. She'd ask her mother later why she'd snooped through the Asquiths' rooms. Della took a deep breath. She was poking and prying through the Asquith estate as much as her mother was, and she could always snoop one more time—through her mother's things—and see for herself just what her mother had written in that notebook.

She turned away and slipped down the hidden hallways once more, memorizing the passageways, plucking secrets as she went—the Asquiths', their maids', and even her mother's, it seemed.

Another muffled conversation met Della through the wall, and she wondered what else the evening might reveal. The voices rose, seeping to her through the crack of a hidden door, and Della no longer cared if she eavesdropped—Weston had tucked away a maid, and her mother was hiding *something*, and she was so very tired of the secrets scurrying out from every shadow in this manor.

A deep voice curled through the gap beneath the door, and Della stepped over, cracking it open and peeking through. One of the twins—Easton, she assumed, since he seemed well enough—stood with a red-haired kitchen maid. The girl's hazel eyes skipped around the room and then landed on the floor.

Della should close the door, back away, and leave their conversation, but decency had left as soon as a butler's hands had searched her, and then the maid's words slipped through the crack—and pierced her.

"Are you going to try to kiss me again, sir?"

Della froze, and Eloise's soft smile from dinner the night before flitted through her thoughts until a new kind of anger burned in her chest.

The Asquith twins were nothing more than pathetic boys dressed in the skin of men.

And Della wasn't about to let herself *or* Eloise marry anyone with straying eyes.

She'd find Eloise and tell her what she'd seen, but as Della stepped back into the shadows, ten small words stopped her.

"I told you it's *not* sir. It's Weston."

Della raced down a passageway, glad the halls hid her from her fiancé. A flame burned in her belly, hot and feeling an awful lot like embarrassment. Of course, it hadn't been Easton. Not when he was engaged to beautiful Eloise. No, it was only *her* fiancé who wandered to pretty maids. Plural.

She could already hear the whispers of gossip, couldn't get them out of her thoughts, couldn't get them to leave her alone.

Dull Della, and all her money couldn't even buy her fiancé's attention.

Not even married and already he couldn't stand her.

Ran away the moment he saw her.

She shouldn't care. But oh, how she did. For one moment, she wanted someone to see her as more than gold and paper bills, wanted to be looked at like her father used to watch her mother—with love—when her mother was still warm and kind, before he'd died and social status had replaced her heart.

Della crumpled to the ground at the end of a long, dark hall, and took a deep breath. She refused to cry, especially over an engagement she hadn't even wanted. Instead, she exhaled slowly and thanked the good Lord she'd found out who Wes was before her mother had forced her to marry him.

She waited a moment, simply breathing, picking the right words to tell her mother so she'd agree this engagement was the worst idea. Even her mother would have to admit a cheat wasn't worth a name—she hoped. Della glanced around, about to pick herself up off the ground, when she realized she'd rushed off too quickly and hadn't paid attention to which halls she ran down. She had no idea where she was.

The hall was dimly lit like all the hidden passages, but a single bulb gave a soft orange glow, and as Della looked around her, she noticed a thin outline in the floor beside her.

She inched toward it and found it to be a small door pocketed into the ground, barely noticeable. A square trapdoor with well-oiled hinges, and as she examined it, Della noticed its latch wasn't completely caught.

She opened it all the way, uncovering steps that led down beneath the manor.

Curiosity pulled at her, and she let it. The stairwell was a nice distraction from thinking of Wes and maids and gossip, so she followed steps that crawled into the earth.

They could lead to nothing more than a vegetable cellar or storage for wine, but in a home that housed a poisoned garden in plain sight . . . She wondered what might hide in its shadows.

The gray stone walls were wet, as if a cold sweat clung to them, and they seemed to close in on either side of Della. She followed them down until the stairs opened to a small room with the same bleak walls.

It took a moment for her eyes to adapt to the darker room,

but as they did, she noticed a lump on the floor beneath a statue of a woman carved from white marble, her face covered by a black cloth.

Della stepped over to it slowly, her soft-heeled shoes not making a sound against the hard bricks under her feet. It was only when she was a handful of steps away that her sight adjusted enough for her realize the lump in the middle of the room was shaped like a person.

She crept closer. Slowly. And as she did, a scream scratched out of her lungs, and it took every solid thought in her head to stifle it, to smother it in the back of her throat so no one would come running and find her here in a dark room, with a body hidden at her feet.

Della stared down, where—eyes closed and so still—Lachlan Asquith's form lay deep underground on an abandoned cellar's floor.

27

El

Three Years Earlier
Winter 1907

Eloise opened the kitchen door, stepping into Asquith manor with Tux twisting between her feet and rubbing against her ankles as she went.

"Oh, get that thing out of my kitchen!" Agnes whipped a towel in Eloise's direction before mumbling something about cat hair in the bread.

"Sorry, Agnes." Eloise scooped up Tux, cradling him in her arms.

Cook turned to Betty—a small woman with black hair, graying at the edges and tied back in a bun beneath her cap—and added, "She better not think that when she's lady of this house she can bring creatures into our kitchen."

Betty nodded as she rolled out dough, but it was Agnes' words that stuck in Eloise's thoughts. *Lady of this house.*

"What do you mean?" Eloise asked, gently squeezing the cat to her chest.

"Oh, you heard me." Agnes flapped a towel toward her

as Betty nodded, agreeing with the head cook. "Don't think when you're the lady of this place I'll let you bring animals in here." Agnes shook her head, flipped the towel over her shoulder, and pushed down on a ball of risen dough. "Betty and I will still be the queens in the kitchen." She winked, her pale lashes fanning speckled and sun-spotted skin.

Betty snickered. "That's right." A smile spread across her cheeks, carving wrinkles beside her brown eyes. "And we've earned that title with the hard work of our hands. You cannot take it away from us."

Eloise shook her head, Cook's four words still circling her mind. "I wouldn't anyhow, because I won't be Lady Asquith." Eloise narrowed her eyes as she glanced between the two women. They giggled like schoolchildren, like they held a secret.

Yet it was Eloise who knew what no one else did.

Lady of Asquith meant Easton's wife.

But she would be Wes's bride. She'd make sure of it.

Two months had passed since she'd shot Easton, since Wes had taken the blame, and the rivalry between the twins grew faster than a foot-a-night vine. Easton stayed away from Wes, but he found Eloise often if his brother wasn't nearby, as if Easton waited around corners for her company. No one but Cook would be so bold to speak what the whole manor saw. Easton searched out Eloise.

But it was Wes she harbored under her ribs. Not Easton.

Agnes smiled, a soft thing that made the old woman's freckles dance, and then she flicked one last glance at Betty, who grinned right back. "You've stolen Easton's heart as quickly as he steals my caramel squares. Oh, to be nineteen and pretty again—wanted by all the young men." Agnes played with a bright red curl peeking out of her cap.

Betty nodded with a sigh and touched a hand to her cheek, leaving floured fingerprints. "Those are good days."

Agnes tipped her head, agreeing with her maid, and then emptied the dough onto the counter in front of her. "Not that growing old isn't good either. Not everyone is so blessed." She brought a hand to her heart. "As we know." Her gaze went toward the back of the manor, and Eloise knew she was looking to Roslin's greenhouse, thinking of her. "But enough of that." She bent over the table, kneading and pressing the sticky dough flat before rolling it over on itself. "You and Easton would be a fine pair."

"Quite a handsome one too," Betty added.

Eloise tipped her head down, avoiding Agnes' and Betty's eyes, not wanting them to see the truth on her face—that there was nothing in her for Easton besides the warm feelings of friendship.

"No cats in the kitchen," Eloise said as she cradled Tux. "We should be going then, I think." And before either of the older women could smile that soft grin of theirs again at the thought of her and Easton together, Eloise left the kitchen and made her way down the long hallways, up the stairs, heading for the attic nook where she hoped to see Wes.

But it was Easton's voice that slipped along the manor's walls and curled around the corner to meet her. "What do you mean you can't find her?"

It was quickly followed by a meek feminine voice. "She . . . she wanted to play a game. I was supposed to find her, but . . ."

Eloise rounded the bend and found Easton with Lucy's newest nanny—a petite woman in her forties with ashy-brown hair and eyes that matched. Her hands were splayed, empty palms out to Easton.

"And now you don't know where she is?" Easton closed his eyes a long moment before opening them and adding, "That sounds like a terrible game to play with Lucy." He sighed. "All right, Addie. Don't tell Father. We'll find her."

Addie nodded, and then both of them turned toward Eloise as if just realizing she was coming to them.

"Lucy's . . . hiding?" she asked, dropping Tux to the floor, where he scampered away from the small group.

Easton nodded. "Not for the first time." He stared at her, his eyebrows pinched, and she wondered if his memory was drifting back to six months earlier when Lucy had slipped into the woods . . . and Eloise had let her.

"Where was she last time?" Addie asked softly.

"In the woods," Eloise answered just as quietly, tugging her shawl tight around her shoulder as if that could ward of the chill sweeping over her flesh, the guilt dripping into her veins.

"The woods?" Addie shook her head, her eyes widening. Her gaze flicked to the end of the hall where a window sat, staring out at the forest, and Eloise wondered if the nanny saw not the trees, but her bags packed and loaded in a car leaving the manor when she glanced to those glass panes.

"She thought she saw a rabbit," Easton said, pulling both Eloise's and Addie's attention to him.

Eloise stared at Easton for a small moment. "I never knew that."

"Was she all right?" Addie asked, and guilt like a river flooded Eloise's veins. Here was Addie who'd known Lucy less than six months asking if the youngest Asquith had been okay when she'd wandered into the woods—not what happened to the previous nanny or what might happen to her now. She asked after Lucy.

Something Eloise hadn't done.

No, she'd turned for the manor and Wes, never caring about a fired nanny or Lucy's wanderings.

Eloise glanced away from Addie, whose attention shifted between her and Easton, looking for an answer, searching for reassurance. But then her eyes found Easton's.

His brows were pulled together, marring the skin between with a deep crease. "She was fine." He shook his head, rubbing the back of his neck, worrying the skin there. "But she needs more than a governess."

"I'm sorry, sir—"

Easton waved a hand to the nanny, dismissing her apology. "It's not your fault. Lucy . . . she needs . . ."

He sighed, and in that small sound, Eloise heard the weight of his little sister clinging to shoulders only just broad enough to be on this side of manhood. She knew that at twenty-two, Easton already felt the gravity of Lucy being under his care one day, and she'd only made it worse when she'd let a pretty nanny lose Lucy to the woods just so Wes might glance *her* way.

"How can I help?" she asked, wanting to ease his fears, wanting to smooth away the sharp line between his brows. Wanting to erase the guilt heating her blood.

He watched her a moment, and then his eyes flicked to Addie, surveying her—the wrinkles just marking her forehead; the gray sneaking into her hair; the plain, pinched look her face held—and then glanced back at Eloise. His lips turned down as if to say, *So it's only pretty maids who catch Weston's eye you're glad to see fired.*

Or maybe it was the guilt making her see that in a quick grimace across his face.

He took a deep breath and answered, "Will you take the main floor and go up from there?" Easton turned to Addie. "You check this one and make your way down. Meet Ellie in the middle. I'll check the servants' quarters." He scratched the back of his neck again. "If she isn't here, I'll search the woods next."

They parted ways with quiet nods. Eloise took the hidden stairwell back down to the main floor. She hadn't seen Lucy downstairs when she'd come in, so she stuck to the private passageways, wondering if the young girl had slipped into one to play.

"When did you get here?" Wes emerged from the secret hall's shadows at its opposite end with a book in hand and a small smile spreading across his face.

She hated to see his grin disappear but answered anyway. "Lucy is missing."

"Again?" He stepped over to her quickly, and she wondered if he were thinking of a nanny with golden hair and a soft laugh too.

"Nothing . . . serious," she answered.

But worry pinpricked his pupils.

Eloise put her hands up, palms facing him as if taming a skittish stallion. "Addie and Lucy were just playing. She slipped away to hide. She's . . . playing still. We just don't know where."

"But inside?" *Not out in the forest?* his eyes said, *Not near the lake?* "In the house?"

She nodded, and a hint of relief swept across his face, softening the creases that had formed on his forehead, easing the tension that ran along his jaw.

"Where have you looked?"

"I haven't yet. Addie is on the top floor coming down. Easton is in the servants' quarters. I'm to check the main floor and then head up. I didn't see her when I came in, so I was checking the old servants' passages."

"I didn't see her out there either." He tipped his head to the wall beyond where the rest of the manor spread out. "I'll help you."

Eloise chewed on the inside of her lip, guilt still slithering through her chest. The day felt too much like when she'd purposely let Lucy disappear, but instead of limbs and leaves, it was hidden doors and dark hallways she searched.

Wes interrupted her thoughts with a quick sentence that added worry to her veins. "What about down?" He pointed to their feet and the old wood below them. "Has anyone checked in the cellar?"

Eloise shook her head. "Why would she . . ." She glanced down. "Do you think she'd go there?"

He lifted one eyebrow as if that were answer enough, and then took her hand—a welcome warmth she leaned into, one she only had because she'd helped get a nanny fired. Would it be Cora he reached for still if she hadn't?

He pulled her down the narrow hall, and she left those thoughts behind.

It was done. And she had what she wanted—his fingers wrapped around hers—and it couldn't be long before he realized his heart belonged to her.

Wes stepped quickly toward the direction of the old cellar's hatch, his black sweater and dark pants leaving him little more than an outline in the dim lighting. They crept through the hidden hallways—together—opening doors and peeking inside, quietly calling for Lucy as they made their way toward the cellar steps. They'd almost made it to the cold gray stone stairs when a muted sound tore through the floor below them as if a boulder split in two.

They ran for the trapdoor that would lead them deep beneath the manor.

Only the clammy walls kept them company as the same sound rent the air again.

And again.

They rushed down the cellar stairs, slowing their steps only enough to be careful not to trip. It would be a hard fall down to a rock-hewn floor.

When they'd made it to the bottom, the room opened to a dimly lit area. And there, off to the side, stood Lucy. A pile of bricks—stacked up and waiting for a project to make them useful—lay at her feet. She held one in her hand, and it looked like it weighed half of her thin bones. Without noticing Eloise or Wes standing behind her, Lucy reared her arm back with every bit of her strength and threw the brick across the room. It smashed into the marble statue of Roslin, ripping a chunk off her stone face. Eloise watched as the severed piece clattered to the ground, landing amongst broken bricks and splintered marble.

"Lucy." Wes said her name softly, gently, and his little sister turned around, staring at him with eyes that burned, with cheeks marred by tears. "What . . . what are you doing?"

Lucy stepped over to him. At twelve years old, she was nothing but arms and legs, gangly in all directions. "She never answers me." Her voice was hard, but even Eloise could hear the tremor in it. And in those four small words spoken from a smaller voice, Eloise heard all the pain Lucy held from a mother gone too soon. The youngest Asquith yearned for Roslin, ran to her statue for comfort, but didn't understand that she hadn't been abandoned by her mother, that Roslin hadn't chosen to leave her daughter. An angry flame smoldered deep inside Lucy, the years stoking its heat. Eloise knew Lucy had a heavy ache of longing, of missing—she felt a smidge of it herself every time her parents ran off, leaving her behind, but nothing like the young girl's. And that hurt that curled up in Lucy's heart gripped her tighter and tighter until it bled out in a few hard bricks thrown at her mother's face.

Wes moved to her, one foot and then the other, barely letting his weight settle into his steps. "I know." He spread his arms out. "I know, and I'm sorry."

Lucy dropped a second brick and came running, stopping only when she crashed into her brother's chest.

He enveloped her in a hug. "I'm so sorry, Lu."

"Why won't she talk to me?" Tears slid down Lucy's pale cheeks, dripping into the hair she'd inherited from her mother. "She talks to Father, doesn't she?"

Wes shrugged before simply replying, "I miss her too." He pressed his cheek against her head and held his little sister tight.

Lucy pulled back. "I don't miss her." She turned and stared at the marble figure of their late mother. "I don't even know her."

"Then . . . what . . . what are you doing? Why . . ." Wes's hand slipped down to hold Lucy's.

"I wanted to talk to her." She turned back to Wes. "But she never answers me." She stared at the pile of old bricks before slowly looking at her brother once more. "So I took her mouth."

Eloise glanced to the figure of Roslin. She'd died shortly after Lucy's birth at only forty-four—still fairly young and beautiful. Lachlan had commissioned the statue to go in her garden, in the very center, at her grave, but when he'd seen it, he'd decided it hurt too much to see her cut from stone, never moving, never aging. Stuck—while the days passed him by. So he'd hidden it away down here where he could still visit it on especially morose days.

But now Roslin's face was cracked and chipped, her mouth ripped off along with half her nose, one eye split down the middle. Eloise slipped off her shawl and stepped over to it. Lifting the thin black fabric, she placed it over Roslin's face like a mourning veil.

When she turned back around, Wes was already shooing Lucy up the stairs with the promise of a slice of blueberry and lemon cake. He watched her go, bouncing up the steps at the prospect of a sugared pastry—no longer concerned with her silent mother—and then he turned to Eloise.

"Don't tell Easton it was Lucy. Please." He glanced to the

shrouded statue of Roslin's broken face. "He's already trying to convince Father she needs to be sent away."

"What do we say then?" Her gaze flicked between the discarded bricks stacked up and the torn statue. "This doesn't look like an accident."

"Say it was me." He shrugged. "I don't care." Wes looked at her, worry pulling his mouth down the wrong way. "Just don't let him know it was Lucy."

It was easier than breathing for her to agree, to erase the frown spoiling his face. She nodded, and a second secret spread out between them like a cobweb, trailing off him and clinging to her, pulling them together.

28
The Heiress

Late Evening
May 11th, 1910

Della quietly stepped over to where Lachlan's body lay in the middle of the cellar on cold stones. A marble statue that looked like it belonged in a graveyard—its face covered with a black cloth as if it were in mourning—loomed over him.

She stared at it, too afraid to look more closely at the still figure at its feet. An inscription was carved into the stone base.

ROSLIN VICTORIA ASQUITH
1855–1899
WIFE MOTHER FRIEND

Della stepped back, her heel smacking the bottom step. She glanced around, wondering if she were standing not in a cellar, but a mausoleum—one where someone had dragged Lachlan's body to his wife's.

Her heart pounded in her veins, so at contrast to the stillness permeating the room, reminding her that she was warm and breathing and alive—and how easily that could end. She could be next. It could be her lying prone and forgotten beneath a manor that buried secrets in its walls.

A small thought ticked through her, pushed her to move. What if Lachlan wasn't quite dead? What if he needed help?

What if he knew who was doing all of this?

She forced her feet to move, her body to bend, her back to bow down low. She reached out, and right when she should've nudged his shoulder, she drew back, too afraid to touch a corpse. Instead, she swallowed hard and whispered his name with a throat seized by fear until it warbled the two small syllables.

"Lachlan?"

When an answer came from his dry, weathered lips, Della screamed. For a moment, for a single sharp inhale, she'd thought his ghost had awoken—with her the closest thing for it to cling to.

But then he sat up, brushing the dust off himself as he did—as if he were just waking from a nap.

"What—" Della's voice trembled, and she cleared her throat. "What are you doing? Are . . . are you all right?"

"Are you?" He turned to her, his cloudy eyes settling directly on her as if he could see through the dim room and his poor vision. "Why are you screaming?"

"I thought you were dead!" Della scooted away as he leaned toward her.

"Dead?" Lachlan shook his head. "No. I wish, but how could I go home to Roslin with the mess these boys have made?"

"What . . ." Della's mouth dropped open. Here she was with her blood racing in her veins and fear speeding through her heart while Mr. Asquith was . . . hoping to die? "Is that why you're lying on the ground? You're . . . wishing for death?" She thought about the poison growing upstairs and a bloody shot in the quiet woods and how, one day, death would come for her.

He sat forward with a groan. "I am lying on the ground because my body is old and my bones ache. It's easier to talk to her this way." He glanced to the ceiling.

Della looked around and then followed his gaze. "To . . . to who?"

"Roslin." He said the word easily, as if it should've been obvious to Della who he meant. "We're beneath her garden. She's just there. Waiting for me." He pointed above him. "If I lie here, it's almost like we're side by side again, chatting in bed like we used to. I loved talking with her, and oh, how I could use her advice."

Her garden. The small words wafted through the still cellar air, clinging to Della—and two quick questions she shouldn't have asked slipped from her mouth. "Why did your wife have a poisoned garden? Is that how she died?" She thought of Wes and how close to death the nightshade had brought him.

Lachlan's dim eyes shot to her. "Poisoned garden? Who told you that?" He shook his head. "My dear Della, it's a garden of medicine. Roslin"—he said her name like a prayer—"Was sick. Cancer of the . . ."

He glanced away from her while drawing a hand up to his chest.

"Oh," Della whispered, unsure what else to say.

Lachlan turned back to her. "Her mother had it too." He sighed, the weight of death drawing deeply from his lungs. "Her garden was our hope."

Della looked up at the cellar ceiling to more gray stone, trying to imagine what Roslin had seen in the fatal foliage. What would she think if she could know how one of those plants had almost killed her son?

"Homeopathy," Lachlan continued. "A little poison to cure the cancer. Or so we'd heard. Or so we'd hoped." His head dropped. "But she was gone before the garden even had a chance to mature."

"Then why . . ." She thought of Wes again, twice poisoned by an ink-tone berry. "Why do you keep those plants still?"

"Lucy," he answered simply. "Roslin's mother had it before her. What if Lucy followed next? I won't lose her too. I . . . I couldn't handle that." He groaned, his hands reaching for the small of his back. "The boys are already more than I can manage." Lachlan turned to Roslin's statue. "She'd know what to do."

And even though Della should've slipped from this cellar, out the manor's front doors, and let the Asquith name slide from her like smoke, dissipating from her memory, never thought of again, she found her curiosity pulling her close to Lachlan, and in a voice as quiet as the gloaming, she asked, "About who's attacking Wes?"

Lachlan nodded. "I've failed these boys."

"Do you know who's doing it?"

Lachlan nodded again and closed his eyes. "It's Easton." He took a long, deep breath and let it out slowly, opening his eyes as he did. "But I don't know why. Wes gave Eloise up for him." He looked at her with his cloudy gaze. "They think I'm blinder than I am, that I don't know what goes on. But I'm still lord of this manor. I know." He tapped a thin, bony finger against his temple. "Wes ended that relationship even though it broke Eloise's heart—maybe both of theirs." He shook his head and sighed. "But she found it again with Easton. He has no reason now to hurt Wes. I don't under—"

"What?" Della cocked her head. "Eloise and Wes? They . . . they were . . ."

"Oh, I'm sorry, dear. I forgot you didn't know . . ." Lachlan reached out, set a hand on hers, his papery skin cold. "It's . . . it's complicated between the three of them. It always has been." He squeezed her hand. "But Wes chose you."

Della's lips flattened into a hard line and her voice dropped. "He chose my money."

"And you, our name." Lachlan leaned toward her again and, as if sharing a secret, whispered, "But love isn't something you just feel. You choose it too."

Della shook her head, wanting to spit out, *Not while he sneaks away with maids.* But she kept the words in her mouth. Who was she to ruin how Lachlan saw his son?

She'd let Wes destroy that himself.

Instead, she tiptoed around two thoughts still circling her mind—a little glass coffin and a murderous brother. The first one was easier to approach, so she asked, "You loved your wife very much, didn't you?"

Lachlan's face transformed as if the thought of his bride had scrubbed away the years and pain. A smile blossomed over his cheeks, reaching all the way to his cloudy, almond-colored eyes. "She was my best friend."

"Is that her heart in my room?" Della blurted out the question. She'd wanted to poke gently at his wounds, but . . . she'd needed to know. There was still an empty glass box beside it.

He nodded.

"Why?" She leaned toward him, needing to hear every small syllable he'd say.

Lachlan shrugged. "It's romantic."

Della wanted to argue, but as he glanced to the ceiling again, realization coiled through her as fast as gossip at a party. She stared at him—at the man who could calcify his wife's heart, lie beneath her grave, under her statue, and hope to chat with her again. "The other one is for you, isn't it? The empty glass box."

Lachlan nodded. "Our hearts harmonized for so long, and mine's been out of rhythm ever since hers stopped singing." He smiled, but it was sad, wrinkling only one corner of his lips. "It'll be nice to hear that melody again."

Della looked away. She didn't understand keeping hearts in a case or burying his wife in their garden or lying beneath a shrouded statue of her, but that . . . that longing to be loved like he'd loved his wife . . .

Not for an estate. Not for jewels. Not for money.

But as a best friend.

She knew that desire well.

And she wouldn't find it with Wes. Not when he slunk after maids. Not if he'd broken his own heart over Eloise—if he had anything more than a wayward heart.

"Why do you think your sons want to kill each other?" Della pulled Lachlan's attention back to her with that single question. "Because of Eloise?"

Lachlan shook his head. "I didn't say they do." He sighed and glanced down. "Just Easton."

Della's pale blond brows rose. "Just." She set her hand on his arm, pulling his attention back to her. "If I'm to join this family, shouldn't I know? Why is Easton after Wes?"

"I'm not as blind as you think I am either." Lachlan looked directly at her, his dim eyes fixed on her even in the dark room. "You don't want to marry Wes."

Della thought about lying, but maybe he did see more than she assumed, so she told the truth instead. "No, I don't." She stared right back at him. "But I am stuck here in this manor while Wes has now been poisoned *and* shot by someone." She leaned close and chiseled her words from a stiff, stiff heart. "I want to make sure I'm not next."

Lachlan patted her hand. "You won't be."

"How do you know?" She eased away from him, staring at an old man who could barely see, and wondered how he could speak so confidently. "How are you so sure it's Easton?"

His voice dropped. "Because three years ago, Wes shot Easton"—he lifted a finger, holding it up—"By accident"—his index finger fell—"In the same exact place." Lachlan touched his own shoulder. "Maybe it's Easton's way of getting back at him before the boys part ways for good. Wes to your estate"—he lifted one bushy gray brow—"If you choose him." Lachlan shrugged as if it didn't bother him whether she wanted his name or not. "And Easton staying here without him."

"But Wes said it wasn't Easton." Della shook her head. "And Easton didn't have a pistol."

"I know." Lachlan took a deep breath, and as he let it out, his shoulders dropped with the weight of his worry. "But if it's not him, it's not just revenge that could end with a half-poisoning and a matching scar—it . . . it would mean someone was trying to kill—" He snapped his mouth closed as if speaking would make it true. "And . . . and I don't know who else it could be."

Della leaned in close to Lachlan until she saw the rich brown of his eyes hiding behind the gray clouds, until he looked back at her, until she was sure she had his attention, and then whispered, "What about a maid?"

29

The Cook's Assistant

Late Evening
May 11th, 1910

Leave me alone or I'll tell your fiancée.

Sadie slipped under Easton's arm with a threat she'd shot at Weston—or so she'd thought—and Easton's name still on her tongue. Both tasted like curdled milk. He reached for her, his fingers grasping her apron strings. It tugged her to a halt, but only for a moment, only long enough for her to hear him say, "Kitchen mouse," in a voice that dripped with venom.

"I have a name," she bit back. She half-turned, ripping her apron ties from his hand and freeing herself from his grip.

"Sadie," he drawled. "I remember." He leaned in close to her, his eyes like cinnamon and fire. And then his voice dropped as he said, "If you want to continue your employment here, I suggest you not threaten me again." He smiled as if his words were sweet, as if they weren't laced with poison. "You won't tell my fiancée anything."

"Yes, I w—"

"That wasn't a question." Easton's words were as sharp as a butcher's blade.

"I care more about Ms. Eloise than this job." Sadie tipped her chin up, her curls spilling down her back, and hoped her words were true. But her aunt's face tore through her thoughts.

"But you didn't care about Ms. Drewitt?" He lifted one jet-black brow, a vicious smile playing at his lips.

Sadie dropped her gaze a moment before lifting her chin, but still, she avoided his eyes. "They . . . Ms. Drewitt . . ." She bit her lip. "It's easy to see she doesn't love your brother."

Easton stared at her, watching the way she fidgeted. He scoffed. "And you think Eloise loves me?"

"I—"

"You're Cook's niece," he said before she could finish answering. He watched her as if he were an owl and she *was* a mouse—his eyes never leaving her, catching every small movement she made. "Aren't you?" Easton reached out, touching her hair, gripping a lock the exact same shade of copper as her aunt's. "Would be a shame if in a few years, when I'm lord, she found herself without employment, without her home." His lips drew a hard line, his jaw clenching even harder. "Wouldn't it?" Easton raised one coal-stained brow.

Sadie swallowed and looked away, her thoughts twisting through her slowly. "Yes, sir," she whispered, her voice soft, meek, with no hint of the blaze burning inside her. She'd let him think he'd broken her.

But she wasn't so brittle that a few hard words could crack her to pieces.

Sadie ducked under Easton's arm and raced out of the kitchen, down the hall. She waited around a corner, glancing to see if he'd storm after her. When no footsteps echoed on the old brick floors, Sadie turned for the stairwell with her heart shivering.

She'd find Eloise now, before fear froze the words in her lungs and that fiery blaze in her chest turned to an icy burn.

Sadie scurried up the stairs, heading for the guest room across from Della's. It was Eloise's for the week, but with the poisoning and shooting, she'd spent more time in Wes's room than hers, having teas and soups delivered there. Should she check his room for Easton's fiancée? She glanced down the hall to where the twins' rooms sat opposite each other, but she had no desire to meet either of them again.

She raised her hand and knocked, praying Eloise was there before her nerves had her racing to her room like a rabbit to its burrow.

"Come in," seeped through the door in Eloise's soft voice, and Sadie turned the brass knob, entering slowly.

She left the door open, prepared for a quick exit, unsure how Eloise would take her news.

"Yes?" Eloise turned from the large window she stood before, the view of Lammore stretching out beyond its glass. She looked Sadie up and then down, waited a moment, but when Sadie hesitated, Eloise asked, "Can I help you?"

"Yes, ma'am." Sadie shuffled her feet. Her mouth didn't like the taste of the words her tongue formed, so she threw them out quickly without savoring their flavor. "Easton kissed me two nights ago." She swallowed hard. "I . . . I didn't want him to." She put her hands up. "And just now, he . . . I think he was going to, again." She shook her head. "But I didn't let him." Her throat closed as if she'd been sipping sand. He hadn't kissed her in the kitchen and yet . . . he shouldn't have been there, shouldn't have cornered her, was wrong for threatening her.

"So, you were the distraction he left for." Eloise turned back to face the lake. "Thank you for telling me." She sighed. "And I'm sorry."

Sadie took a step toward her with a hand reached out, as

if Eloise were a friend to comfort and not a lady whose fiancé had kissed *her*—a kitchen maid. "You're not upset?"

"With you?" Eloise shrugged, her face still to the lake and not Sadie. "No." She glanced back. "With Easton?" She lifted one shoulder again. "Maybe. I'm not sure."

Eloise was calm, and Sadie hadn't expected that. It pulled her thoughts back to the greenhouse, to the door that had slammed, and she wondered if it'd been Eloise watching when Sadie thought it had been Weston who'd kissed her. "Did you already know?"

"What?" Eloise turned to face Sadie fully again. "No."

"He told me he was Weston when he kissed me or I would've told you sooner."

"Two nights ago, you said?" Eloise's lips twisted as if she were thinking, calculating.

Sadie nodded. "Yes, ma'am."

Eloise smiled, but it barely touched her lips, was pinched at the corners. "Thank you—"

A knock at the open door pulled Sadie's and Eloise's attentions to the hallway.

"Ma'am." Violet peeked into the room with a large wicker basket in her hands full of folded clothes.

"Ah, Violet, thank you. Come in." Eloise stepped over to Sadie, setting a gentle hand on her arm. "And thank you, Sadie. I'll take into consideration what you said." She nodded to the door, and as Sadie slipped out, Violet watched her with eyes the exact shade of the lake after a storm had raged.

The heat of the other maid's gaze pressed on Sadie's back as she walked down the hall. She glanced to her once before turning the corner and found Violet glaring at her for one long moment before stepping into Eloise's room.

Sadie shuddered, wondering why Violet looked so angry.

Sadie already had Easton to contend with. She didn't need another person to avoid. Perhaps she could seek the other maid out later and find out what bothered her. Had she done something at the picnic to upset her?

Sadie thought through the day. It'd been long, and she could hardly think of anything other than Weston being shot or Easton cornering her in the kitchen. Perhaps it was nothing more than the day's stress and the accusations that had flown around the hunt making her think Violet was upset at her.

Sadie headed for her room, for sleep and a night to clear away the chaos of the day. Tomorrow she'd find Violet and ask if something was wrong.

Or perhaps, Sadie thought as she neared her door, perhaps the maid was just overwhelmed as well, and her glare had been nothing more than everything piling up on *her* shoulders too and spilling from her face. Nothing personal, nothing to do with Sadie at all. Accusations *had* swooped across that picnic blanket quicker than a barn swallow, putting everyone on edge.

Sadie pulled a key out of her apron. She'd made sure to lock her door since finding the note on her bed. The thought of someone sneaking into her room sent chills sweeping up her spine. She had nothing to hide, no evidence of an accidental poisoning even, but it was her room. A small, meager place, but *hers*.

She unlocked her door, and as she opened it, her eyes immediately went to her bed where that note had stood propped up. When she found nothing there, the tension that had curled around her spine all day unwound, letting go of each small vertebra slowly.

It hadn't been until that moment that she realized just how much she'd been expecting another note, another threat.

Would it always be like this in Asquith manor?

She slipped into her room, closed the door behind her and turned the lock before undressing and changing into her night clothes.

Sadie let the day's trouble melt from her mind as she got into bed, but when her hand slipped under her pillow and met a small piece of paper, she shot up as if bitten by a black widow.

Carefully, Sadie lifted her pillow and found a piece of parchment with her name flourished across the top in the same writing as before.

She sat with the note in her hand and unfolded it slowly. Nine small words glared at her in black ink.

You don't belong here.
Leave before it's too late.

Sadie stared at the paper for too long before crumpling it up and throwing it across the room. She watched where it landed and then looked at her apron hanging on the hook beside her door, the other note—and her key—in its pocket.

She'd locked her room.

And someone had still found a way in.

Her thoughts flew back to two nights ago, when Weston—no, Easton—had popped out of a hidden door across from the golden greenhouse.

How many more secret places hid in Asquith manor?

Was there one leading into her room?

She glanced around, and the tiny hairs at the nape of her neck rose. An itch of being watched bore down on her. Her heart pulsed too heavily in her chest, and she jumped out of bed. She searched for a joint, an outline, something that might show her a disguised door hidden away like a trap.

She had locked her door. She knew it.

And yet, there on her floor, was the balled-up paper with

her name written in curling letters and nine little words that held so much weight.

Sadie forced herself to thaw, to move. She rushed to the walls, pulled at the seams in the wood until her fingernails ripped—all while the crumpled note watched her, stared at her, screamed that someone wanted her *gone*.

She tore her small room apart—dresser shoved askew, rug overturned, books toppled off the short case—searching for a hidden way in. When she found none, she slowly, mechanically put her place back into order as if cleaning the area could clear away the worry in her mind. She worked slowly, setting her room to right, focusing on the small tasks—avoiding the threat watching her from penned parchment. When she'd finished, she finally turned back to that paper, faced it and all its ugly words.

She picked it up.

Her heart crawled into her throat.

It throbbed in heavy beats.

And then she threw the note into her desk drawer where it couldn't look at her any longer.

But she'd get no rest while those words hung in her thoughts.

Leave before it's too late.

30

The Fiancée

Late Evening
May 11th, 1910

It's always Weston. You and him. Circling each other like dogs in heat.

Easton's words from one year prior had slithered back into Eloise's thoughts the moment Sadie's confession had left her cherry-red lips. The crass words had stung back then, stuck with her for twelve long months, and now snaked their way to the front of her mind.

And where's that leave me?

For once, Easton had told her the truth. On the day he'd poisoned Wes the first time, he had told her exactly what he'd do.

Am I to befriend the maids while you and Weston conspire together?

And he'd done it. Even though she'd given him a sliver of her heart, a hope at a future together—just two days ago. He'd thrown her aside as soon as they'd had a single fight.

Easton had gone right to chasing a maid as fast as Wes had run to his heiress.

And where did that leave *her* with two brothers who had always felt like home?

She shouldn't have cared that Easton tossed her to the side too. She'd only agreed to his engagement to make Wes jealous, to make Wes run back to her. Yet she had held on to the small dream in her offered hand as tightly as she'd thought Easton had gripped it back.

He'd called her priceless, and she'd heard his voice say *hope*.

Eloise watched as Violet tucked away her freshly laundered clothes with her thoughts and heart tangled. Anger should've burned through her chest, but instead, Eloise found hurt curled up there—though she'd no right to it. She knew that even in that moment, if Wes turned from his heiress and back to her, she'd split Easton's heart without a second thought and not care how it scarred. Again.

And maybe he knew that. Maybe that was why he slunk after a maid and sought revenge on his brother with a berry and a bullet.

Maybe it was all her fault.

"Ma'am." Violet set her wicker basket down and turned to Eloise.

"Yes?" Eloise let her thoughts slide away and plastered a smile across her lips.

"Are you all right?" Violet's icy eyes flitted to the open door where Sadie had disappeared and then back to Eloise. "It's only . . ." She stared at her face, and Eloise wondered what she'd seen on it as she'd put the clothing away. "You seem like something is wrong. Did Cook's new maid bother you?" Violet's black eyebrows shot up, and she almost looked . . . hopeful? "Did she do something?"

Eloise shook her head, not caring if there was contention between some maids, but she'd also not let Sadie take Easton's blame. "No, she's done nothing. It's . . . Easton." Eloise sighed. "As always." She shouldn't have let his name slip out, but if this gossip sliced through the manor, it was only Eloise who could be pierced, and she wasn't so soft that a few words would wound her.

Violet tipped her head, her hair falling to the side like silk. "Easton?" Her voice was light, a question hiding in the two syllables, but Eloise owed this maid nothing, so she gave her just that.

"Are those Wes's clothes?" Eloise nodded to the basket at Violet's feet, where a small pile of Wes's clothing sat. His sweater from the hunt was on top, waiting to be sewn up. Eloise couldn't heal his shoulder, but she could stitch his sweater for him where the bullet had pierced the soft fabric.

"Yes, ma'am." Violet grabbed the worn wicker handles and picked it up. "I was headed there next."

"I can bring it to him." Eloise took the basket from Violet, intending to sew his sweater before bringing it to him tonight, but the maid held on.

"It's my job, ma'am." She tugged on it. "I can do it." Violet held on tightly.

Eloise pulled on the basket, ripping it away from the maid. She stared at her.

And she hadn't forgotten the way this maid's cold eyes had glared at her from across a picnic blanket, hadn't forgotten the words Violet had shot at her while Wes sat bleeding at the hunt.

Maybe it was Sadie. Or Eloise. They could be lying for each other.

Did this maid think she was conspiring with Sadie to kill Wes? Was she trying to stop *her* from going to his room, as if she had any power over her?

She would end those foolish suspicions now. And let this maid know who was in charge.

"You." Eloise stared at Violet, took in her smooth hair and

black dress, her polished shoes and stark white apron. "You accused me of shooting Wes."

Violet flinched and looked away. "I . . ."

Eloise stepped toward her until the wicker basket in her hands nearly pushed into Violet. She saw how everyone had floundered at the hunt, had vomited rushed excuses, but she'd no inclination to explain to a maid where she'd been or what she'd done. She was competent and clever, and the whole manor knew it.

"If I wanted Wes dead"—she dropped her voice, letting it darken and churn like the lake before a storm—"He would be already." She watched as Violet's bright blue eyes widened. "I wouldn't be stupid enough to give him too few berries." She took another small step toward the maid. "And I wouldn't have missed his heart." Eloise kept it to herself that she hadn't shot a gun in three years, probably *would* have missed, but everyone in this house, aside from Wes, thought she had perfect aim, so she'd let them continue to think that. "Do you understand?" she added, and even Eloise wasn't sure if it was a threat spilling from her mouth or not.

"Yes, ma'am." Violet dipped her head, but Eloise caught the fury in the pinch of the maid's lips.

"You may go."

Violet paused only a moment before she slipped out the door, her steps hard on the wooden floors.

Eloise waited until Violet left and then closed the door, clicking the lock into place. She leaned against its frame, drawing in a deep breath, letting her shoulders fall with its weight. Her gaze fell with them, down to the basket in her hands.

Eloise shook the day off her, straightened, and walked over to her wing-backed chair. She put the laundry down and sat heavily, turning to the large window, watching Lammore lap against the shore. Words churned through her thoughts as she stared at the gentle waves. She needed to confront Easton, but first she needed to untangle the feelings swarming inside of her, and she should talk to Wes too, see if he knew why someone would want to harm him if it really wasn't Easton like he thought. Eloise turned to the basket holding his laundry, glad for an excuse to go to him that didn't look like groveling. She missed him—the way his arms would wrap around her waist when he hugged her, how he smiled when he won a game—always a shy thing that curled his lips so slowly. Gently. And his broad grins when she'd win. She missed the smell of him—the deep scent of warm vanilla and the rich, sharp cedar of his soap.

She picked up his sweater from the laundry basket—her favorite one, the color of creamed coffee—remembering the hard lines of him that it always outlined. How it would cut across his shoulders sharply before tapering to his waist.

The blood was, thankfully, washed from it. Eloise traced her fingertips over the fine, soft wool and pulled it close, holding tight to the traces of his scent, wishing it were *him* she still held.

31

The Cook's Assistant

The Dead of Night
May 11th, 1910

It was the creak in the floorboards outside Sadie's bedroom that woke her from an already restless sleep. One quick rap on her door followed by shuffling paper had her jumping from the warmth of her bed and padding across the room, her bare feet cold on the aged wood.

Her hand was on the brass knob, about to turn it, when she saw the note halfway slipped under her door, peeking into her room. Staring at her.

She looked at it unmoving, and then forced herself to melt, to reach down and pick it up, to open the door and see who it was slinking through the night, leaving her threats on thin paper and dark ink.

It was the last thought that had her twisting the handle and flinging the door wide open to an empty hallway. There were no lights illuminated, no candles lit, only a slice of moon tipping its head into the window at the hall's end, but it was enough silver light for Sadie to see two things—no one was there, and this note didn't bear her name on its front like the others.

Yet there was no mistaking that it had been made for her. It had found its way to her room, and whoever had left it had made sure to wake her before they'd disappeared into the night.

Sadie clutched it in her hand before unfolding it slowly, waiting to see what threatening message this scrap of paper held.

But this letter had no menace, and its penmanship bore no marks of anger. Instead, it said two soft, short sentences.

We need to talk. Meet me at the manor's south entrance.

Perhaps the person leaving the letters had come to regret ever sneaking into her room and scattering papers like petals on a grave.

Sadie's mind picked through the manor's layout. The south entrance was the same one the Asquiths and their guests had gone through to reach the picnic by the woods. There had been no time marked on the paper, but the knock on her door had Sadie thinking the person meant *now*.

It wouldn't take her long to get there, and Sadie was tired of wondering who was behind these notes.

She tugged on her dress and apron, her slippered shoes and cap, not bothering to tie her hair back, and quickly lit a candle. Its warm glow brightened the dark night and bolstered something inside of her. She was finished with wondering why someone wanted her gone, done imagining who could be behind the letters.

And she never wanted to see another scrap of paper bearing her name with a threat again. She held the note in her hand and lifted it to the candle, touching it to the flame, watching it burn as quickly as she torched her fears.

She'd find out tonight who was behind all of this. Now.

Sadie crept down the hall quietly, with only her single lit taper to lead the way. She snuck through the manor's many halls in the dead of night when no one but the owls had any right to be awake, making her way past closed doors, never meeting another soul as she went.

As Sadie neared the south entrance, though, she stopped and turned, deciding to slip into the kitchen for two small things. Her fingers brushed the wooden counters dusted with traces of flour before she snagged a pencil and Agnes' butcher paper. Her aunt often wrote little directions on it and tore off sheets of the brown paper for Sadie. Tonight, she would leave her own letter for her aunt. Sadie scribbled it quickly, and then stepped through the room, picking her way over to the knives. Sadie grabbed a small one, the cold metal glinting in the silver moonlight. She tucked the blade within her grip, holding it close to her skirt where it could hide within the folds. She was a fool for following a knock and a note in the middle of the night—but she wasn't *that* foolish.

The knife shot courage through Sadie's veins as she left the warmth of the kitchen, snuck down the long halls, and reached the south entrance. She tucked the blade at her waist between her dress and apron, and reached out, brushing her fingers on the door's handle. She stopped when her hand wrapped around its icy metal.

An itch crawled down her spine like a spider scurrying slowly over each vertebra.

The previous note's cold words shot through her thoughts.

You don't belong here. Leave before it's too late.

She should wait until morning. The soft sentences in the note from tonight were probably a trap.

Why else would someone meet her when no other person was around, when the world slept, when only the moon kept watch over her?

But Sadie was tired of jumping at every sound and hated how the sight of paper and ink-toned words could send her blood thrumming through her veins.

And she was so very, very weary of wondering, of fearing.

She turned the handle.

And stepped into the night with her candle guiding the way.

A light breeze met her, blowing off the lake. It threaded the night's brisk air with the smell of fresh water and the scent of fallen, cracked oak from the forest.

Sadie sucked in a breath, let the crisp smells lace through her.

She stepped across the grounds, the lush grass wet with the first tendrils of dew. From where she stood, she could just see the kitchen's back door where the henhouse and the pig's pen sat off to the right. Soon, she'd be there, collecting the morning's eggs and heading back inside to the kitchen's toasty hearth with the yeasty scent of bread rising as her aunt prepared breakfast.

It was a good life at Asquith manor . . . if it weren't for the threatening notes or unwanted kisses or a garden full of poison. She pulled her small knife out from the band at her apron and held it in a firm grip close to her body, hiding it between the folds of her skirt—just in case.

But her aunt had found a home in the odd manor, had even found her uncle Henry within its walls. Sadie wasn't so sure she'd ever discover the peace they had. Not there within its stone and wood and secrets. She let out a small breath.

Perhaps a simple life in a simple cottage was all Sadie really wanted—

A light cough pulled her from her thoughts, tugging her once more to the woods before her. The thick trunks and thin limbs huddled close with the manor looming at her back. The lake watched from a distance.

Sadie's eyes shot to where she'd heard that soft clearing of a throat. The timid sound echoed in her mind, and she wondered how such a quiet noise could speed her heart so quickly.

It kicked a heavy rhythm under her ribs.

Blood spiraled through her veins.

Adrenaline chased it.

They were here—the person who had left her letters and threats in drops of dark ink.

Sadie took a deep breath, loosening her hand from its tight grip around her hidden knife.

A figure stepped out from behind a thick tree, the moonlight silhouetting them.

She dug her heel into the dew-covered grass.

And as they stepped closer, her hands shook. She dropped her candle. The wet ground snuffed it out quickly, leaving her under a night filled with shadows and a single question.

It slipped from her lips quickly, on shaky syllables. "It was you?"

32

The Heiress

Early Morning
May 12th, 1910

Della Drewitt was beginning to know the hidden hallways better than the rest of the manor. She woke before the sun, unable to sleep well with her thoughts tangled between the walls of this home and the people within it. She'd tossed all night, dreaming of a silver pistol and berries like ink—their flowers that bowed down low—of calcified hearts that no longer beat, and a mother that snooped as she scribbled away hidden notes on tucked-away paper.

Sneaking through the secret halls, Della mapped out how they carved passages through the rooms with only the bright moon to keep her company. Pale beams streamed in from thin, slanted windows at their ends. Occasionally, the lake peered at her through the glass. In other halls, it would be the forest watching her from outside those panes.

Lachlan in his cellar had shared more about life with the Asquiths than she'd anticipated, and Della wondered what other stories she could unveil in the early morning before the sun awoke, before the manor's secrets scurried back to their shadowed corners.

Footsteps, soft and hurried, tapped around a bend. Della pushed open the closest door and slid through it as quiet as a field mouse under a red hawk sky. She found herself in a servant's room. An older lady lay on her bed with copper curls across a linen pillow. Her eyes were closed, and her chest moved slowly, breathing in deeply. A man lay beside her, his arm flung over his eyes, hiding his face. Della froze, her attention caught between the sleeping couple and the hidden hall. She peeked quietly through the crack to see who else slunk through Asquith's passages in the early-morning twilight before life stirred.

A shock of crisp white on a black skirt told her it was a maid, and as the woman stepped closer, Della caught jet-black hair and a flash of ocean-bright eyes under the dim electric light.

Violet.

The maid threw quick glances over her shoulder, and with her focus behind her, she never saw Della's pale eyes staring from a crack in the wall, a door barely open.

Violet scurried past, and as she neared, Della noticed the maid's hand closed tight around something.

She let a moment linger after the swish of Violet's skirts passing, and then crept out again, following those hurried steps at a distance with curiosity tugging her as sharply as the moon's pull on the tide.

Della waited around the next corner as Violet pulled open a thin door and stepped inside.

Ten minutes passed, and Della almost left. It could be Violet's own room for all she knew. Instead of going, the maid could be coming. Perhaps she'd met up with Wes and was returning from a place where they'd talked and laughed and kissed until the early-morning light. The thought twisted embarrassment through Della's veins, and she nearly went back to her own room, where a hardened heart waited for hers to turn to stone as well.

But a soft creak of rusty hinges stopped her.

And Della watched as the dark-haired maid snuck back into the hidden hallways. Violet tossed glances up and down the passage with bright doe eyes as Della slunk back behind the corner.

She waited a breath, two. Three deep lungfuls. And then peeked around the edge of the wall, hoping she wasn't about to come face-to-face with a maid she had stalked through dim corridors.

But there was nothing to mark that Violet had even been there aside from a strong trace of vanilla that didn't belong in the dusty air. It mixed with the scent of aging wood, making the hallway seem as if it had once worn the skin of an old library.

Della tiptoed over to the door Violet had gone through and cracked it open slowly. A simple room met her. A small bed sat in the middle, its covers tossed down. A desk snuggled close to a short bookcase against the wall. It was a fairly empty place, but tidy. Della stepped inside and closed the hidden door behind her, watching as it fell seamlessly into the wall. If she hadn't just entered through it, she never would've realized anything had been there. She pulled a pin from her hair and dug a notch into the wood, marking where it latched so she could find it again after she had figured out what Violet had been doing in here. Two clean gray kitchen aprons hung by the door, letting her know it wasn't Violet's own room.

Names spun through her thoughts, but she couldn't seem to pluck any of the cooks' from them. Why would Violet slink into one of the cook's rooms before the sun arose? Della looked around, searching for anything abnormal in a manor already filled with the strange.

But nothing was out of place aside from the bed covers pulled down where someone had been sleeping—should *still* be sleeping. It was early, even for a cook that would wake before the household to start the bread for the day. But the bed was empty. A blanket the same shade as freshly made rose tea draped off cream-colored sheets. Della brushed her fingertips along the soft woolen fabric as she rounded the mattress. And then she noticed a small slip of paper sitting in front of the pale pillow. Flourished across its front was a name in looping letters.

Sadie

Della thought back to the hunt. Violet had hurled that name across the picnic to a red-haired cook after Wes had been shot. And that night, Wes had stepped close to that same copper-headed maid—Sadie—and she'd asked if he would kiss her again.

Della turned back to the letter and picked it up, the paper crisp in her hand. She unfolded it and read four little words that sent a shiver along her skin, though they hadn't even been for her.

You'll regret coming here.

The period dented the parchment as if it'd been pressed down in anger. Droplets of ink were splattered beside it. Della glanced to the hidden doorway where Violet had slithered through. Had that snake of a housemaid left this note for a kitchen's cook? The letters swooped across the paper as if from a woman's hand, and Della tucked it into one of her skirt pockets. If Violet were threatening one of the cooks, Della would keep the evidence. Was she jealous? Did Violet know that Wes wasn't slinking around with only her?

A grimace graced Della's mouth, turning her lips in a too-familiar way. Violet had no right over Wes, had no claim to jealousy. It was another thing stolen from Della by a maid that took too much. And what else would Violet do? Was she the one targeting Wes? Jealousy was a flame, and fire spread quickly. Della would have to smother it before Violet's blaze burned a kitchen maid and a wayward fiancé, and quite possibly, Della herself.

She glanced around the room, searching for more traces of Violet and her fiery words—more evidence to show Lachlan that her suspicions were correct. She skimmed her fingers along the books on their case, opened a few and let the pages flutter, seeing if anything was hidden between spine and ink. When nothing fell out, she went to the desk and opened one drawer, then another. There was nothing out of the ordinary of combs and pencils and trinkets until the third drawer. There, Della found another note with the same sprawling handwriting and Sadie's name stretched across the paper. It looked as if it'd been crushed.

Della plucked it up, smoothed it out, and opened it carefully.

You don't belong here.
Leave before it's too late.

Della stole it, sliding the paper into her pocket with the other one, a sharp grin sliding across her cheeks.

She'd been right—perceptive, like her father had always said.

And now she had the proof to see Violet thrown out of Asquith manor like the pest she was.

33

The Housemaid

Three Days Earlier
May 9th, 1910

The Night the Guests Arrived

Violet stepped down one of Asquith's many halls, heading for the manor's main greenhouse, while her mind stayed in Caroline Drewitt's room. She'd fluffed pillows and spread-out linens, dusted chandeliers and scrubbed windows until the dark storm clouds over the lake nearly reached in through the clean, clear glass. Now all that was left for her to do was to collect an armful of flowers and arrange their blossoms in delicate Delft-painted vases around the house as the guests were *supposed* to be settling into their rooms and warming themselves after their rain-drenched arrivals.

"Lachlan . . ."

A woman's voice Violet didn't recognize trailed like woodsmoke through a cracked doorway, curling around her and turning her attention to Lachlan's study. Was that Caroline? Had she left her room to talk with the lord of the manor? Perhaps

Violet could listen in and overhear something that would help her convince Weston to ditch Della.

Rumor had it that the Drewitts *had* earned their money through unsavory means. Maybe Caroline would let something slip while she was at Asquith for the week, and if Violet couldn't convince Wes to rid himself of a dull, ugly heiress, maybe she could convince him they were crooked enough to cast aside. There *was* still something about Caroline's window, open to the storm, that tugged at Violet, something that whispered the woman wasn't quite . . . normal. She'd be doing both herself *and* Weston a favor showing him who the Drewitts really were.

"Lachlan," the woman said again as if she didn't trust his dim gaze to truly be paying attention, "What's the meaning of this? Your son—*my* daughter's fiancé"—at the mention of Weston, Violet stepped closer and peeked into the study—"Was out there with the pigs and the mud and the chickens . . ." She waited a beat. "And *another* lady." Caroline Drewitt stood on the opposite side of Lachlan's desk, her jeweled fingers flinging out toward the nearest window, her back to Violet.

And the way she said "another" made a shiver slip over her skin. Did Caroline know Weston was with *her*? Would he be upset if the truth of them didn't come from him? But she hadn't been outside with him . . . So who did Caroline mean?

Lachlan shook his head. "Let me guess . . ." His old, thin lips twisted to the side. "Short dark curls? Darker brown eyes? A glare for Weston?" He rubbed a hand along his chin. "And probably a black dress?"

Caroline nodded, her bright blond hair, only just touched by grays, sliding across her back. "Everything but the glare." She placed a hand on one hip, her blue dress a fine satin that Violet wished to drape across her own waist. "And that's exactly the problem, Lachlan. I didn't catch everything they said, but I heard plenty." She took a deep breath as if enough air might douse the fire building within her, sizzling out in her rigid movements. "I won't stand to hear of Della tossed aside. We had an arrangement."

"Dear Caroline, that was just Eloise—*Easton's* fiancée. Nothing to fret over." He smiled, his papery lips curling at the edges like old parchment.

"It didn't look like *nothing*." She took a step away. "Make sure it isn't. And make sure it doesn't even *look* like it. If it got back to the city . . ." Caroline took a deep breath. "If word got out that Della . . . it would . . ." She shoulders fell. "It would ruin Della's life." And then Caroline turned around quickly, storming toward where Violet hid. "Make sure it doesn't. Or I will."

Violet jumped away from the cracked door but not before seeing Caroline's angry face or hearing her last words. "Don't make me regret this, Lachlan."

Violet scurried down the hall before the study door could open and Caroline catch her eavesdropping. Bitterness coiled as tight as a snake through Violet's chest. Della Drewitt had everything Violet hoped for: money and status, fine silken gowns and jewels that glittered like starlight, bubbly drinks and the means to travel beyond a manor and its lake. What more did that heiress need? She didn't need Weston, and it most definitely would *not* ruin her life if he chose someone else—and not Eloise, but *her.*

Yet a new worry tore through Violet's chest. She knew Weston and Eloise had been close once, but he'd assured her their relationship was over. She didn't know the details, but she knew it had broken up badly. He hated to talk of Eloise and how she still crawled after him, wouldn't even let Violet mention their past, even if she'd only asked for reassurance that he didn't still want the woman.

Fear tugged at her heart. It was nothing but greed, Violet decided, that made Della or Eloise want to steal Weston from her. They both had more money than Violet could've ever hoped for without Weston by her side. What did either of them need him for? It was Violet who needed the Asquith name. And, as Violet stomped down the brick path toward the greenhouse once more, she thought of ways to make sure the heiress didn't settle in too comfortably into Asquith manor. Violet would keep her eye on Eloise, too. She needed Eloise to stay with the right brother. If she could do that, perhaps she could find a way to rid herself and Weston of either of the other women before the week ended. She'd have to—one way or another.

She neared the corner by the greenhouse with her thoughts spinning around a thieving heiress and a dishonest fiancée, at dreams fading at their edges—and stopped short as a familiar voice whispered, "Shouldn't you be by the hearth, kitchen mouse?"

It was the last two words in a voice she knew so well that sent a sinking feeling into her already heavy chest, as if her lungs had flooded with water and she'd soon be choking on the weight.

Weston said "kitchen mouse" to someone while *she* had always owned the nickname "my bird" from his lips. Had Della already stolen an endearment from him? She supposed it fit, at least. The heiress *was* as plain and fat as a mouse.

Violet waited, with her heart lodged firmly in her throat, but only a shuffle of feet answered at first, and then a soft voice said, "Just coming to collect some huckleberries for dessert, sir."

Violet peeked around the corner to see not Della Drewitt but the new kitchen maid. The woman lifted an empty wicker basket between herself and Weston. Violet nearly stepped out from around the corner she hid behind, not willing to let another maid or heiress or even a pretty childhood friend steal a nickname from Weston when all his endearments belonged to *her.*

But then Weston smiled, and that broad slice of his mouth directed at a red-haired maid stopped her. She knew that smile—the one that said *Oh, I like you.* It had always been hers. Why . . . *why* would Weston look at a cook's assistant with a grin that belonged to her?

Violet's dreams of silk gowns and petite pastries served to her by her own flurry of maids started to feel fluid—watery—as if they were melting before her. Worry cut through her chest—deeper than when she'd stood outside Lachlan's study listening to Caroline's concerns—and all because of a pretty kitchen maid. That was more dangerous than an ugly heiress with a fortune of gold. Money was one thing to contend with. Weston had enough, even without inheriting, that she was sure she could convince him to give up the heiress. But . . . a pretty face? Violet knew quite well how quickly *that* could snag Weston's eyes.

"Sir belongs to my father," Weston said, unaware of Violet watching, listening, drinking down every word exchanged. "And then I suppose it'll be my brother when he's in charge of this place."

"Weston," the kitchen maid simply repeated, and Violet watched the other woman's movements, the language her body spoke. Was the other maid glad for his attention?

"And you are?" Weston asked.

Violet spied on them as he stepped close to the other woman, saw how his eyes never strayed from her.

"Sadie," the maid answered, and Violet burned that name across her soul, seared it into her mind. She wouldn't soon forget it.

Weston moved closer to Sadie, and whispered, "You're at the wrong garden for huckleberries, kitchen mouse."

Violet sucked in a breath, held it, let it burn as sharply as those words scorched her.

The nickname ran through her thoughts, consumed her

mind. And she heard little more than its sound in her ears as Weston placed one hand on Sadie's elbow and they walked away. Together.

He opened the main greenhouse, where the flowers Violet was still supposed to collect bloomed, and as Weston led the other maid in—his body close to Sadie's—Violet felt her heart wilt with fear as the future she'd so carefully constructed started to wither as well.

She waited a moment, her feet desperately wanting to follow, but she knew Weston well enough to know that if he caught her, he'd be angry. He was broad grins and warm embraces, but he was also quick tempers and tightly held grudges. She'd seen his dark moods up close once, and she didn't care to have them directed at her ever again.

You're so much better than your brother, she had said one evening when they'd found a stolen moment together between his leisure and her chores. *You should be the one to inherit. Not him. He doesn't deserve it.*

His whole face had changed. His smile had slid from his lips quicker than his eyebrows had crashed down into a scowl, and in a voice that growled more than a beaten dog, he'd snapped, *Don't ever talk about Easton like that again.*

She'd leaned away from him with her own eyebrows knitting together. *But it's true. You're better than he is.*

He'd stormed off after that, leaving her wondering why a compliment could upset him so much. He hadn't talked to her or so much as looked at her for a solid week then. And as she served one tray followed by another, made up beds morning after morning, she'd decided that a life away from serving was worth her pride, so she'd apologized even though she'd done nothing but speak highly of him. And after a sorry or two or three, he'd welcomed her back with warm arms, several heated kisses, and eight small words. *I won't hold it against you, my bird.*

So, Violet hovered with one foot around the corner and her body aching to chase after them, to see if he'd replaced her as soon as an attractive new maid had arrived.

It was that last thought that had her finding herself in the greenhouse, tiptoeing behind plants and listening as Weston whispered, "You're very pretty," to a red-haired maid with soft green eyes and rosy lips that formed a surprised little circle.

Weston stepped close when Sadie said nothing, his polished boots inches from the other maid's shiny black shoes. It would take nothing for him to reach out and sweep Sadie into his arms. Violet knew because he'd done so countless times with her, tucking her close, kissing her softly, whispering promises she held on to as she scrubbed silver dishes until they shone with her warped reflection.

"You must know it," he added, and Violet watched as Weston leaned closer, trying to get the kitchen maid to look at him.

Sadie shook her head—as if she didn't know her pale beauty nearly rivaled Violet's own dark looks. "You're engaged, sir—"

Violet almost exhaled in relief, for once glad that Weston's engagement was something good. Perhaps it would keep this kitchen maid from reaching too far, from taking what was already claimed.

But then Weston's fingers were on Sadie's chin, tipping the other maid's head up. "Eyes like honey and jade, and lips like cherry blossoms."

Violet swallowed hard.

"You're engaged. You shouldn't be saying such things," Sadie whispered, looking away from him.

No, he shouldn't be—not to a kitchen maid, Violet thought. But not to an heiress either. Only to Violet.

He'd made promises to her. He'd been taken long before his sham of an engagement. Weston shouldn't . . . he shouldn't be talking to Sadie like that. Or Della. He . . . he shouldn't—

He'd made promises.

"Engaged to someone who doesn't even want to marry me." Weston tipped his head, watching Sadie, and Violet hid herself away as he whispered words he'd told her often. "Even as a second son, I could have a lot to offer to you, though."

Violet's veins heated, the blood running in them pounding until it crashed through her. The drumming in her ears made her miss Sadie's quiet reply.

Violet didn't care about Weston's love. But those promises were *hers*—his name, his money, a better life than a maid's.

They belonged to her.

She nearly left. Della Drewitt had already frayed the corners of Violet's dreams, and now a kitchen maid was unraveling them altogether.

But when Weston's hand caught Sadie's elbow and spun her to him, Violet couldn't look away.

Without a word, she watched as Weston pressed his lips to Sadie's.

And then Violet was running from them, scrubbing the image of their embrace from her mind. Dread spiraled through her, and a single thought sunk into her chest as the greenhouse's door slammed behind her.

Della Drewitt wasn't Violet's biggest problem.

Sadie was.

34

The Fiancée

Early Morning
May 12th, 1910

Eloise stepped through the kitchens with the morning's breakfast scraps in a pale blue bowl she cradled. Cook had tried to stop her, had said disposing of them wasn't her job, but Eloise wasn't just a guest—she was family. She wanted to help, to be a constant presence in the manor, and since Sadie had slept in, Cook had only fought Eloise for so long. Agnes had lunch and then afternoon tea and, most importantly, dinner on the boat to prepare for, after all. So, Eloise stepped outside with the sun streaming through the clouds, searching for ruffled feathers and clucking little beaks.

A fat white hen found her first. Eloise crouched down, dropping crushed eggshells before the bird. "Hello, Sophie, still alive and uneaten, I see." She picked up a handful of leftover blueberries from the bowl and scattered them like seeds in front of Sophie.

Mattie and Flora, their wings flapping in deep blacks and rich browns, joined Sophie while Eloise dumped out the remainder of the kitchen scraps for the three girls to feast on. She sat watching the happy hens as they gobbled up bits of fruit and sausage, as they scratched the grass for wayward bugs without a care for anything but the food before them.

If only Eloise had so few worries. But two brothers intent on nearly murdering each other weighed her down. Not even Lammore crashing gently at the bank beside her could ease the tension crawling through Eloise's chest like an infection, spreading to her lungs, rotting the flesh under her ribs.

She sighed as she stood up, leaving the chickens to their meal, and headed for the lake's edge. Lammore was a deep blue today under a sky the exact shade of a robin's egg, thin white clouds spanned its surface like cracks. A light breeze tugged at Eloise's short curls and sent the smell of fresh, clean water into the air. It should be a nice evening out on the lake tonight, full of celebrating aboard the Asquiths' boat as the sun set. *Should be*. If a pair of twin brothers weren't ruining everything because of revenge.

Because of you, her thoughts whispered back, and Eloise shook them aside, not wanting to face that truth.

She stepped into the lake instead, letting the cool water seep over her soft, slipper-like shoes. Eloise closed her eyes and sank down as the lake pooled around her. "Oh, Lammore." She breathed in deeply, let it back out just as heavily. "I don't know what to do." She dipped her hand into the water, pulling it up. "Everything is such a mess." And as she let the water drip between her fingers, worry wove through her veins. "And I'm afraid it's only going to get worse. They won't stop until—"

A stomping through the forest beside her tore Eloise's thoughts to the trees, and she opened her eyes to find Easton splitting a scar through the brush. His chest heaved as he moved, sucking in sharp breaths.

Eloise stood. She and Easton had ended the previous night with sour words that had left a twist in her gut and guilt quickly slithering in its wake. She should make things right with him.

She lifted a hand, and when Easton saw her, he paused, and then his steps turned to her slowly. They met in the middle, the forest behind him and the lake at her back.

"You're out early," she prodded gently, trying to gauge his mood. Should she bring up what Sadie had told her? How he'd gone off in search of a maid to distract himself from her and Wes and their tangled engagements?

But did Easton's sneaking with Sadie really matter to her? He'd only sought out a kitchen maid because *she* had thrown it in his face that her heart was still clinging to his brother. Everything was a mess, so Eloise let the previous night slip away, choosing forgiveness even if it wasn't asked for. She desperately needed some herself—from him, from Wes, from the whole Asquith family—and she hoped if she freely gave grace away to the family she'd fractured, that maybe . . . maybe it might return to her one day. So instead of anger and accusations, she simply asked, "What are you doing out here?"

Easton took a deep breath, staring at her, hesitating as if he, too, were poking at the tender and frayed friendship hanging between them. And then he answered her with a single small word. "Hunting."

Her eyes immediately went to his forearm, where the slashes of bright red to mark his kills were absent. "Didn't catch anything?" She stared at his hands, at his blood-tinged fingertips. "Or was it a runt?"

When he cocked his head, she nodded to the empty patch of skin on his arm, then his hands.

"No." Easton shook his head. "I mean, yes . . . it was a runt." He shrugged and glanced away. "I threw it to the pigs."

"Oh," Eloise said, and then silence lingered between them, and she felt the weight of their words from one night prior settling into the quiet, heavy air.

Eleven short ones in his deep voice. *To turn you against me right when . . . you gave me hope.*

Followed by too many spoken in her sharp tone. *You and I both know I went crawling back to him several times. He doesn't want me.*

And all the unsaid sentences they both knew so well. She could craft novels on her want for Wes and papers outlining her suspicions regarding Easton. How all she'd spoken and everything not said must've sunk into Easton's skin, burrowed into his bones. Words festered far too easily. And Eloise had always thought too little for how hers might poison him. What wounds did Easton carry because of her?

So, for once, she held back, stayed quiet and swallowed her thoughts, stopped herself from unraveling the threadbare fragments of their friendship.

"I . . ." Easton tore a hand through his hair, his eyes shooting between the woods and her and the manor. "I have to go."

"Oh, of course." She took a step to the side, moving out of his way. "But you'll be on the boat tonight, right?"

Easton froze, tension rolling through his body. He didn't look at her when he asked, "At the party celebrating . . . our engagement?"

"And Della's." She didn't add Wes's name. Neither of them needed to hear her voice curl around those three small letters. "You've always loved being out on the boat."

"Ellie." Easton sighed, and his shoulders dropped with the movement as if they were trying to drag him down into the dirt and bury him under the earth. "I . . . should be going." He turned to face the manor, giving her his back.

"Right." She nodded, even though he couldn't see it. "I

suppose you need to freshen up." It was true. He was caked in dirt and bits of blood. It coated his hands and shirt. Leaves had caught in the treads of his boots, and his pants bore the signs of snags from the forest's brambles. Nothing like the crisp tuxes the Asquith brothers would wear tonight to complement their fiancées' shimmering gowns. It was to be a night of decadence and glitter—and hopefully a reprieve from a week of old pain and fresh wounds.

He took a step away, and she called out, "I will see you tonight, though?" It was one thing to watch Wes smile at the heiress. It was another to do it alone. For all the grief and damage they'd caused one another, she wanted Easton at her side. "Please."

He paused, let out a heavy breath, and then slowly, in a voice more broken than Eloise expected, answered, "All right."

And then he was gone, trudging across the lawn and slipping into the manor, leaving her with tension tangling along her nerves and nowhere for it to leak out. She flicked her gaze from the manor to the forest and then to her oldest, dearest friend. What did Lammore think as she watched the chaos two brothers and a single woman could wreak? Would she keep their secrets—their fights and kisses and threats? Or would the lake spill all her knowledge, throwing it to the shore as easily as her waves crashed against its bank?

35

The Heiress

Morning
May 12th, 1910

Della skipped breakfast, having no interest in seeing her mother or her fiancé just yet—or anyone in this place but Lachlan, really. She'd go to the lord of the manor with the notes she'd found, but . . . not yet. She needed proof Violet was bitter enough about Wes chasing after someone else to be the one to target him, not just leave threatening notes for another maid. That could be nothing more than anger because of a biting word or jealousy over her position. Della needed evidence that tied Violet to Wes's attacks. Only that would clear Della's own name and make sure no one thought *she* was the jealous, jilted lover. She needed actual proof that it was the housemaid behind everything. And she had none yet. So, she'd slink around the manor, plucking clues like ripe apples.

Della opened the lounge's door, peeking her head in first to see if that wayward maid was there. When no one greeted her, she slipped inside and helped herself to a black coffee that smelled like strength, and a still-warm buttered croissant.

"So, this is where you've been?"

An itch ran down Della's spine, and she turned around to see her mother standing in the doorway with a gaze that traveled Della up and down.

The older woman stepped inside with pinched lips tugging themselves to the floor, deepening the lines beside her mouth. "Hiding away and sneaking treats." Her eyes flicked to Della's waist—only a moment, but long enough for Della to catch it.

She shrunk inside herself, her shoulders curling forward. Della could creep through a manor full of poison and secrets and calcified flesh, tucking information into her pockets as she went. She was clever enough to solve Wes's would-be murder, and yet she'd not quite found the piece of her that could stand up to her mother. It wasn't even her inheritance and the threat of it being taken away that stopped her. It was fear and love and always chasing after being enough. She'd been whole with her father—perfect to him as she was—but always, *always* one small step away from her mother's approval.

Chin up, Della.

Shoulders back.

You could afford to lose five more pounds, you know.

That's not how a lady chews.

If only your teeth were straighter and nose smaller. You didn't get that from my side of the family, I'll tell you that.

Everything was outside perfection even as her insides were withering away. All a show. Smile when you're sad. Like each other if people were around. She wouldn't want to upset the socialites' view of the Drewitts or give the gossip columns even *more* to talk about. They already had enough. If only Della would—

She shook her head, wondering why her thoughts sounded so much like her mother's voice, and when that had begun.

"What are you doing skipping meals when you're a guest

of the Asquiths?" Her mother raised a single blond eyebrow plucked to perfection. "Do you even know how embarrassing that is for me?" She clicked her tongue. "I had to tell Lachlan you had a headache and how it must be the air out here, and yet I find you in their lounge stealing pastries? What if it'd been your fiancé to walk in on you? He'd think you were avoiding him."

Della took a bite of her croissant—slowly—letting the flaky pieces stick to her lips and flutter down in front of her. After swallowing, she smacked her mouth together once, watching her mother's lips flatten in disapproval. "It's not stealing when they set it out for us."

"That's it?" Her mother tossed her hands up. "That's all you have to say? You've missed more meals than you've attended." She pointed a finger at Della. "You better show up tonight on the boat! Do you hear me?" And then her mother was storming through the doorway, but she stopped before leaving and glanced over her shoulder. "And wear your red dress with the sash covering the waist. I've heard rumors your fiancé might be straying to a former sweetheart—a petite and *beautiful* former sweetheart—and I do *not* want you encouraging him to break this engagement because of your—" She stopped short and tipped her head up, staring at the ceiling, taking a deep, deep breath. "You'd never find another suitor." And then her mother was gone, having spit one last barb at her, and Della was glad to see her go. She knew she should've asked about the notebook her mother kept tucked in her pocket or why she'd been snooping through the Asquith estate, but one short conversation had already dried up her pride and parched her heart. And she wasn't sure she wouldn't wither altogether if she had to stay in the same room with the older woman a moment longer. Maybe she would marry Wes—cheat though he was—just to get away from her mother.

The older woman's words trailed through the room, dissipating slowly.

You'd never find another suitor . . .

"Maybe I don't want a suitor," Della mumbled to herself, and then she thought of Wes. "And maybe *your* choices aren't actually suitable."

She turned to the table.

And snatched another croissant.

Della stood beneath a trapdoor tucked into the top floor's ceiling. She stared at its deep brown wood and the sturdy ladder that reached up to it from the floor. One by one, she curled her fingers around the rungs in front of her and stepped up, gathering her skirts and piling them over her elbow, and then slowly, Della made her way to the top, pushing on the trapdoor and smiling as it groaned open at her touch. She crawled through it and found herself in a small, angled room with cedar walls. Dust motes floated through the morning sunlight streaming in from a window sitting above a cushioned bench.

Open books were strewn about the small room. Five sat across the top of a small table. A few more lay sprawled along the edge of a bookshelf, crammed between closed novels standing upright. A handful more dotted the floor. They all lay face down with their spines cracked, holding pages, their stories waiting to be picked up and sunk into once more.

There was an old quilt, frayed on its ends, draped across the bench. Della tiptoed around books littering the wooden floors and stepped over to it, running her fingers along cloth softened by the years. In a manor full of poison and hardened flesh, the attic seemed a cozy reprieve, and even Della could picture herself coming up here on foggy mornings, plucking a half-read book and diving into its words beneath a window that watched the lake.

She sat on the bench, its cushion lumpy and dipping in places from use, and glanced around the room. Aside from the books, there was little else up there. Not even drawers on the desk to sift through. Della drummed her fingers along the windowsill, wondering if she could slink through the hidden hallways once more and discover Violet's room before the boat party tonight. The maid's room had to be in the servants' quarters near Sadie's, and she already knew where that was. Della reached into her pocket, touching the two letters with the kitchen maid's name flourished across them. She kept them close, not trusting that there wasn't someone else sneaking through the manor, and if they'd found these in her room . . . It would look like evidence against *her*, not Violet.

She should get up, look now while everyone was preparing for lunch, but the attic was peaceful, so Della stayed, staring out at the lake that lapped its shore with unhurried waves.

A flash of white in a sea of greens and browns snagged her attention, and Della stared at the forest where Violet slipped between trees that huddled as close as gossips. She leaned closer to the window, her breath fogging it and blurring the view. When she wiped it away, she saw Violet trudging through the brush, covered in dirt and muck, and heading for the manor. The maid clutched a wicker basket in her hands with a tight grip and shot too many glances over her shoulder, as if she couldn't stop staring back into the tangled trees and all the secrets they whispered together.

36

The Fiancée

Noon
May 12th, 1910

Eloise strode into the dining hall five minutes late, and yet lunch hadn't been served. Lachlan sat at the head of the table, sipping a glass of water and chatting with Caroline Drewitt as if everything was all right, even though his place was bare of a plate and food. Wes waited with his attention split between the clock and the servant's door. A question hid in the tilt of his head, but when his gaze snagged hers, he looked away, avoiding her eyes. His fiancée was nowhere to been seen. And neither was hers.

Eloise sat opposite of Wes, but he stared down at the empty table rather than talk to her, and that was fine by her. Too many emotions pooled in her belly, too many thoughts swam in her head, and he'd know them all if he read her eyes.

So, she kept her face turned from him just as he did and looked to Lachlan instead. "We should have a late dinner tonight, instead of a sunset cruise, don't you think?"

"Hmm?" Lachlan focused his cloudy eyes on her. "A late dinner?"

Eloise nodded, well aware of how Wes's attention had shifted to her, how he traced her movements. "Cook is obviously busy and could use the extra time."

"Oh, yes, sorry about the delay, Caroline. Cook is usually so punctual." Lachlan glanced to the grandfather clock ticking away in the corner of the room, and Eloise wondered if he could even see its face and hands and numbers.

"If we delay dinner, she'll have the extra time she must need for all the preparations," Eloise went on, pulling the conversation back to her. "And we could do fireworks. I know you have some tucked away." She split a smile across her face. "Wouldn't that be grand?"

"Oh!" Caroline leaned forward, her blond hair spilling over until the loosely curled ends grazed the table. She wore a deep blue gown that brought out the sea in her eyes, and a black fur shawl—too warm for the spring air—wrapped around her shoulders. "Fireworks? Oh, we must."

Lachlan's mouth pinched, and out of the corner of her eyes, Eloise saw Wes's head cock. She snuck a peek at him and saw his gaze dart between her and his father.

"My funeral fireworks?" Lachlan shook his head as he chewed on the inside of his cheek, his wrinkles dipping and hollowing out the skin there.

Caroline turned to him. "You have fireworks for your funeral?" Her pale brows lifted. And then she grinned as if she were guzzling champagne he was pouring out for her.

Lachlan smiled, but it was a lonesome thing that curled his thin lips. "When I'm finally reunited with Roslin, I want my family happy. I want them to celebrate for me. And to take my life as an example that everything around us is so fleeting." He looked at Wes. "Love your wife while you can. Cherish her." He scanned the room with his dim eyes, as if searching for Wes's fiancée, and when he didn't find Della, his attention landed on her. "Be willing to die for her—and I don't mean a physical death, but your wants for hers." He turned back to his son. "I'd tell her the same if she were here. And so would Roslin if she could. It's a happy marriage when you give up self and seek good for the other."

"Oh, how romantic." Caroline sighed, and then tipped her chin up, and though Eloise knew little of the woman, even she could read the pride hanging off Caroline's lips, her smile saying for her that she'd made the right choice in choosing an Asquith for a son-in-law.

If only Caroline Drewitt knew that Lachlan's sons scratched and clawed and fought—with each other, with Eloise, with anyone that stepped too close—to get what they wanted.

"But surely," Eloise said, directing the room back to plans for the night, giving Cook the extra time she needed, "you'd have a few fireworks to spare for your sons' engagement celebrations?" She smiled at Lachlan. "It would be a lovely reminder to start our married lives off as you hoped, as you and Roslin had." She snuck a glance across the table. "Wouldn't you agree, Wes?" And even Eloise wasn't sure why she was asking him. If it were their names still paired would he treat her like his father wanted? Would she return it to him? Or would they secretly always be searching for their own selfish desires?

Before he could answer, Easton stepped into the dining room with a scowl marring the skin between his brows. "Still alive, I see," he drawled, turning to Wes.

"That's not funny." The words shot from Eloise's mouth before she could stop them, but she was so tired of the cuts to one another, the anger, all the little swipes of revenge.

Easton started to open his mouth, but a door crashed open, and Violet stepped through, a tray brimming with food in her hands.

"Sorry, sirs, ma'ams." Wisps of her black hair slipped out

from beneath her mobcap, and her pale skin was flushed as if she'd run all the way from the kitchen to them. "Cook sends her—"

"Tell her not to worry." Lachlan raised a wrinkled hand, flapping her words away. "I know she's overly busy preparing for tonight."

"It's not—"

"But Eloise had a wonderful idea," he went on, "and I think just what Cook needs." He smiled at the maid. "Tell her we'll postpone dinner until after sunset. We've a motion for a candlelit dinner on the lake and fireworks as well." He winked at Caroline and then Eloise.

"Oh, how lovely," Mrs. Drewitt said as she clapped her hands together.

"But . . ." the maid started, still standing at the edge of the room.

"Violet"—Lachlan spread a hand toward the empty table—"If you please." He tipped his head to Caroline. "Our guests are hungry."

Violet clamped her mouth shut, but Eloise noticed how her lips flattened into a hard line as she served the plates.

They ate with only Lachlan and Caroline keeping conversation. Eloise had too many thoughts spinning wildly through her mind while Easton and Wes barely acknowledged each other.

Both avoided meeting Eloise's eyes, and she preferred it that way.

But as Wes finished his last bite, he stood and slipped out of the room without even saying a "goodbye" or "see you tonight," and somehow that felt more like a deep breath than Eloise had expected it to. She would've thought it'd feel like a knife to the ribs, not relief.

She turned to Easton at her side and watched him—the way he stabbed his meat, the gulping and hurried sips he took, how he bit down hard as if something were bothering him—and she wondered if she really, truly knew either of the twins after all these years.

"What?" Easton set his fork down. "Why are you staring at me?" He looked at her. "What is it?"

"I want to make things right with you." Two words of his from that morning had echoed through her thoughts since he'd said them. He'd left the woods and slipped into the manor and his answer had rung in her mind, tangling with all the other noise in her head.

All right.

"How?" He arched one dark brow.

"We'll give each other something," she whispered, not wanting Lachlan or Caroline to hear them, but a quick glance in their direction proved them to be deep in their own conversation.

Easton watched her warily, his eyes narrowed and flicking over her. "Like what?"

"Like you end things with your maid." She said the words softly even though she had every right to let them bite.

His gaze shot to Violet standing on the edge of the room. "There's no—"

"I'm not dumb, Easton." She leaned toward him, close enough for her warm breath to graze his ear, and dropped her voice. "And neither are you."

"Fine." He shrugged as if shedding his skin. "Fine, all right?"

"I want to see you do it." Eloise sat back. "Today. Before the celebrations tonight."

Easton let out a deep breath. "And what do I get?"

She stared at him. He was cleaned up from the woods—his skin scrubbed, his face shaven, his jet-black hair brushed and slicked off to the side. "What do you want?"

He turned to her, and his eyes were burning—toasted cocoa and fired cedar. "I want the truth."

She stiffened, and then, slowly, forced herself to relax. "About what?"

Easton turned in his seat until his knees brushed her and he faced her completely. His voice turned as soft as velvet as he asked, "Do you think you could ever be happy with me?"

"Of course—"

"The truth, Ellie." He looked down, avoiding her eyes. "Could you be as happy with me as you would've been with him?" Easton didn't say Wes's name. It was as if even whispering it had become an incantation that would curse them both.

But it seemed to Eloise that they were already headed for ruin, so when his gaze slipped up to hers, she answered honestly. "No." *Not after the last few days, not after this morning,* she thought. *Probably never.*

His shoulders slumped. "And all because I gave him half a berry years ago when I was a foolish boy?" He bowed his head down. "You've never forgiven me for that."

"Break it off with the maid and you're forgiven."

He looked up at her. "That's it?"

She nodded.

"And we could start fresh?" His canine tooth peeked out to snag the soft skin of his lip where hope hid. "Why?"

"Because I've my own faults I need forgiveness for." She swallowed.

"Ellie, you—" Easton stopped, the rest of his words clinging to his lips.

"See." The corners of her mouth curled in a weak, watery smile. "We both know it."

And they did. She was as ugly and messy and cruel as the brothers. They'd all taught each other well over the years. She could scratch and claw and cause as much damage as half a berry and a bullet could. And as she and Easton stared at each other with not enough words to make up for the years, they both knew it. She was as monstrous as he was, and she wondered if either of them could truly find forgiveness.

37

El

Three Months Earlier
February 1910

Eloise sat in the crook of a large maple tree near the fringe of the forest, cuddled in a quilt as Lammore watched from a distance. She'd stolen Wes's blanket from the attic and wrapped it around herself to ward off the late winter's chill. The scent of cedar wood and the small traces of vanilla from him that clung to the fabric enveloped her, competing with fresh pine needles and the crisp, clean wind whipping off the water. It would snow before the night ended—Eloise would bet on it. Ice already edged the lake, and as her hands stiffened in the cold, she wondered why she'd agreed to join Easton and Wes while they chopped up a fallen tree for firewood. Tux lay in her lap in a round puddle of fur and warmth, purring contentedly. Eloise ran her fingers over his back and then tucked them under his body, his heat thawing her better than the blanket.

"Isn't this Henry's job?" Eloise snuggled into the bend of the tree.

"A little labor won't hurt Weston." Easton lifted an ax, bringing it down on a slice of wood until it cracked in half.

Wes shook his head. "He's just cranky because I'm beating him." He paused a moment before adding, "Like I always do." And then he winked at Eloise.

And she didn't miss the underlying words he didn't speak with that quick closing of his eye.

Neither did Easton.

Wes meant *her.*

He jabbed at his brother about winning her without outright saying anything—everything always a competition between them. Even her. Or maybe it had started with her.

He moved his chess piece. And I couldn't let him take the queen.

But Wes had assured her that she wasn't a game. He'd promised he wouldn't play with her, but he'd made no mention of including Easton in that oath.

Only six months had passed since Easton had asked her to marry him, since she'd run off to Wes instead. The wound wasn't so well healed that Easton could joke about it. Eloise knew that. And so did Wes.

She shook her head at Wes only to have him mouth, *What?*

Her eyes answered that he knew, and she was well aware that Easton spoke their quiet language, that he caught all they didn't say.

But Easton only bowed his head and lifted his ax again. His jacket slid back enough to show the gun slung underneath it, a leather holster hanging over his shirt with sleek, silver metal meant for protection out in the woods. She glanced down where the firearm Wes had given her lay beneath the tree, still in the holster that should be on her ankle. The twins insisted she bring it whenever she was going into the forest, but she slipped the gun off every chance she could. Its silver barrel and alabaster handle always reminding her how *she'd* been the one to shoot Easton.

"I hope you know what you've *won*, Weston."

And then it was the brothers speaking as if she weren't right there watching them, hearing every word they uttered.

"I do." Wes smiled at her, but Easton's face was grim, his jaw clenched and lips flat. "A heart." Wes winked at Eloise before turning to the stack of wood waiting to be chopped.

Easton smoothed out his face, the anger disappearing quickly, and in a voice colder than the winter's air, he said, "If you break it . . ." He waited for Wes to turn around, to face him, so his brother could drink in each small syllable he uttered. "I'll kill you."

"Easton." Eloise sat up, leaning over to stare at the brothers below her. "I'm fine." She shook her head. "And he wouldn't."

Easton let his ax slip down, his fingers curling around the end of the handle—his grip so tight his knuckles turned white. "I just want you happy." He ignored the way his brother's gaze narrowed at his words, and turned, staring at her with eyes like fresh coffee—heated and dark.

"I . . . I am," she whispered, half wanting him to know she truly was and half not wanting to hurt him even more.

He nodded then turned back to his wood pile—to pretending she hadn't cut him down as easily as a dead tree six months prior, or that Wes hadn't chopped him to pieces right after. It was one thing to be rejected, Eloise thought, and quite another for Easton to watch his brother walk away with the person that had felled him.

And she couldn't deny that the scars she'd carved into him still lingered. She didn't want them to fester, so she turned to Wes and glared at him for chafing at sore wounds.

"This is pretty." A light voice broke through the silent tension lingering between the three of them. "I like it."

Eloise looked down to see Lucy at the base of the tree she sat on in a dress not meant for a winter's day. The girl huddled over something in her hands.

Eloise gently picked up Tux. He uncurled slowly before stretching and jumping from her hands, landing on the ground with ease. She shimmied down after him and turned to the youngest Asquith. "What is?"

Lucy didn't say anything, but she held up a shiny, slim gun with an alabaster handle.

And then pointed it at Wes.

He dropped his ax, letting it clunk against the cold, hard ground, and stretched his hands out. "Lucy . . ." He said the fifteen-year-old's name softly, gently. "Put that down."

Eloise took a slow step toward her. "That's . . . that's mine, Luce." She reached her hand out. "Please give it back."

"It's pretty, though." Lucy stared at it, then tried closing one eye as if looking down its sight to where Wes stood on the other end. She cocked her head, her rich brown hair spilling over her shoulder.

"Lucy." Easton's voice was a sheathed sword—strength restrained—its biting blade oh so close but held back. He took a deep breath, pulling the sharp edges from his words until their syllables softened. "Give it back to Eloise, and I'll have Cook make you some hot chocolate."

Lucy stared down the barrel at Wes. "Right now?"

He nodded. "Yes, just give that back to Eloise. It's not a toy."

Her eyes—the same fiery ones burning in Easton—narrowed. "I'm not a little kid. I know that!"

Easton chewed his words and took a step toward Lucy. "Then stop pointing it at Weston."

The girl spun, her dress and hair flinging out with the movement, and then she faced Eloise. "Fine."

The single thin barrel from her own gun stared at Eloise,

Lucy's gaze right behind it. She took a half step back and almost tripped over the cat curling around her feet. "Luce . . ." she whispered, but her voice caught in her throat as her vocal cords vibrated with fear instead of sound.

Easton crept up behind his little sister, and Eloise kept her eyes on Lucy rather than him.

Between a prayer on Eloise's lips and an exhale from her mouth, Easton's hand shot into the air. Lucy cried out as the forest turned into a jumble of pale pink skirts and strong arms, a deep shout and a shot screaming from a slim gun with a white handle.

Tux jumped at Easton as he fell hard to the frozen ground, dragging Lucy with him. A hiss spit from the cat's mouth a moment before one slid through Easton's teeth.

And before Eloise could see what had happened, Wes was beside her, his hands grazing her body. "*El!*" His fingers trembled along her arms. "Are you okay?"

Easton looked at her from the ground, blood marring his cheek in four clean lines. He held a crumpled Lucy in one arm and a spent gun in his other hand, and as he stared at her, she'd never seen his pupils so large, the black devouring the golden brown almost entirely. "E-Ellie?"

"I'm . . ." She swallowed hard and brushed a hand over herself, running her fingers down the black fabric of her dress. "I'm . . . I'm fine. Nothing." She swallowed again, hoping it would ease the tremor in her voice, slow the panic in her veins. "Nothing bleeding but the sap." Beside her, dug into the maple tree's trunk, was a crushed bullet. And then she glanced at Easton's face. "And . . . and you."

"Dumb cat," Easton spit, but she heard the relief in his voice, in two words that had no right sounding like a deep breath.

Eloise glanced down to where Tux stood with his back arched. He hid next to her feet, his growls loud behind her skirts, and it wasn't until Lucy pulled herself from Easton's grip that the cat stopped howling at him. Eloise laughed, and as it burbled up her throat, she wondered if shock was gripping her tightly. "I . . . I don't think he likes you anymore, Eas—"

"You hurt me!" Lucy screamed, turning a hard gaze at her oldest brother, her warm eyes so very cold.

Easton returned the icy stare, his voice just as frigid. "You nearly shot Ellie."

"I didn't mean to!" She took an angry, shallow breath as tears pooled, spilling down her rosy cheeks. "Easton scared me!" Her neck and face and collarbone were splotched with raging red marks. Lucy's fair skin showed every emotion tearing through her. "He pushed me!" She turned and sprinted through the woods, heading toward the manor, leaving Eloise with her heart pounding too hard.

Silence split the air. Easton stood, sucking in a deep, deep breath, even as Eloise's lodged in her ribs. He stepped over to her, gently grabbing her wrist and uncurling her fingers, before placing her gun in her open palm.

"Take better care of this." He paused for a single inhale before his arms wrapped around her, the scent of him—freshly split oak and hints of spicy tobacco—drowned out the smell of sulfur and sweat-soaked fear. He pulled her in tightly and whispered, "I thought . . . I thought she shot you."

Tux, still at her feet, swiped a paw at Easton as he held her.

"Get out of here." He kicked out, pushing the cat away. It yowled and then, just like Lucy, ran for the manor.

"He was just protecting her, you know." Eloise gripped Easton as tightly as he did her, only loosening her hold as the adrenaline slipped from her veins, and he let go of her in inches, his fingers clinging to her before slowly parting.

When he glanced to the manor with his brows knotted together, staring hard after his sister, Wes finally stepped up, putting himself gently between Eloise and Easton—not quite prying them apart—and she was thankful he'd waited, had given his brother that small comfort of reassurance rather than the constant fighting over her.

"How'd she get the gun?" Wes's words were soft, and Eloise knew he was looking for an excuse for Lucy.

She'd heard the words Easton hadn't spoken—what he really meant as he'd stared after their little sister—and knew Wes had too.

We can't help her here.

And it wasn't the first time Lucy had had an outburst that could've hurt someone—*or worse*, Eloise thought with a hard swallow.

But the girl was still theirs. Eloise had plucked up this family, claimed them as her own in all their mess. And Lucy was one of them. She'd not let her go easily.

"It was my fault." She bent, picking up her empty holster at her feet. Eloise lifted the edge of her skirt and wrapped it around her ankle before tucking the gun away once more. "I left it at the base of the tree." She glanced to the ground where the maple's roots dug into the earth. "I didn't want it on me. I don't like—" Her gaze shifted to Wes as their secret nearly slipped out. *I don't like it. I don't even use it. I don't want it.* "I don't like to climb with it. It was my fault, Easton, not hers."

He closed his lids and pinched the bridge of his nose. "Father won't—*can't*—overlook this." Easton opened his eyes and regret lingered there. "He—"

"You heard El," Wes interrupted, his attention darting to the manor where their little sister had run off to. "It wasn't Lucy's fault."

Easton took a deep breath in and let it out slowly. "There are other places that can help her better. She—"

"*We* can figure it out." Wes set a hand on his brother's arm. "Together."

Easton pulled away. "You don't understand. She'll be *my* responsibility. She'll—" He stopped and tried to tip his chin up, straighten his spine, but his shoulders fell instead as if they wanted to pull him down deep into the earth.

"Then give her to me," Weston said quickly. "Let her be my ward when you're lord." He leaned toward his brother, his expression filled with hope.

Easton stared at his brother, his dark eyes burning slowly. "You won't get her the help she needs."

"You're just trying to get rid of her!" Weston's voice was sharp, as deadly as a dagger.

After a moment, Easton dropped his head, and he didn't look at his twin when, in a hollowed-out voice, he whispered, "You don't know everything, Weston. You don't always know what's best."

"I'm . . . I'm sorry, Easton." Eloise stepped close, pulling the attention to herself. She placed a hand on Easton's shoulder, and he stiffened beneath her touch. "It *was* my fault."

Easton turned away slowly, letting her hand slide from him. He had just embraced her, but now that the fear of her bleeding away was past, it seemed his emotions hardened once more like armor slipping over his skin, iron over his heart. "She shot a gun at you, Ellie." He rubbed the base of his palm against the hard line of his jaw, scrubbing at the skin there. "What if . . . what if it had hit you?"

"It didn't." Eloise spread her arms out, let the brothers see her healthy and well, no holes in her dress, her body. No splashes of crimson. No ragged flesh. "It didn't. I'm fine."

"This time," Easton answered, and Eloise heard the pain in his voice, the way it trembled the ends of his words.

Wes shook his head. "There won't be another time."

Easton turned to him. "She needs so much more than we can—"

"She needs us." Wes said the words softly, but they fell with the weight of an ax.

Guilt crept through Eloise. This was her fault. She'd left her gun lying in the open, and now what would Lachlan do when he found out? Lucy hadn't meant harm. Eloise knew the youngest Asquith well enough to know Lucy hadn't realized what a single brass bullet could do.

Easton took a deep breath. "It's not your call, Weston."

"And it's not yours either."

"Enough." Eloise stepped between the brothers. "Lucy didn't mean to hurt anyone." She glanced at the manor standing tall through the trees. "And she's in there confused and crying." She turned back to the twins. "You can stay here and bicker when it's your father's decision what happens with her"—she glared at the brothers as the adrenaline released its last hold on her veins, replacing it with shaky limbs and a heart stuttering down its pace—"But I won't. Lucy needs someone, and if neither of you can see that, I'll be the one to go to her."

She turned on her heel, leaving the brothers with their claws and teeth snapping.

Eloise found Lucy with red eyes and tear tracks down her cheeks. She sat at the end of a hidden hall on the main floor, curled up on the wooden boards with her knees to her chest and her hair sticking to the sides of her face.

Eloise approached her slowly, tiptoeing around the trapdoor that led to the cellar, until she squeezed herself beside

Lucy and sat. She pulled off the quilt still wrapped around her shoulders and spread it over their laps.

"It wasn't your fault, Lucy," she whispered.

The youngest Asquith sniffed and wiped the back of her hand beneath her nose. "I didn't mean to hurt anyone."

Eloise wrapped an arm around her. "You didn't."

"Easton pushed me." Her lips twisted, pulling the wrong way until a grimace marred her face. "He hurt me."

"He didn't mean to either." Eloise tugged Lucy close. "He was just scared."

"Is he going to tell Father?" She looked up at Eloise with wide eyes framed in dark, wet lashes. "Am I in trouble?"

Eloise was quiet. She didn't want to lie to Lucy, but she also wanted her to calm down. If she could soothe Lucy, perhaps then Easton could see that they could handle his little sister themselves. "I think we'll try to keep this our own secret," she finally answered, hoping it was true.

Lucy's focus dropped down to the floor. "Easton has a secret already."

"What?" Eloise tipped her head, trying to see the girl's face. "What do you mean?"

"It's Mother's secret. She had it first." Lucy pointed to the trapdoor at their feet, and only then did Eloise see it wasn't fully latched. "And . . ." The girl took a shaky breath before leaning forward. She sat on her shins as she pulled the trapdoor up all the way. "And . . . and so do I." Lucy swallowed hard, her thin neck bobbing. "But I don't want it."

Eloise scooted to the edge of the trapdoor, pressing close to Lucy. She followed the youngest Asquith's gaze and peered at cellar steps that sunk into the earth. Their cold gray stones were dark in the unlit stairwell, but there, at the bottom, Eloise saw a pair of shiny black shoes and pale white legs. An ankle splayed in the wrong direction. Fingers bent backward and a neck twisted too sharply.

Eloise stared down at the broken body of a maid.

"Why won't Betty get up?" Lucy whispered.

Eloise found the Asquith brothers still arguing in the forest, their pile of firewood half split and forgotten.

She took a deep breath, letting the adrenaline that had sent her racing out to the twins—and away from the cellar steps—drain from her veins. "Something . . . something's happened."

Her eyes flicked to Easton, wishing he wasn't there—that he didn't have to know—and then her gaze found its way to Wes. "Lucy—" Eloise stopped, the words clinging to her ribs like sap, gripping themselves to her heart. She tore them from her mouth in a too-quick sentence, peeling each syllable from her teeth in jagged little sounds. "There was an accident. She . . . she—"

"Is she all right?" both brothers said at the same time.

Eloise nodded. "Yes . . ." Her lips twisted, tasting the lie like soured cider. Lucy wasn't all right. She was inside, crying and confused, tucked in her room where Eloise had left her with a promise that everything would be fine, that Betty was just . . . She wasn't even sure what she'd told Lucy. Sleeping? Had that been it? Had she said that the kitchen maid had simply been sleeping? Did Lucy believe it? Eloise wasn't sure just how much the girl understood. Or didn't. She looked from one brother to the other, and guessed how each would respond. "It wasn't her fault, but—" And then two words tumbled from her mouth faster than a maid down cellar steps. "Betty fell."

Silence hung between the trees, and all Eloise could hear

was her own heartbeat. It was as if that confession had torn itself from her own chest, as if *she'd* been the one to bump into a kitchen maid coming up stone steps.

Both twins were staring at her, intensifying the feeling, jumbling her thoughts. Everything tangled on her tongue, refusing to leave her lips. "Your father," finally slipped out and then all her thoughts and words unraveled from her chest. Lucy's confession from Eloise's mouth fell at her feet on the forest floor between two brothers.

Wes stepped close and folded Eloise in his arms. "Calm down, El." He glanced to Easton once before turning his head back, peering down at her, and Eloise read what the quick look meant.

She's not okay. She's still shaken up.

But this wasn't about her. She wasn't trembling from nearly being shot.

It was a creamy neck cracked at a sharp angle that shook her fingers.

Hadn't they been listening?

Had she told them clearly enough?

Betty fell.

And the stones were too hard.

"Breathe, Ellie." Easton came closer, standing behind Wes, his face stern as he peered at her over his brother's shoulder.

She listened to Easton for once, breathing in deeply.

She held it until it burned in her chest, and then exhaled gently, slowly, and let her words follow its example. "Lucy ran to Roslin." Eloise paused, gathered her thoughts. "To her statue. She was scared because of the gunshot, afraid she'd be in trouble." She ignored the way Easton's lips twisted, and then carefully picked her next words. "She wanted her mother. She wanted comfort. *We* should've been there." Guilt ripped through her blood. "But we weren't." It clung to the thin bones in her chest. Lucy was innocent. This was her fault—their fault. The three of them.

Eloise shouldn't have left her gun on the ground. Easton should've known better than to yell at his little sister. Weston shouldn't have picked that time to fight with his brother. They'd scared Lucy, confused her, sent her running when they should've been soothing.

This was their fault.

"She ran to the cellar," Eloise whispered. "But she didn't see Betty coming up the stairs." She gripped Wes's shirt in sweaty fists.

"Is Betty all right?" Easton asked the question slowly as if he wanted the answer to take its time as well, as if he already knew.

"She's . . . dead." If there had been a breeze lacing through the leaves, Eloise was sure it would have stolen those two hushed words.

Wes leaned back and looked into her eyes. "What?"

She stared at him rather than the red crawling up Easton's neck. "She . . . she tried to push past Betty, just nudge her aside, but Betty went backward instead. Lucy was upset, but it . . . it wasn't her fault. She didn't mean to. She would never—"

Wes nodded quickly. "She wouldn't," poured from his tongue just as fast. "It was an accident."

"Do you hear yourselves?" Easton stood still, his back rigid, his voice as cold as ice, and Eloise wasn't sure it would ever thaw again, not after two small words she'd spoken. Two small words that had burned the back of her throat as they'd smoldered from her mouth.

She's dead.

Wes let go of Eloise slowly before twisting around, his heel digging into the dirt, and faced his brother. "Yes." He ground the single word out between his teeth.

"Betty had a sister." Easton glanced from Wes to Eloise and back. "She sent her money every month."

"Then you'll make sure she's cared for. Betty's sister won't want for anything." Wes chewed the inside of his cheek, hollowing out the skin there. "But right now, I'm worried for *our* sister. She needs—"

"She needs something—someone better than *you*!" Easton took a deep, deep breath. "Or me," he added after a moment. "We can't help her here. How is that not obvious to you? She needs to be somewhere she can't hurt anyone." He paused, his head shaking as if he could fling away the last two hours from his memory. "Anyone . . . else." He didn't raise his voice, but it still shattered the quiet forest air. "And I'm not lord of this manor yet. I can't pay off Betty's family to ease your guilt."

"Father will listen to you," Wes said softly.

"He doesn't even have to know what really happened," Eloise added. "He doesn't have to know Lucy was involved. Betty just fell. You could suggest we care for Betty's sister . . . out of . . . kindness."

"I would do the same for you, Easton." Wes stepped over to his brother, one hand out as if to pat his arm. "If you had—"

"But I didn't." Easton's fist curled, and each vertebra in his spine stood static as if they'd locked into place, as if he would never relax again. "I wouldn't. I'm not—"

"She's our sister." Wes's voice dipped, the three small words a plea too big for steady speech.

Eloise stepped over to the brothers, putting herself between their bodies. She turned to Easton, looked up at his dark eyes, but he was staring at Wes with fire in his gaze, and then she spoke the few words she knew would convince Easton. "This would kill your father. If he knew . . ." She placed a hand on Easton's chest, trying to draw his attention to her. "It would kill him."

Easton's eyes flicked to her, just for a second, and then his shoulders slumped. After a minute, a heavy, "Fine," slipped past his lips, and he looked at his brother again. "It was an accident. But this isn't the end of—"

"I know." Wes let out a deep breath of his own, one that stirred the back of Eloise's hair. "Thank y—"

"Don't." Easton's jaw clenched, the muscles tight and popping out. "Don't you dare thank me for this." He turned away from them. "Something still has to be done about Lucy."

"I—"

Eloise turned and set a hand on Wes, stopping his protest. She shook her head. They had what they needed from Easton for the moment. They'd leave Lucy's future to argue over another time. For now, they had an *accident* to uncover and the truth of Betty's death to bury deep.

38
The Housemaid

Afternoon
May 12th, 1910

Violet huffed as she slipped into the kitchens, dropping off a basket of lemons from the greenhouse, their sunshine color popping against the dark brown of the woven wood in her hands.

"I've my own work to do, Agnes." She nodded down the hall. "The boat party isn't just food. I've the silver to polish and the tablecloths to iron, and that's all before I even get onto the boat to dust down the rooms. I'm sorry, but I can't be gathering your ingredients all day." She arched a dark brow at the cook.

"I know, Vi, and thank you." Agnes chopped thin stalks of green onions before pausing, spinning around, and stirring a pot quickly. She pivoted back to the cutting board before Violet could blink and was chopping again. "It's just"—her eyes darted to the hall before flying back to Violet—"Sadie." The name was a whisper on her lips, barely audible above the crackling of the fire in the hearth.

Violet stepped farther into the kitchen.

The silver could wait.

"What about her?"

Agnes shot a look around the room again. "Well, she . . . she hasn't come to help me today."

"Skipping work on the day of the boat party?" Violet clicked her tongue. "Of all days to abandon you, Agnes." She lowered her voice. "Lachlan won't be happy if he finds out."

Agnes set her knife down and reached a hand toward Violet. "He can't know. She's a good girl, Vi, she's just . . . She made a mistake."

Violet thought of the red-haired kitchen maid with rosy lips and a face that wasn't as innocent as it looked. "Oh?" she said softly.

"I . . . I can trust you, right, Vi?" Agnes nodded, her copper curls falling from her cap and bouncing. "Yes, you've always been a good girl, too." She smiled at Violet, but it quickly left her mouth, her lips turning into a grim line in its place. "I need your help with Sadie."

"Of course." Violet pinched her eyebrows together, hoping it looked like worry written across her features. "What happened, Agnes?"

It took a long time for the cook to respond, but Violet knew the best thing to do when fishing was to wait quietly. So, she did. And Agnes offered Sadie up—flayed on a silver dish—without the need for Violet to bait. "She . . . she didn't poison Wes. It wasn't her, but—" Cook's mouth snapped shut as if she hadn't meant to say so much.

Violet's brow shot up, and she held silent, but when Agnes didn't continue, she whispered, "But?"

The cook's eyes flickered to the hall, and then she turned back to Violet and dropped her voice. "She thinks she did. Poor girl went to the wrong greenhouse the other night." She shook her head. "But I made sure. There was no nightshade left."

"Nightshade?" Violet couldn't help how the single word slipped from her mouth. It'd been whispered all week along with the question *who?* And here was Cook sharing with *her* how Wes had been poisoned. By Sadie. She clamped her lips closed and waited for Agnes to continue.

"No, no." Agnes abandoned the onion shoots on the cutting board and stepped around the kitchen island. "It wasn't her, Vi. She didn't poison him." She twisted the front of her apron in her hands as if keeping them busy would stop her from spilling too many secrets. "You believe me, right?"

"Of course." Violet smiled, and she made sure to soften the corners of her lips, not let them turn too sharply. "How can I help?"

Agnes reached out, taking hold of one of Violet's hands within both of hers. They were warm and calloused, and she squeezed tight. "I can't leave the kitchen." She let go and swiped a hand to the mess around them. Burbling pots crowded the hearth's stove and half-chopped vegetables littered the counters. Pastries, rolled only partway, were spread out on one corner of the island while the rest was cluttered with utensils: butcher blades and dough cutters and paring knives. "There's too much to do. If you see her, please tell her I said not to worry, everything is okay, and to please come to me. I know she needed a break, but . . ." She stared at Violet with hazel eyes flecked with gold, the skin under them tinted with dark purple as if bruises had burrowed beneath her bright gaze. "I need her help now. Would you do that?"

She patted Agnes' hands still wrapped around one of hers. "Of course."

"I think she's just overwhelmed." She nodded to herself and took a deep breath. "She just needed some time to gather herself is all."

"Understandable, too," Violet responded, letting the edges of her words curl with affection. "If she thinks she poisoned poor Weston."

"But she didn't." The cook let go of her hand slowly. "She didn't."

Violet nodded. "I know, Agnes, I know."

"So, you'll tell her to come?" Agnes scurried back through the kitchen, picking up her knife to chop and slice and mince some more.

"If I can find her." Violet let one more gentle smile sweep across her cheeks.

Agnes' lips curled up softly. "Thank you, Vi, and thank you for the lemons." She tipped her head to the basket on the counter. "I told Lachlan when you first showed up that you'd be a lovely addition to the manor, and I was right. You've always been a good girl and a great help to me."

"But I'm not a little girl anymore, Agnes. I'm grown." She swiped a hand down the front of her. "And I've changed." The words raced out without her thinking, and as soon as they'd left her tongue, she wanted to gobble them back up. Agnes had always been kind to her, and here she was plotting against Sadie, her niece. She *had* changed, and she wasn't so sure Agnes would approve of the woman she'd grown into. Violet swallowed hard and pushed those thoughts away.

It was Sadie's own fault for kissing Weston, for trying to steal Violet's future.

But Agnes didn't notice the emotions flitting across her face. The cook simply turned back to the work piling up around with only three words in parting. "Haven't we all?"

Violet nearly sprinted down the hall as she left the kitchen. She'd wanted a way to get rid of Sadie the moment her lips had met Weston's when they thought no one had been watching.

She couldn't go to Lachlan, though. It wouldn't do any good for her to tattle on Sadie herself. She'd look like a jealous sweetheart to Weston if it came back to him that she'd been the one to get rid of the cook's assistant. And she wanted to stay in his good graces when he finally tossed aside that heiress.

Luckily, as she made her way toward the dining room, where the plates for dinner waited for her to polish them until her hands ached, she remembered they had a guest with a penchant for gossip. All Violet had to do was let a few scandalously delicious words of who, what, and why slither into Caroline Drewitt's ears, sounding a lot like *Sadie*, *nightshade*, and *jilted lover*, and she was sure they'd fly through the manor, making their way to Lachlan as swift as tree swallows.

And perhaps Caroline would even be so upset at Weston's wandering that she called off the engagement to Della. The sooner the heiress—and Sadie—were out of the way, the closer Violet's dreams were. She could almost brush her fingertips against them again—and they felt like soft silk and smooth pearls. All it would take was a few small words whispered into the right ear.

Violet turned around, no longer worried about polishing plates. If she succeeded, someone else would be scrubbing the silver, and she'd be free to drink and dance and dine on sugared desserts and sparkling drinks, to drape herself in delicate velvets and elaborate laces. She could almost feel the trace of satin on her skin. If only her words could leak through the manor before the party. Violet dreamed of hanging off Weston's arm as they boarded the boat, of kissing him under the fireworks-sparkled skies.

She headed for Caroline's room where she was sure the lady was preparing for the party—tugging on gilded jewelry and glittering gems that would complement Violet's smooth skin and dark looks so much better than an old woman's wrinkles.

Soon, she thought. Soon she would have anything she'd want, everything paper bills could buy, and she'd be happy. Happier if it'd been Easton—as the heir—that she'd snagged, but Weston would do. He was better than a life as a maid at least.

"Ahem." Footsteps echoed behind her. "Violet?"

She stopped and turned around, knowing that voice so well. "Weston." She flung her arms around him. Her dreams were so close, and she no longer cared who might see them.

He was already dressed in a black tailcoat and tuxedo jacket with a white formal shirt beneath for the party tonight. Matching slacks, polished shoes, and a bow tie like fresh milk finished his outfit. The men would be dressed in their finest formal wear—all in inky blacks and creamy whites—for the boat while the women would don soft silks and pretty colors, and oh, how Violet wished for a dress the same shade as the lake on a clear day—a deep blue that glittered and would bring out her ocean eyes, a watery fabric with gems that twinkled like a sunbathed sea.

"My, how handsome you look." A smile bloomed across her face, her lips grinning against the fabric of his crisp shirt. "But you'd look so much better with me on your arm tonight."

He stilled for a moment, and then—slowly—peeled her from his waist, setting her back a step. "Violet." He let go of her arms and scratched the back of his neck, the side of his jaw.

She swallowed hard as he looked away from her. Something was wrong, and a deep worry curdled in her stomach at the way his voice had tripped over her name. "Is everything okay?"

He stared at the floor as he answered. "Is it ever?"

"What's going on?" She stepped toward him, even as he inched away and nearly bumped into the wall behind him. "Has someone done . . . something?" She thought of the nightshade, of Sadie, of a shot in the woods. "Are you—"

"No, I'm fine." He waved a hand, dismissing her worry. "It's just . . ." Then he breathed in deeply and let his words spill out in a rush. "I've chosen the heiress. I'm sorry, but it has to be this way. This"—he flicked his fingers between the two of them—"Has to end."

Violet's voice lodged in her throat, and she choked on its vibrations, until a single quiet word squeaked past her lips. "No."

"I . . . I never meant to hurt you." He put his hands up, palms facing her as if in surrender, as if he hadn't just gutted her.

Her mind raced, but all she could think to say was four blunt words. "You promised me things."

He nodded. "And I meant them." His attention drifted from her to the library's doors splayed open behind him. "At one time." Then his eyes found hers again. "But"—he shrugged—"Life."

"You mean an heiress." She spit the words at him, but he didn't even flinch.

"Yes." He took a step toward the library. "I am sorry. I really am."

She reached a hand toward him, her fingers grasping air. "But—"

"Don't." He shook his head. "You won't change my mind on this."

Anger burned in Violet's gut. He'd made her promises—velvet dresses with buttons down her back that a maid of her own would have to fasten, golden rings and gems that would wink as she crossed a room with all eyes on her, bubbly drinks that spilled over with laughter, a life of ease and excess—that's what his lips had promised each time they'd kissed hers, even if his mouth had never said those exact words. And she wouldn't let it all be taken from her with a simple sorry. She glared at Weston, but only pity hung in his eyes. She didn't want it, didn't need it. She was more than a poor, simple maid.

"I'm better than a fat, ugly heiress, Weston!" She sliced her words from a sharp tongue, letting them stab whoever they could. "And you'll regret this."

39

The Fiancée

Late Afternoon
May 12th, 1910

Eloise stood against the library's wall, Tux at her feet, as he always was these days. He meowed once, but she reached down, shushing him softly so a maid with rash words wouldn't notice her listening. The doors were open, and they let Violet's angry barbs slide along the air to her.

". . . a fat, ugly heiress, Weston, and you'll regret this!"

Eloise was surprised to hear Violet's voice at all. She'd thought she could make Easton confront what he'd done with Sadie, and instead, had found him facing another maid.

Footsteps stormed away, down the manor's long hall, as Easton slid into the room amongst the books and dust and quiet.

"Weston?" Eloise's lips twisted to the side. "Really, Easton?"

Tux hissed, a growl clawing up the back of his throat as Easton stepped close.

"Oh, shut it," he said to the cat.

Eloise reached down, stroking Tux's back, calming him. "Hush."

A hiss split through the space between her and Easton instead.

"That thing has never forgiven me for pushing Lucy." He touched his cheek as if remembering the scratches Tux had given him the day a bullet missed her. "I was saving your favorite person's life"—Easton reached down and tapped one finger on Tux's head—"Dumb cat."

Tux hissed again.

"Enough, you two." She nudged the cat with her foot until he scampered from the room and then turned back to Easton. "You fight with that cat as much as it fights with you. It's ridiculous."

Easton shrugged.

And Eloise shook her head in response.

They were quiet a moment, the silence comfortable, but thin—as if once the lightness Tux had brought between them dissipated, it would never return.

Eloise broke it first. "You told that poor girl you were Wes?" She didn't wait for him to answer and instead added, "You told Sadie that too." Easton looked so startled at the mention of the kitchen maid's name that she almost spilled everything she knew right then and there. "Why?" she asked instead.

An indifferent mask shadowed Easton's face quickly, and he popped a hip against the closest bookcase with a shrug falling off one shoulder, his arms crossed. "Why not?"

"That's it?" She stepped toward him, her dress for the party swishing around her feet in heavy folds as she went. It was made of fine, thick fabric and was a red so dark it bordered on the shades of black and dried blood. The top barely brushed her shoulders, swept across her collarbone. The edges of her skirt and sleeves and neckline ended in intricate lace reaching across her skin. "Just because you could?"

"Fine." He stared at her, his eyes cinnamon and fire. "Petty revenge." Easton peeled himself from the bookshelf and pivoted around her as if they were dancing, his steps careful, his eyes on her. "Just like you've always thought."

"You thought you could tarnish his name"—Eloise narrowed her eyes at him—"For me. If it got out?" She watched as he lifted a single shoulder. "You wanted to ruin him for me?"

He took a slight, short bow, and when he stood, answered, "It was . . . worth a try."

Eloise turned away from him, giving Easton her back as her thoughts spiraled through her head. And then something—a slight gap in the wall—caught her attention. The library's hidden door was split open just a fraction. She took a step toward it.

And saw the sharp outline of an eye staring back—watery blue and too much gray.

"Della?" Eloise crept over, her soft shoes not making a sound against the room's thick rug.

The door cracked apart all the way, and Della Drewitt stepped out in an emerald green dress that hugged every curve along her body and flared out at her feet. Gold glittered at her ears, down her neck, along her fingers, and wrapped around her waist in a thin chain. Her blond hair was piled high and pinned back, and Eloise wondered if Della knew just how beautiful she looked.

A jealous maid's words hung in the library's air. *Fat, ugly heiress . . .*

But Della wasn't either of the things Violet's angry heart had screamed.

"Can we help you?" Easton asked, interrupting Eloise's thoughts. He glanced at her, his eyebrows raised and asking one question. *How long was she there?*

Eloise shrugged as the heiress stepped into the room.

"Oh, hello." Della tiptoed away from the hidden passageway's door and into the library. "I seem to be lost."

"You've found the old servants' halls, have you?" Easton stepped to Eloise's side and draped his arm across her shoulders, wrapping her in the scent of split oak, fresh tobacco. Eloise stilled beneath his touch.

"So that's why you have hallways pocketed behind the walls?" Della glanced back, her long gilded earrings swishing with the movement. "To not see the staff as they work?"

"Old times tucking them away like that." Easton glanced to the secret door as it swayed slightly on its hinges, yawning into the library.

"Oh." Della followed his gaze. "I *was* rather confused."

Eloise smiled, but it was tight across her lips. How much of her and Easton's conversation had Della caught as she'd hid like a cat around a corner? She glanced at Easton and the pinch of his lips told her he was wondering the same thing. "We don't mind seeing the servants now, though, do we, Easton?" She elbowed him in the ribs, pushing him off her and letting him take her words as she knew he would.

He ignored her jab and faced Della. "Do you need help?"

She nodded. "Yes, thank you." She pointed a thumb over her shoulder. "I was rather turned around in there."

Easton stepped over to Della then past her. He closed the hidden passageway but not without peeking in, Eloise noticed, and then he ushered the heiress out the library doors with a few mumbled directions. When he returned, Easton's voice dropped to a whisper. "So, you've given me the truth and I've sent off the maid, are we to start fresh then?"

Eloise thought about it for a moment. "I want one more thing." She stepped close to him and lifted a hand, laying it on the stark fabric of his shirt, and looked up at him. "Will you give me a small, simple truth too?"

Easton cocked his head, staring at her. "What do you mean?"

"Well, you said 'petty revenge' earlier as to why you gave Violet Wes's name, and it made me think . . ." She paused, letting her words linger between them.

"Of?" he asked.

She shrugged. "Oh, just of that nightshade a—"

"I didn't poison him." Easton stepped back, letting her hand fall from him.

She shook her head, her loose, short curls dancing along her jawline. "I don't mean now. I didn't mean . . . this week."

He watched her, his eyes roaming over her face and trying to read its quiet conversation. "So, you no longer think I did it?"

Eloise lifted one shoulder, the lace there pulling along her skin. "Does it even matter anymore?"

He nodded slowly. "It does to me." And then his hands wrapped around her upper arms, and he looked her right in the eyes. "I want you to think well of me, Ellie."

"Then, no." She glanced down, let her lashes fan against her cheeks, and for once, let the truth fall from her lips. "I don't think you did . . . this time."

"Now you've given me two truths when you asked for one." He leaned back and was quiet until she looked up at him. "What is it you want to know?"

"Well . . ." She bit her lip, one single side tooth popping out to snag the soft skin. "I never did win against Wes with that game, and it's bothered me ever since. I asked for your help one year ago and you said you would've given it to me if only I'd asked you first." She glanced down. "So I'm asking you now." Eloise played with the lace that fell from her sleeve and stretched across the back of her hand rather than look at him. "How did you do it? How'd you get the key from your father?"

Easton laughed, a short, sharp bark from deep in his chest. "Father would never part with that key."

"Then—"

"Come, dear, sweet, smart Ellie." His fingers slipped from her arms and his grip found her hand. He tugged her to the open doors. "And I'll show you the one thing that's eluded you, the one thing at which I beat both you and Weston."

There was nearly a bounce in Easton's steps as if they really could start fresh with a simple promise and two secrets spread out. Eloise followed him as he pulled her along down Asquith's halls, stopping only when they entered one of the hidden passageways and stood before a trapdoor in the floor.

He paused, staring down at the worn wood. "The truth is, I never did find the key." He glanced back once, his eyes finding hers in the dim light, before he bent down and lifted the small, square door that would bring them to the cellar. "Follow me." And then he was stepping down the old stone stairs.

Eloise trailed after him slowly, remembering the last time she'd been there, four months earlier when she and Wes had been side by side without a million words and an heiress' fortune splitting them apart.

When a maid's neck bent the wrong way.

As she reached the bottom, she glanced around, but the cellar was empty. No polished shoes. No ankles splayed too harshly. No empty eyes from a maid gone too soon. Eloise closed her own, wiping away the memories of Betty. When she opened them again, only Roslin's statue greeted her, Eloise's black shawl from years ago still draped over her face, giving the statue the appearance of a ghost in mourning in the dark room.

"Easton?"

His back was to her. He stood so very tall and so very still, facing the covered marble of his mother. Mumbled words fled from him, their corners softened until she couldn't understand their syllables, but it sounded like a prayer, like a plea, like a secret he spoke to the dead.

Then louder, without turning around, he said to Eloise, "I know Wes didn't do that." He tipped his head to the shawl covering a broken face made of stone. "Even though he said it was him. But—" Easton stepped up to the statue, running his fingertips along the smooth marble arm to his right. "Lucy's outburst isn't why we're h—"

"It wasn't—"

Easton held up one finger, never looking away from his stone mother, and stopped the lie from falling off her tongue. "I know it was her, but I didn't bring you here to talk about Lucy." He finally turned to her, pressing his shoulder against the alabaster arm and leaning on it, one knee bent, an ankle crossed over the other. "You asked for a truth from me, so here it is." He shifted around and pushed against the marble arm until the sound of stone scraping stone echoed through the small cellar. Roslin's statue slid to the left where Eason had shoved it, and a thin opening appeared where she'd been, looking too much like the mouth of a great black beast.

"Here." Easton wiped his brow with his sleeve and then spread his hand toward the dark doorway. "There's always been a second entrance to Mother's poisoned garden."

Eloise stared at the opening in the dimness."So, you cheated?"

Easton nodded as he grinned, his teeth flashing white in the dark cellar. "But I won."

40

The Heiress

Night
May 12th, 1910

The stars glimmered above Della as the drinks sparkled. Everything on the boat shone in the dark night. Jewelry and smiles and smooth words all bright and shimmering. Even Della found herself enjoying the cool air, the way the lake sloshed, how the boat swayed softly as she leaned against its railing.

"That was a lovely dinner," her mother said as she stepped up to Della with Lachlan at her side.

"It was wonderful, wasn't it?" The lord of Asquith manor smiled, and deep wrinkles cut themselves into his cheeks. "I'll give Cook your regards. I know she's been busy. I heard even poor Violet had to take on some of the work. I'll tell them both thanks from you." He patted his full stomach. "And from me."

"Tell them to give me the recipe for our own cook to use." Caroline patted the pocket on her skirt. "I'll be sure to write it down exactly!" She giggled, and Della wondered if the pale, bubbly drink half gone in her hand wasn't her first. "I don't remember the last time I had duck that delicious." She smacked her lips, and as Lachlan closed his eyes around a laugh, Della's mother leaned in close to her and whispered, "You didn't wear the red dress I told you to," in a low voice. "Don't ruin this, Della. It won't be just an engagement broken. It'll be your rep—"

She stopped as Lachlan's laugh died and his cloudy gaze searched for them once more. Her mother wiped the frown off her face in less than a breath and turned back to him with an easy smile plastered across her mouth.

"Lachlan." Della tipped her head to the old man. "Mother. If you'll excuse me."

"Of course," Lachlan answered as her mother's eyes flashed, flitting quickly from Della to her fiancé across the room, and she didn't miss the message her mother silently spoke. "But don't retire to your room"—Lachlan leaned toward Caroline so his dim eyes could search her mother's face—"It must seem excessive to stay the night on the boat with the manor still in view, but I was afraid it would get late and—"

"Nonsense." Caroline patted Lachlan's arm. "Why should we not enjoy it out here? I think it's lovely to spend a night out on your lake."

"Excuse me, but why shouldn't I go to my room just yet?" Della smiled, but it pulled stiffly against her mouth. A moment ago, she'd been content with the breeze brushing past her and the slap of water against the hall ringing in the night. But a moment ago, her mother hadn't been there, and now all she wanted was to tuck herself away from everyone.

"Fireworks, Della," her mother answered. "You would've known that had you joined us for lunch." Caroline's eyes pierced Della, pinning her like an insect.

Della merely smiled with tight lips again and said, "Oh, until then," to Lachlan.

He nodded and put an arm out to her mother. "Shall we?"

She set her hand on his wrist, her rings glinting like the stars. "A moment." Her mother grinned. "I'll meet you over there."

Lachlan gave a short bow and then shuffled over to where Wes stood.

Her mother turned to her. "We need to talk." She narrowed her eyes at Della. "Where have you been scurrying off to all week? First your fiancé was accidentally poisoned and then he was *shot*, and every time I turn around you've been off secreted away, hiding from me. I haven't even seen you since this morning. I've been worried something's happened to *you*."

Della thought about answering her truthfully, the worry creeping into her mother's face *did* look sincere at least, but three words stuck in her mind.

Scurrying. Secreted. Hiding.

Everything her mother had been doing as well.

"I could ask you the same." Della tipped her chin up, thinking of the notes her mother scrawled in a little—

Notes. Della twisted the strings of her purse. A small, circular handbag dangled from her wrist, hiding the notes Violet had left for Sadie behind gold fabric. Or the notes Della *thought* Violet had left. What if they had already been in Sadie's room when Violet had entered? What if Violet had gone in not to leave a message, but for something else? What if she'd been looking for Sadie and simply left when she hadn't found her in her room.

What if her mother had left the notes?

It'd been a long time since Della's mother had written a letter herself—that's what she had servants for, she'd once said to Della, and then lectured her on the indignity of calloused fingers and ink-stained skin.

Would Della even recognize her mother's own handwriting now?

She glanced to the older woman's pocket into which she'd seen her mother slip a notebook several times this week.

"What are you talking about?" Caroline asked, bringing Della's attention back to the boat, to the sway of the water, away from angry letters meant for a kitchen maid. Did her mother know about Sadie and Wes?

"I saw you snooping through one of the Asquiths' rooms, digging in a desk, and writing in that little notebook you hide away in your skirt pocket."

Caroline took a step back. "What—"

"What is it you're hiding, Mother?" Della lurched forward, intending to reach out and grab the notebook from the pocket Caroline kept it in, but her mother smacked her hand—harder than an old woman had a right to.

Della snapped her finger back, keeping them from her mother's reach.

"You could just ask to see it." Caroline pulled out the small, leather-bound book, and handed it to her idly.

Della flipped it open and found . . . drawings.

Pencil sketches with an occasional description jotted down. Pictures of a calcified heart, shrunken to the size of jewel and dangling off a chain; of a pale dress whose skirt looked like the flowers drooped down on Lake Room's door; of earrings that sat snug and shone like poisoned berries.

Della flipped through the pages, each one with a different drawing that reminded her of something in the manor. So the notes *had* been from Violet. Not her mother.

"That one." The older woman stopped her on a brooch that looked like a dagger, its hilt curling and delicate. "That's when I was *snooping* and *digging*"—her mother rolled her eyes—"through the Asquiths' desk." She lifted one shoulder. "Lachlan had a letter opener I found quite inspirational. Oh, they have a deliciously dark style here, don't you agree? I thought we'd take some of it back to the city with us. How jealous"—she smiled and it curled all the way across her cheeks—"Everyone else will be when they see us. Even rude old Mrs. Hardcastle will have to choke out something nice to say about *us*, Della!"

"Fashion?" Della shook her head. "That's what you were doing? That's—"

"What did you think?" Her mother snatched the small notebook back, tucked it into her pocket once more.

"I thought . . ." Della's mouth gaped open, and her mother shot a hand out, flicking it up against the bottom of Della's chin with a snap, closing her jaw shut.

"You thought the worst of me . . . like you always do."

"But what about 'the girl'?" Della leaned in close to her mother. "You said, 'Now what to do about that girl.'"

"How did you—"

"Sadie?" Della lowered her voice. "Violet?"

"Who are they?" Caroline glanced around as if two socialites might pop out of the water. Leave it to her mother to not learn a servant's name. "I was talking about *Eloise*—the girl who's been nursing *your* fiancé back to health all week." She pinched her mouth together until her lips were two paper-thin lines. "I know she's a childhood friend of theirs and engaged to the other Asquith boy, but . . . I don't trust her."

"Eloise has been nothing but kind to me, Mother."

"If you say so . . ." Caroline sighed. "Don't forget the fireworks, Della. Just tonight, could you please stand beside your fiancé? Maybe talk to him even? At least don't let *that girl* be on his arm."

"She's Easton's f—"

"So everyone says." Her mother turned then, ending the conversation, and lifted a hand. She waved to Lachlan once before leaving Della alone in the cool night air as it gusted off the lake.

Della meandered around the large boat, ignoring her mother's parting instructions to find Wes, and followed the railing that wrapped the hull's sides. The steamboat was three stories tall as far as she could tell, but she supposed a kitchen and some other rooms could be down below. From the water, it rose up. The top level was smaller than the rest and it sat open beneath the stars with only a gilded rail to keep from falling. The next level was closed off and full of bedrooms. The lowest, where she stood, housed a dining area with a dancing space spread out at the back and the thin walkway where she stood that wrapped around the edge of the boat. A gramophone sat to one side of the dance floor, letting music spill and crackle and swell over the chilled air.

Eloise in a dark red gown and Easton in his formal wear at her side stood near the dining area talking. Eloise fed him a dessert from her fingertips between sips she took from a thin glass full of a sparkling drink. Della wondered if they'd step out and sway beneath the stars when they finished—and wondered if she'd ever find something like that for herself.

Their conversation earlier in the library when she'd been spying on them slipped back to her—and that awful maid's stinging words along with it. *Ugly. Fat.* Two words that were too sharp for how bluntly they shot from Violet's lips.

But she'd heard enough of Eloise and Easton's conversation to realize it hadn't been Wes wandering to a thieving maid, and Della wondered how Eloise stood so calm, so close to Easton, smiling at him even, when he'd been straying from her and wandering to Violet *and* Sadie. Della had hid outside the library doors after Easton and Eloise had found her watching them, eavesdropping long enough to discover it'd been Easton with *both* maids.

She shook her head and kept walking. It wasn't her business. It seemed Eloise already knew of it and had taken care of the problem too. And as Della thought about it, she realized it did little to change things for herself. She still wanted a husband that hadn't agreed to marry her just because she had a large inheritance.

Della should be able to breathe deeply knowing her fiancé wasn't a cheat, but . . .

She didn't want a fiancé at all. At least, not one her mother picked.

She wanted one that chose *her.*

Della traced a finger along the purse string wrapped around her wrist. Inside the bag were little notes from a disrespectful maid. Should she keep them? Show the Asquiths who Violet really was? Or toss them over the railing and let the lake carry them away as she forgot this manor and all the oddities in it—both in the people and in the house?

Wes found her leaning against the rail at the front of the steamboat before she could decide what to do. A black cat with white markings was curled up in his arms.

"It's a dark night," he said, popping a hip against the golden railing and staring at a sky that harbored only a thin sliver of moon. "The fireworks should be bright."

But she couldn't think of a glittering sky when a ball of fur purred within his arms. "Why do you have a cat on a boat?" She thought of her own back at home—a pale fluffball with fur the color of champagne.

Wes shrugged as if it were normal to board a steamboat with a cat—of all animals—and sail the waters. "He snuck on. I found him just now shivering under a table." He scratched the animal's neck. "Poor thing. Couldn't leave him like that. What if he got scared and took off? I wouldn't want him falling over the edge." He nuzzled the cat. "The lake is deep." Wes glanced to the dark water. "He could drown."

Della didn't know what to say to that, so she reached out, petting this cat's silken fur and missing her own. "She's friendly."

Wes grinned. "*He* likes everyone but Easton. Won't even go near my brother without hissing at him. He acts like Eloise is his favorite"—he pulled the cat close and nuzzled his face against its cheek again—"But it's actually me, has been since he was a baby and I found him hiding in the chicken coop looking for warmth."

Della smiled, and then silence hung between them for an awkward moment as she discovered his company was *nice*.

She wasn't sure how she felt about that, so she pushed the thought from her mind and filled the lingering quiet with, "Your father said I shouldn't retire before the fireworks." Della glanced at him. He had the same formal jacket his brother and father wore, the black helping him blend into the night while the shirt stood out starkly, the cut sharp and tailored tightly to his torso. Della shook her head, tossing that last observation aside where it could sink below the water.

Wes nodded. "He's right. You have to see them. Father has been saving them for some time, and Henry is preparing them now." He turned toward Della. "Would you like to watch them with me?" He smiled at her, but it was a sad, soft thing that barely curled the corners of his lips, and Della wondered what made him so melancholy on a night reserved for celebrating. Had it been all the *accidents*—as her mother had claimed—wearing down on him, or was it that he wanted this engagement to work but she'd been aloof and distant all week? She thought back to the last few days, weeding through moments she'd thought had involved him but had really featured Easton, and found that Wes had truly been nothing but kind to her.

"Perhaps," she answered, and when he smiled again, something soft blossomed in her chest, feeling an awful lot like the first tendrils of friendship.

"That would be—"

"Ahem," a cold voice behind her interrupted. "Care for a drink?"

She turned around to find Violet glaring at Wes before her angry face whipped to her. The maid held a tray of tall glasses filled with a lavender drink that sparkled.

Violet plucked one up and held it out to her as Wes juggled the cat into one arm so he could grab a drink.

He sipped it slowly as Della put her hand up, palm facing the maid. When she said a simple, "No, thank you," to Violet's outstretched arm, a cold liquid splashed across the front of her dress.

Della gasped as glass shattered on the polished floor.

The cat jumped from Wes's arms at the same moment Violet said, "So sorry, miss," with a smile cutting one corner of her lips.

"Oh!" Wes's attention shot from Della's wet gown to the cat as it ran away. "Uh, here." He pulled out a handkerchief, handed it to her, and then turned to the maid. "Get something to clean this up."

Violet scurried away like a little cockroach, that smile still spread across her cheeks.

"I'm so sorry," Della said at the same time Wes did as well.

He glanced at her as she patted her dress with his handkerchief. "For what?"

"Your cat." Her dress was ruined. She sighed and gave up, giving him the small square of fabric back.

He shrugged. "He'll probably just find Eloise. It'll be okay. I'm almost sure of it." He lifted his hand—he'd managed to hold on to his drink. "Saved this, though." His eyes flicked to Della's wet dress. "Oh, sorry. That was rude—"

Della shook her head. "The maid is the only rude one here."

Wes glanced to where Violet had run off, his eyes narrowing. "It did look like she'd done that on purpose."

She had, Della thought, but she'd not whine to Wes about a maid who couldn't control her temper. *Fat. Ugly.* Violet's words wound back to her, clinging to her like a cold sweat.

But she wasn't rash like the maid. She was patient, and she had all she needed to show the Asquiths who Violet truly was. Della touched her wrist where her purse string hung.

"I'll have a talk with her," Wes said, interrupting her thoughts. He scratched the back of his neck.

"No need." Should she tell Wes that Easton had used his name and tossed aside Violet under it? That that was why the maid was so angry? She glanced to where Easton was finishing the pastry Eloise had given him, and decided she'd had enough of the Asquiths' secrets, of their lies and drama. She kept her mouth shut, staying out of it, and instead tipped her head to the floor above them where their bedrooms waited. "We'd planned to stay the night anyway. I'll just go change."

Wes nodded. "Until the fireworks?"

"Until the fireworks," she repeated and was surprised to find she was looking forward to watching them with him. "I hope you find your cat again."

His lips curled up. "I'll find *you*."

Della tipped her head at Wes, unsure what to say to that, and then stepped away, wondering when her mouth had remembered how to smile again.

As the first fireworks cut across the sky in sapphires and emeralds and amber golds, Della stood alone.

I'll find you, Wes had said, and yet she waited by herself at the front of the boat back where he'd last seen her.

Lachlan was on the top level where her mother's loud laughter fell over the railing. Out and open beneath the sky, they'd have the best view, but Della was happy to leave them there, and keep herself from their company.

Footsteps sounded behind her, and she glanced around, a small blossom of hope unfurling in her chest unmerited.

But it was Eloise walking up to her fiancé, not Wes looking for Della.

She watched them as Eloise curled her arm around Easton and whispered soft words in his ear. They took the stairwell, arms squeezed tight around each other's waists, and headed up to the top floor to meet her mother and Lachlan beneath a glittering sky.

And once more, Della was alone.

It's for the best, she thought. She didn't need a friendship with Wes—or anything else. Let her learn now that his promises were empty before any more warm tendrils wound around her heart.

She watched the fireworks split the expanse above for some time and wondered if she'd always be standing alone.

As the last light fizzled across the dark sky, fading slowly, it left only the pinpricked stars and a small sliver of moon. Della's eyes adjusted slowly. She closed her lids, hoping to help her sight adapt. The echoes of fireworks splashed across her vision as she waited. The soft sloshing of the lake below and the scent of gunpowder kept her company, and for a moment, Della was content to stand and be still and soak in her surroundings.

Until a scream sliced the quiet air. High-pitched, far too familiar, and warbling with fear so deep, Della felt the spike in her heart, the tremble in her veins.

Her fingers shook.

Her eyes shot open.

And she ran as fast as her dress and heeled shoes let her, chasing her mother's cry, but as she charged up the stairs, four people raced down toward her.

Lachlan, Easton, Eloise . . . and her mother.

"Mama!" she cried, feeling young and full of worry—like a child needing to be held, needing to cling to her mother and make sure she was well and safe. They'd had their hurts and wounds, arrows shot from one to the other over the years, but they'd fractured to small splinters the moment her mother's scream had pierced her ears. She'd only ever heard Caroline's voice pitched in horror like that once before—the day her father had died.

Della couldn't lose her mother too. They had far too much to mend between the two of them.

"Are you all right?" Della sucked in quick breaths as she reached for the older woman.

"The water!" Caroline screeched, and she, too, stretched her arms out for Della.

They embraced, holding each other up, as Lachlan passed them with Easton behind, and Eloise—eyes red-rimmed and looking like she'd been crying—nearly tripping on his heels.

"Henry!" Lachlan bellowed, his voice clearer and louder than Della had ever heard it. "Go!"

"What's happening?" Della squeezed her mother.

"In the water," she whispered back, her eyes blank and not quite looking at her. "Just . . . just floating there."

Caroline blinked and then turned, racing down the rest of the steps and pulling Della along with her.

When they caught up to the others, Henry was already there. The same gruff butler with a wide build and thick arms that had searched her for a pistol at the picnic was now wet. His head popped over the railing as he climbed the ladder on the side of the hull. Henry's dark brown hair was slick against his forehead and a grimace deepened the lines around his thin lips. Easton bent, reaching for something on Henry's shoulder and pulling up. Eloise had a hand over her mouth and tears streaming down her cheeks while Lachlan held a fist to his chest and yelled for the others to hurry, hurry, *hurry*.

"They weren't accidents, were they?" her mother whispered as Henry climbed over the railing.

The others crowded around him, but Della caught glimpses—black slacks and a ripped white shirt, a shoulder drenched with blood. The water mixed with the thick, sticky fluid, turning the crimson to pale red—not quite pink, not fully scarlet—a bullet wound not yet healed.

Della's pulse tied a noose around her neck, strangling her. His waterlogged and too-still body suffocated her voice. But one single syllable clawed up her closed throat, weighing a thousand heartbeats.

"Wes."

41

El

Fourteen Hours Earlier
Early Morning
May 12th, 1910

Eloise stood between Lammore and the woods, wondering what the lake thought as Lammore watched the chaos two brothers and a single woman could wreck. Would the lake keep their secrets—their fights and kisses and threats? Or would the water spill all her knowledge, throwing it to the shore as easily as her waves crashed against its bank?

Easton had slipped inside the manor to clean himself up after his hunt, and Eloise supposed she should do the same. She had sat at the edge of the lake after feeding the chickens before she'd spotted Easton, letting the water hold her, and now her shoes squelched with each footfall and her dress lay heavy and sopping around her legs.

She took a step toward the manor, leaving a trail dripping in her wake. The three fat hens pecked at the ground, and something ticked through her thoughts when she saw them. Six small words that didn't quite make sense.

I threw it to the pigs.

Eloise tilted her head, watching as Sophie, Mattie, and Flora finished the scraps she'd tossed them. They squawked as the last specks slid down their gullets, and then wobbled back to the henhouse. The three friends had gobbled up all the food before any of the other chickens had had a chance to turn the corner and see it.

Or the pigs, who would've gladly eaten anything: vegetable ends and bits of crushed fruit, leftover buttermilk and scraps of meat. Even fresh runts from an early-morning hunt.

But Easton hadn't had a kill in his hands. And he hadn't made it to the pigpen when she'd spotted him.

He'd only just stepped out of the woods.

So, what had he been doing in the forest before the sun had barely crested the horizon? And why had he lied?

Eloise took a step toward the trees and followed the scar Easton's boots had left in the brush.

She moved quietly as she walked deeper into the woods until the foliage blotted out her view of Lammore. And as the lake disappeared, the hairs on the back of Eloise's neck stood up slowly, one by one, as if each were trying to warn her, telling her to race back to her oldest friend and safety, step her feet into the soft, rolling waves again. She knew—felt it deep in the marrow of her bones—that Lammore was everything good and that her waterlogged secrets were held tightly. But the forest, it was full of nothing but bloodshed and lies, brass bullets and lacerations. Eloise's skin prickled as the brush crunched beneath her sodden shoes. But she delved deeper into the trees, following Easton's trail. She stopped only when her skirt snagged on thorns. Droplets flung off the wet fabric as the briar caught her.

And then Eloise saw a long copper curl tangled in the bramble with her.

She took a step toward it, and her foot landed on something soft beneath the leaf litter.

Eloise froze, knowing the ground shouldn't feel like that, shouldn't give way before it crunched. She bent slowly and pushed aside freshly turned dirt and dead leaves and little beetles that scurried to hide.

It was a forearm she found first. With a muddy handprint wrapped around pale, pale skin.

Eloise shuffled away.

Her heart kicked within her chest.

Her body fought to freeze, to numb itself, to let the fear still her bones, but she moved back slowly. Eloise's hands felt as if they would crack as she forced them to skim the ground, to scrape away thick globs of muck and silt.

Her fingertips touched something soft and fuzzy with a hard ridge beneath. She wiped away the damp dirt, and it took longer than it should have for her to realize she brushed an eyebrow. Eloise smoothed away more sludge as a scream clawed the back of her throat. When a muck-smeared hazel eye met hers, opened and staring at the sky—unseeing—she clamped her mouth shut. Pressed her lips tightly together. Suffocated a shriek.

Ice tore through her blood. She sucked in quick breaths—too shallow. Never filling her lungs. Squeezing her chest until she gasped on slips of air.

Eloise stared down, frozen on her knees with fear in her veins.

Sadie lay before her, too cold and far too still.

Blood turned the kitchen maid's copper curls scarlet and sticky.

Eloise forced herself to brush aside the dirt, and more blood spilled itself across Sadie's stomach. Metal glinted there. A sharp blade bit the girl's belly.

Eloise jumped back, and her eyes went from the knife to the muddy handprint around Sadie's arm. She held her own palm up to it without touching the dead maid's body. The print swallowed her hand, big enough for the fingers to wrap around Sadie's arm. A man's handprint. A mud-slicked mark lingering to tell the truth.

Oh, Easton. Eloise grabbed her sodden skirt, lifting up the edge. *What have you done?*

And then she wiped away the only evidence of who had killed Sadie Fischer.

42
The Housemaid

Night
May 12th, 1910

Violet stepped past the dance floor with a tray in her hands as the last fireworks fizzled. She headed for the boat's dining area. Flaky desserts drizzled in warm honey and topped with piles of fluffy cream sat on gold-plated dishes dotted with fresh berries.

They should've been for her.

But no, Weston had to ruin everything she'd striven and fought for. With a few small words, he'd destroyed all her dreams, and he wouldn't get away with it.

She'd had the small satisfaction of tossing a drink on his heiress, but it wasn't enough.

"Henry!" a voice screamed over her thoughts, and in the time it took for her to turn her head, Lachlan tore down the steps with the rest of the guests tripping behind his feet. Even the cat chased after Eloise as if afraid to be left behind.

They rushed to the back of the boat, and Violet froze with the dessert held before her, staring at the commotion and bodies pressing into one another. She quickly stepped over to a table and dropped the tray, and then slowly, carefully, she made her way over to the noise, the shouts and frantic cries. Her polished shoes *click-clapped* against the dance floor as she crossed it, but not a single person glanced her way. No one noticed her sneaking up behind them.

Violet was only a few feet away when a loud, thick silence draped over the night. Everyone froze as they gathered in a half circle around the railing, their backs to her.

Caroline Drewitt took a half step away from the others. "They weren't accidents, were they?"

Henry popped over the side of the boat, carrying a load on his shoulder as he climbed the hull's ladder.

And as Henry heaved himself up, that heiress whispered, "Wes."

The single word sunk into Violet's skin, burrowed into her chest, and her hardened heart melted, making its beat race through her veins.

They lowered Weston to the ground, Henry holding his weight and Easton guiding, until he lay on his back, wet and unmoving. Blood seeped from his still-fresh wound. His shirt had torn apart, and any skin on his shoulder that had healed was ripped open once more. His blood mixed with the water. Rivulets of pink dripped down his chest, his arm. More scarlet bloomed on the white shirt, fanning out like poppy petals.

"Weston," Lachlan cried, dropping to his knees. "My . . . my son." His hands skimmed the younger twin's cold, wet face. Lachlan bent over him, his mouth forming a wail though no sound came out.

Violet caught a glimpse as tears leaked from the old man's cloudy eyes, and she looked away, unable to hold his pain, to cry with him, to care.

Weston lay dead not ten feet away, and yet anger *still* burned in her belly. She should snuff it out, let it wither, but like a spark that caught and grew, she couldn't douse the fire in her chest. He'd destroyed her dreams. He deserved it. This was justice.

"Who?" whispered Caroline as she clung to her daughter's arm. "Who would do this?"

Easton bent, crouching beside his father while Henry knelt on Lachlan's other side, and put an arm around the old man. He stared at the floor, avoiding his brother's body, and Violet wondered what it must be like to stare at a dead reflection of yourself.

"Who would do this?" Caroline said louder, her voice trembling around the short syllables.

On the old woman's other side, Eloise stood, her body shuddering, her head shaking. Her short curls skimmed her clenched jaw. She swallowed, looking as if she were about to throw up. Even her skin, usually a rich and warm color, was pallid—ashen almost—as if everything bright in Eloise had been sucked away.

"Who did this!" Caroline's voice rose in pitch and volume. "I . . . I demand an answer!" She clutched her daughter, and even Violet could see the nail prints left in Della's arm.

The heiress gently pulled her mother's hand off her skin, uncurling each jeweled finger slowly. "I"—Della paused and took a deep breath, cleared her throat until her words lost their tremor—"I know who."

And then the heiress turned, her watery gaze locking onto Violet's ocean eyes.

"Her."

43
The Heiress

Night
May 12th, 1910

Della turned away from Wes's motionless body, from Lachlan curled over his dead son. Two small notes weighted heavy in her purse, and her mother's question rang in her ears.

Who would do this?

Della lifted one finger and pointed it at the dark-haired maid. "Her."

Violet took a step back. "What?"

"You heard me." Della narrowed her eyes at the maid's wide ones. "You did this." She tugged at the purse string tied around her wrist. "You were jealous—of me, of that kitchen girl Sadie. You—"

"Sadie?" a rough voice whispered behind Della, one she didn't recognize. She turned around to see Henry slowly standing up.

He'd not spoken at the picnic as he'd searched her, and his voice had a warm lilt to it even amidst this cold, callous night. "What about Sadie?" His dark brown brows crushed together. "My wife—Cook, I mean—we've not seen her since last night." He glanced once to Wes's body and quickly back to Della with fear hiding in the twist of his lips. "Aggie said she left a note. Said she'd gone to the south entrance but would be back and she was sorry if she was late. But . . ." He swallowed, his Adam's apple dipping slowly. "But she hasn't been back. You don't think . . ." He looked at Violet and then back to Della. "You don't think she's a part of any of this, do you? Aggie just thought she needed a break. The stress of coming here the week of the party and all. It was just a tad too much. She just needed a break. She's a good girl. She . . . she . . ." His words trailed off, but they stuck in Della's mind.

Sadie had left for the south entrance—the one that faced the woods, where the forest crept close to the manor. She spun away from Henry, facing Violet once more. "Please." She shook her head, her pale blond eyebrows pulling together tightly, pleading with the maid. "You didn't hurt her too, did you?"

Red crept up Violet's neck, flushed her cheeks. "I didn't hurt anyone!"

"I saw you." Della's glance drifted in the dark night, where—somewhere out there—the forest loomed, and out of the corner of her eyes, she saw Lachlan turn his head to face Violet. She wondered how much he saw. Could he see his son's killer standing only a few feet away?

"Whatever you saw, it wasn't me." Violet took a step back.

"I saw you come out of the woods this morning." She opened her purse and pulled out two small notes that spelled a confession. The papers were creased and soft, and she stepped over, handing them to Lachlan, staring at the old man and his many wrinkles—stories of a long life written on his face. Della read both joy and heartache in his crow's feet and smile lines, and she hated adding to the sorrow splashed across his mouth, his eyes, his posture. She focused on Wes's prone body instead, but that was worse, so she simply said, "She left these for Sadie," and stepped away, back over to her mother, holding her tightly once more. "I saw her put them in Sadie's room."

Lachlan held the notes in shaky hands, staring at each small paper before handing them to Easton. "Read them for me."

Easton took them slowly, and in a voice that cracked at the edges, said, "'You don't belong here.'" He paused. "'Leave before it's too late.'" He quickly looked at Violet, and Della wondered what he thought. "'You'll regret coming here.'" He flipped them over. "They say Sadie's name on the other side."

"No," Henry whispered as all eyes turned to the dark-haired maid.

"She was mad at Wes for agreeing to marry me, so she poisoned him at dinner." Della turned to face the small group and held up one finger, pointing it at Violet. "She was the one who'd given him his plate." She shook her head. "When that didn't work, she shot him in the woods and claimed to be collecting morels then, but she'd missed his heart." Della took a deep breath. "And now, tonight"—she glanced to Lachlan still bent over Wes's body—"I'm so sorry, but Violet poisoned him again." Della thought back to the lavender drink Violet had offered him. The one she tried to get Della to drink as well, had dumped on her when she'd refused it. "I think she wanted to poison me tonight too."

Caroline gasped, loosening her grip on Della, and stomped past her with a storm raging in her steps. Before Della realized what her mother meant to do, a smack tore through the night, and Caroline's red handprint was left splayed across Violet's pale cheek, her rings slicing delicate skin.

"How dare you!" Her mother reared her arm back again, but Della stepped forward and grabbed it, tugging her mother back, pulling the older woman to her side.

"I'm not done," Della said in a low voice, and turned to pierce Easton with eyes narrowed to thin slits. "This is your fault too."

"What?" His mouth hung open as everyone's gazes bounced between him and Violet.

"You used his name." Della looked at him with disgust penned across her features, written in the curl of her upper lip. "You told that maid you were Wes and then promised her your name—one that wasn't yours to give. It should be you lying there. It would've been if you hadn't been a coward, if you hadn't slandered your brother's name instead of your own." She thought again of the drink she'd refused not even a handful of hours earlier. Would Easton's fiancée have declined it on a night they'd been celebrating? "But it might be you *and* Eloise dead if you had. It's all . . ." She shrugged, wishing an answer hid in her empty hands. "It's all just . . . such a tragedy."

Lachlan curled farther over his dead son, his eyes rimmed red and wet, as Henry asked, "How do you know so much?"

"I'm observant." Della's eyes flicked to each person's face. "I watch and pay attention."

"It's true." Her mother held on to her. "I've always said she was smart. Perceptive. And she is. She should be a detective herself! She—"

"Mother." Della brushed away her father's words on her mother's lips. "Wes is dead. Now's not—" *Now's not the time*, she wanted to say, even if her mother's words—*She should be a detective*—sparked something deep inside of her. Della shook her head. They'd have time later to figure each other out, to find what path Della would take—with or without her mother's money. For now, she had to prove her theory correct. "Check the forest." Della's mouth curved into a frown, and she glanced to Henry. "If you find Sadie, you'll know I was right." She turned to Violet. "She did all of this because she thought Wes had kissed another maid, and because she thought he'd tossed her aside"—she sharpened her words, letting them fly across the short space—"For a *fat, ugly* heiress."

"That last bit is the only true thing you've said. You are fat and ugly, and Wes didn't want *you*. Maybe it was you! Maybe you killed him!"

Della shook her head. "But I knew it wasn't Wes sweet-talking you. It was Easton." She turned to him. "Tell her. I'm right. It was you all along."

He said nothing, but slowly, without looking either of them in the eye, he nodded his head.

Violet screamed, a violent sound that shattered the air. And before Della could cover her ears, she was pushed to the ground. Her head snapped against the wood and then the dark-haired maid was on top of her, scratching and clawing and screaming. "You're a liar! It was you!"

"Henry!" Lachlan bellowed.

Della put her hands up to block the maid, but her mother reached over, grabbed Violet by her long silken hair, and wrenched her off, dragging her away.

Della sat up, and Lachlan yelled, "Get her, Henry!" over Violet's shrieking. He clutched at his chest. "Tie that maid up!"

Heat and pain and little droplets of blood beaded along Della's cheeks where Violet had scratched her, but she ignored them. In the chaos, no one saw what Della witnessed. Everyone around her watched the maid. Her mother held Violet by the hair while Eloise and Easton clutched each other—Eloise with tears spilling down her face and Easton with a face filled with guilt. Even the cat's wild eyes stared at the chaos from behind Easton's feet where it hid, its front paws on his legs, begging him to pick it up and keep it safe as Henry roared. He clamored to Violet and grabbed ahold of her, gripping her tightly as she bucked and kicked.

But no one glanced at poor Wes lying still, or Lachlan over his dead son with his bony, wrinkled hand grasping for his old, worn heart. No one saw his eyes close in pain. Or his last gasp for air.

No one but Della, and in a small moment between shock and grief for a man she knew too little, she wondered if he were reunited with Roslin. His words slipped back to her in an echo of his voice.

Our hearts harmonized for so long, and mine's been out of rhythm ever since hers stopped singing.

And Della hoped he was chatting with his best friend once again.

44

El

Late Evening
May 11th, 1910

The Night Before the Boat Party

"You." Eloise stared at Violet after pulling the laundry basket from the maid's clenched hands. She glanced at her from head to toe, Eloise's eyes flashing over Violet's silky hair, black dress, and polished shoes before she pinned her with a look that burned. "You accused me of shooting Wes."

Violet flinched, her head snapping down to avoid Eloise. "I . . ."

"If I wanted Wes dead, he would be already." From the moment Wes had hit the floor at dinner the first night, Eloise had assumed Easton had been the one to poison and shoot him, and then, when the thought that maybe it wasn't the older twin seeking petty revenge ticked through her thoughts, Eloise had been determined to find out who had done it, and yet this maid had accused *her.*

She ground out angry words from an angrier heart, putting Violet in her place, and hearing her own voice spit venom in what seemed awfully close to a threat. “Do you understand?” she asked at last, and she didn’t like the way Violet’s mouth pinched in tight lines as if the maid thought she was better than Eloise, as if Violet had any claim over the Asquiths when they belonged to *her.*

She dismissed the maid curtly, glad when she obeyed without another word. It’d been a long day and she still had to go to Wes, but she needed a minute to let her fury bleed from her veins. Violet may have inadvertently given her a reason to see Wes that didn’t look like groveling, but something still needed to be done about that maid’s attitude. She’d noticed the quick, cutting looks from those icy eyes more and more these days.

Eloise took a deep breath and let Violet slip from her mind. She was another day’s worry. Tonight, Wes was trouble enough.

She held the old wicker basket with his laundry in it in both hands.

But she’d need more than a moment before seeing him. Too many thoughts churned in her mind and too many feelings skimmed the surface of her skin. She set the basket beside her wing-backed chair and sat, watching Lammore lap against the shore and wishing she could run out into the night and sail her waters. Tomorrow, she’d celebrate the start of a new life with Easton on the lake, but tonight . . . Tonight she missed Wes. Everything about him burned inside of her: his warm arms wrapping around her, his shy smiles and broad grins, even the scent he wore—the warm vanilla and sharp cedar soap that lingered on his skin.

She reached down, grabbing the sweater he’d worn on the hunt—her favorite one. The creamed coffee color of it always contrasted sharply against his dark eyes, drawing them out. And she hoped it might smell like Wes—that she could wrap herself in him and dream a little longer of a life stolen away. She'd mend the bullet hole in a moment, but first, she wanted a minute to mend her own heart. To hope. To dream.

Eloise slipped his sweater on, and even though it'd been scrubbed free of his blood, it somehow still smelled like him. She curled her arms around herself, her hands hugging her shoulders, and traced her fingertips along the fine, soft wool, pulling him close, holding on tight to the traces of Wes in the fibers of his shirt.

But as she ran her fingers over the downy fabric, realization shot through her, and the understanding that followed was far faster than a brass bullet biting a shoulder.

There was no hole.

The sweater wasn't shot through.

She thought back to the hunt. She'd found Wes already shot, sweater off, and blood splashed against his torso, dripping down his arm. She had thought he'd ripped the sweater off to get to the wound and try to pull the bullet from his flesh. His fingers *had* been soaked in his blood, but what if he'd taken it off to shoot himself, to give himself his brother's scar? What if he'd planned to slip his shirt back on, hiding a wound that would heal slowly?

Her conversation with Wes the first night of the engagement party week, when the storm had raged, crept back to her.

Let Easton marry her, Eloise had shot at him.

He doesn't need an heiress, he'd whispered back.

And you do?

Wes had looked down then, avoiding her eyes. *For now.*

And then, she'd asked him to tell her the truth. *Are you playing a game, Wes? What does that mean?*

Eloise's mouth dropped open, and as she sat with his sweater wrapped around her, she finally realized what he'd meant.

It had been *him*. The whole time. A long con at least three months planned out—since he'd tossed her aside and she'd run to his brother.

It had been Wes behind the poisoning. Who knew better than him how much nightshade his body could handle without too many repercussions, without dying? He knew exactly how long it took for nightshade to kick in. She thought back to that dinner. *Wes* had served Lucy her plate with mushrooms, knowing it'd cause an outburst. *Wes* had insisted she skip dinner after that, had told her to eat dessert in her room.

He'd known what was about to happen . . . and hadn't wanted Lucy to see.

And who else but her and Wes knew *exactly* where Easton's scar was?

Eloise touched the soft fabric at the shoulder, at a space she knew too well, and she was sure of one thing. She and Sadie weren't supposed to have seen Wes's bullet wound out in those woods.

They'd ruined his plan when they saw him with a fresh wound and covered in blood.

Wes had been planning his brother's murder.

And Eloise could think of two reasons why.

You're going to marry Easton Anthony Asquith, he'd said only a few days earlier. *It's the only way forward for all of us.*

And in Easton's deep voice, *She needs to be in a place that can help her more than we can.*

There was only one person that Wes loved as much as he loved Eloise.

Lucy.

And Wes had told Easton he'd fight for their little sister.

He'd told everyone—that night at the dinner party before his poisoned body had hit the wooden floors—that he'd do whatever it took to keep Easton from sending Lucy away.

He meant take his brother's place.

And no matter the promise Easton made to her when she took his ring on her finger, Eloise knew Easton would never actually let Lucy stay at Asquith manor. Not after Lucy nearly shot her, not after the girl *did* kill Betty, even if it'd been an accident. Eloise hadn't made him promise because she thought he really would. Easton knew she didn't love him, so she had needed a plausible reason to accept his engagement and make Wes jealous enough to come back to her.

Only Wes hadn't.

And she wondered now if her taking Easton's hand had started Wes's scheming. Or had he been conspiring even longer than that?

In one terrible swoop, if Wes had played his dark game cleverly enough, he would've won everything he wanted—his sister at home as his ward and Eloise's hand in his. All he'd had to do was fake his death with his brother's body and clothe himself in Easton's name.

But he hadn't planned on her beating him, on Eloise figuring it out, even though she'd told him she would.

It's not a game this time, he had said to her in a voice as deep as a grave.

But it is something. Her words had been clipped when she'd shot them back to him. *And I'm going to figure it out.* She'd always been as smart as him. This time, she'd proven it, and she couldn't let Wes kill Easton. They were brothers. Blood. If Wes bore Easton's name, he'd hear his brother's death for the rest of his life each time those two small syllables called for him.

Eloise would have to stop that from happening.

45

The Fiancée

One Month Later
June 16th, 1910

Eloise fixed the skirt of her velvet dress, its color so deep a red, it bordered on black. Matching lace swept across her bare collarbone. She wore no jewelry but a thin black ribbon wound around her ring finger.

"You're still going to do it?" Lucy tucked her head into the door where Eloise was getting dressed. "You're going to marry Easton?"

Eloise nodded, and the wildflowers tucked into her short curls fluttered around her face. "Could you help me with the back?" She turned away from Lucy, showing her the buttons that traveled the length of her spine.

The girl's footsteps pattered against the wooden floors, and then one by one, she fastened Eloise's dress. When she'd finished, she was quiet.

Eloise turned around to find Lucy's head bowed low and tears wetting her cheeks. She bent and cupped the girl's face in her hands. "What's wrong?" she asked, even though Eloise knew that Lucy missed Wes, that she mourned her father still.

One month wasn't nearly enough time to heal.

But Lachlan wouldn't have wanted them to waste away their lives in ink-colored veils and black armbands. And the whole manor agreed. After three deaths and one arrest on Asquith grounds, they needed a little hope that life would get better, that it wouldn't always be so dark, even though Eloise herself wasn't so sure.

"He wants to send me away." Lucy sniffed, wiping her nose with the back of her hand. "Mother stole Father from me. And Wes too. And now—" She crumpled to the floor in a pile of creamy lace. "Easton wants to get rid of me!"

Eloise sat, wrinkling her skirts, and pulled the girl to her lap, cradling her in her arms though she barely fit. "Oh, Luce, no." She held her tight. "You aren't going anywhere. He promised me."

"Really?" Lucy looked up with rosy cheeks and wide eyes. "I don't want to leave."

"You aren't." Eloise hugged her tightly. "This is your home as much as it is mine now. You aren't going anywhere. I promise."

A knock at the door had Lucy jumping up and wiping the tear tracks from her face. She scurried out of the room as the new lord of Asquith manor stepped in.

"You're not supposed to see me yet." Eloise walked over to him on bare feet, grabbing a bouquet of dark jade roses.

Their fragrance filled the air around him. "I thought I'd escort you to the lake."

"You don't think it's too . . . morbid to marry there?" She leaned into him, wrapping her arms around his waist. "You don't think it'll remind everyone of . . ." She let her words fall to the floor, unable to finish the sentence.

"The lake is a part of you, El." His arms curled around her, pulling her snug to him. "It always has been." He softened his voice. "I think it's where we were meant to marry."

She rested her head on his chest, in the small crook where jaw and jacket met.

A hiss spilled from his lips, and Eloise pulled back, looking up into bright brown eyes beneath brows pulled tightly together. "Does it still hurt?" She brushed her fingers over a small space she wished she didn't know so well.

And then his hand was over hers, cupping them both gently against his shoulder. "Yes, but not there."

"It'll be an ugly scar you'll carry," she whispered. "Will that bother you?"

He shook his head, and pulled her to him again, his smooth-shaven cheek rubbing against her hair as they held on to each other. "Will it bother *you*?" And she knew he wasn't speaking of his marred flesh.

"It should," she answered softly. "But it doesn't."

46

One Month Prior
May 12th, 1910

The Night of the Boat Party

As the first firework popped in the night sky, Eloise pinned Easton against the steamboat's gilded railing. She kissed his cheek, his neck, unbuttoned his shirt.

"Ellie?" His voice was low, rough.

Her hands skimmed his skin, and she flattened her palms against his chest, feeling his heartbeat, noticing it speed up.

"Eloise . . ." He said her name cautiously, his tone dipping even more.

She didn't answer, and instead let a hand slip down to lift up one corner of her skirt.

"Ellie, what are you . . ." His words turned slow. "What are you doing?"

"You . . . you killed her." Eloise fumbled with the edge of her dress, her hands shaking. "You killed Sadie."

"How—" His chest heaved, and he grabbed her shoulders as he sucked in short, ragged breaths. "No, I—I didn't."

She looked straight into his dark, dark eyes. "Don't lie to me."

His grip slipped down, wrapping around her upper arms, pulling her hands to her sides and away from her skirt. "It . . ." He swallowed, his Adam's apple jerking with the movement. "It . . . was an accident." Easton pulled her close. "I swear, I didn't mean to."

"She was *dead*." Eloise whispered the last word. "There was blood all over her. There was . . . a knife." And even though she didn't want to know, she needed to, so she asked in a quiet voice, "Did you stab her?"

"She . . . she . . . she fell." He tried to squeeze her thin arms, tried to force her to look at him, but she wouldn't. "I just . . . I barely pushed her—" He snapped his mouth shut. "I didn't know she was holding a knife." He swallowed again. "She fell and it just . . . It was her own fault!"

"*You* killed her." Eloise stared hard at him. "You did that!" She took a deep breath, hoping it'd ease the adrenaline racing through her veins. "You—"

"She . . . she was going to ruin us." Easton dropped his head. "I didn't . . . I didn't know you'd start over with me if I stopped with the maids. You'd said, 'All right,' and I'd lost you before and I was so, so afraid I'd lose you again." He looked up at her, his pupils large in the dark night. "She was going to ruin everything. I just meant to scare her. I promise!" His head bent low again, his shoulders joining.

"She'd already told me," Eloise whispered. "She'd already told me everything."

Easton's head shot up. "What?"

"And then you covered it up. You covered her up." It wasn't a question, not when she knew intimately, not when she had been the one to brush aside the dirt over Sadie's body in a shallow, makeshift grave he'd buried her in.

He stared straight at her, his gaze so consumed by his pupils that his eyes looked black. "You covered up Lucy's. You covered up Betty." He swallowed hard, his breathing rough and too fast. "And you promised you'd do the same for me."

Eloise shook her head. "Wes promised you that." She let out a long, slow stream of air. "And this isn't the same."

"It is! I—"

"Lucy can't help how she is." Eloise reached under her skirt again. She wrapped her hand around cold metal and an alabaster handle. "You don't have that excuse." Lucy hadn't meant to hurt Betty. She was still such a small child in her mind, and she didn't quite understand what had even happened with the old kitchen maid.

But Easton had killed Sadie in anger, in a threat. He'd meant to make her fear.

Eloise's grip tightened.

"It doesn't matter anyway." She softened her voice, even though her next words would cut just as deep on a whisper as they would a scream. "You're already dead." Her fingers trembled as she raised her hand. Eloise had to marry Easton. And Wes had to die. For Lucy. For Sadie.

She took a deep, shuddering breath. Eloise had ruined the plan Wes had set into motion and Easton had killed Sadie, but Eloise could fix both. The family wouldn't get the chance to cover up the kitchen maid's death as an accident or retire Agnes and Henry to ease their guilt. It wouldn't be Betty all over again. Eloise wouldn't marry a murderer.

Instead, she'd give Sadie redress and finish what Wes had started. He'd take Easton's place without feeling his brother's blood on his skin every time Easton's name was used for him.

She would bear that guilt herself, knowing she gave a forgotten maid with copper hair and cherry-red lips the justice due her.

And together, she and Wes would protect Lucy.

"I'm sorry." Eloise lifted her gun to a small space of skin she knew so well. "You can't have just a scar now. You need his wound." She swallowed hard as his hands slackened. "It won't hurt long. The nightshade is already kicking in."

And under a sky shot with fireworks, Eloise let her bullet bite his shoulder a second time. It reeled Easton back, tossing him over the golden railing and into the dark lake.

Into her oldest friend, who kept all her secrets.

EPILOGUE

Della sat in her chair, the city spread out beside her just beyond a meticulously cleaned window, but it was the letter in her hand that she couldn't stop staring at.

Dear Miss Drewitt,

It would be a great honor to have you as our guest at Stirling Estate. I've heard of your fame after the terrible incident at Asquith manor. All the papers write about how you helped catch a murderess maid—how because of you, the police had enough evidence to convict her. You gave that family closure, and we would be honored to have you and your sharp mind. You are cordially invited to Clare Isle for a week of intrigue with a select few, starting on the 30th of September, 1911. All needs will be provided for. Please bring nothing but your astute intuition and keen eyes.

Sincerely,
William Rolland

Della leaned back, falling into the velvet fabric of her wingback, wondering what "a week of intrigue" meant as a soft meow chirped for her attention. She glanced down to find her cat, Ophelia, sliding into the room, her champagne fur sticking out in all directions as she padded over to her. Della smiled softly as Ophelia stretched, reaching her front paws up, begging her favorite person to hold her.

She bent, about to pick up Ophelia when a small memory rose above a night of chaos. One of another cat—black and white—reaching its paws up, begging Easton to hold him. Della froze, her arms outstretched.

And then Wes's words the last time she'd talked to him whispered in her mind and haunted her like a ghost.

He likes everyone but Easton.

Della's thoughts unspooled.

Won't even go near my brother without hissing at him.

Her hands shook.

He acts like Eloise is his favorite, but it's actually me.

With movements like a marionette, she picked up Ophelia. A soft mewl cried for her attention, and Della snapped back to her own room in her own house in a city far from Asquith manor as if a spell had been severed. She shook her head.

It had just been a cat. A terrified cat on a terrible night. Nothing more.

Not a cat reaching for his favorite person.

She was sure of it. Even the police had agreed with her.

It was just a silly, scared cat clawing for whoever was closest.

Nothing more.

Ophelia settled on her lap, smothering the invitation under her fur. Della pulled it out, focused on it rather than the questions tucking themselves into the corners of her mind.

She was being ridiculous. The police *had* agreed with her.

She tossed her doubts aside as easily as she flicked the invitation in her hands onto the table beside her.

It flipped as it landed, and there on the back, scrawled in a man's harsh handwriting, were two small words, barely visible at first, but as the sunlight hit them, they blazed to life.

And Della couldn't look away.

Help me.

Acknowledgments

One of my favorite parts of writing a book is the community of people that helped bring it into your hands. Without them, *A Rather Peculiar Poisoning* would be hidden away on a computer file—probably half finished. Many thanks to all the people that read its early drafts, gave me encouragement, helped fix plot holes, brainstormed with me, or simply stood by my side for years while I dreamt.

Endless thanks to my amazing agent, Sophie Cudd, who picked this story up from the slush and found it the best home. I am awed at your skill in a part of the publishing world that I know so very little of, and I'm endlessly thankful for your wisdom, your kindness, and for your championing of this book. What a lovely whirlwind this has been—all because of you.

Thank you to Nicole Luongo for choosing this book. I'll never forget when we first talked and you told me you read my story in a single sitting, even forgetting your coffee. As a coffee lover, I think that one of the highest compliments. Never did I imagine someone would one day binge a book I wrote. That will always stay with me. Thank you for your continued cheerleading.

Many thanks to Annie Chagnot. Your kindness and insight through edits were spot on and so appreciated. This book is stronger because of you, and I'm so glad it landed in your lap. Thank you to my copy editor, Lee Tipton, for your thorough notes. I'm so grateful for your attentiveness to this story. Thank you as well to SarahElizabeth Lee and the entire team at Park Row Books for all your hard work, from finding the perfect title to helping this newbie author navigate all the behind-the-scenes things that it takes to put out a book. You all are a dream to work with!

To Ande Pliego, thank you so much for your support over the years. I'm so very glad we met. It's been such a joy to navigate debuting with you, and I'm positive this book never would've been completed had you not read it in chunks as I wrote it and encouraged me with each chapter to keep going.

Thank you to Christina Ferko and Elise Warner for being some of its first readers and proofreaders. Christina, you caught all my misspellings and typos. Elise, you helped me fix one of my biggest plot holes. I'm so grateful to the both of you, and I can't wait to see your books on shelves.

Kayla Olson, Emily Bain Murphy, and Autumn Krause, there are not enough words to give you to say all that your friendship and support have meant to me over the years when I had no book deal and only hope. I think without the kindness from the three of you, I would've given up on dreams of publishing years ago. You are the people who make the writing community so great.

To Rachel Andrews and Dennis Andrews, what can I say? Rachel, you have been my best friend and such an encouragement to me for over twenty years. The pictures you sent me of you reading while cooking and cleaning and going about your day because you wanted to know how the story ended are happily lodged in my brain forever. I'm so thankful God put you in my life back when we were baby college students. Denny, thank you for your knowledge of firearms, for being my biggest surprise fan, and for Tux. That epilogue was born from a seed you planted.

To my kids, who are my favorite people and biggest cheerleaders: Elijah, thank you for naming Tux. Here's your payment—your name in print and my endless thanks. Hannah and Noelle, thank you for loving my words and telling me this is your favorite book. To my younger ones, thank you for your joy with each celebration even when you didn't always understand. And to my littlest, thank you for your quick chubby hands that were always reaching for the computer and giving me all the resulting typos. Every "lkdhlkkhkj" that I had to delete was so worth it to have you by my side as I wrote.

David, I could write an entire book with all the things to thank you for in it, and still, it wouldn't be enough. You've been by my side through everything—every rejection and all the tears, each celebration and all those (happy) tears. Every note you wrote me filling me with encouragement is still safely tucked away and revisited often. Thank you for being my first proofreader and for waking up early before work when the sun wasn't even up just to make time to read my words. You have always been the biggest blessing in my life, and without your support and love, this book wouldn't exist. The only good parts of any of these characters were plucked straight from you.

Most importantly, thank you to Jesus Christ, my hope. Without Him, I have nothing.

And finally, to all the readers, thank you so much for spending time in this story. It means the world to me that there are people out there reading my words. I so hope you enjoyed your time at Asquith manor.